A SHINING IN THE SHADOWS

A SHINING IN THE SHADOWS

BEVERLEY LEE

THE GABRIEL DAVENPORT SERIES

II

Published by Ink Raven Press
Copyright © 2017 Beverley Lee
All rights reserved.
ISBN-13 978-0-9935490-2-1
ISBN-10 0-9935490-2-0

DEDICATION

For Emma and Adam. My best creations.

CHAPTER ONE

Night followed night followed night. An endless cycle of unimaginable cold and blood and loneliness.

I thought back to the beginning, as I often do. The first feeling on opening my eyes? Euphoria. I thought I had been prepared to die, but when it comes right down to it, who is ever ready for that? What I remembered was hazy, like it had happened to someone else. Like a flickering away on a screen as I passed. I remember the way Clove's hair fell over my face, silky and slightly damp from the pre-dawn mist. The shiver that ran down my spine at the touch of his chilled lips. I remember breathing so fast, thinking each inhalation could be the last. I wondered if it would hurt.

Something else had happened too, before the blinding, white-hot pain took me to a primal place out of my own consciousness. I was floating, but still tied to my own body, like a balloon with a trailing string.

He took me on the hilltop overlooking The Manor, laying my body down on the wet grass as the pain twisted me into a seething mass of raw nerve endings. There was no ceremony or prettiness, just my eyes to the stars as his fangs sliced open my throat. I cried. For the boy I once was and for the man I would never be. Death came to meet me in a soft blanket of black.

Then his wrist against my lips and the first drips of blood on my tongue. Nothing magical happened. I know I gagged and spluttered, spattering his face. But he forced the gash against my mouth, massaging my throat with ice-cold fingers until I swallowed. And then the need hit me, flooding my senses. My senses, which a moment ago had been drifting towards nothingness, were now *burning*; I didn't know where one ended and the next one began. I grabbed his forearm, clinging on with a strength I didn't know I had, my mouth locked against his wrist, my tongue delving into the wound. Horrified at what I was doing, yet begging for more. His face was impassive as he watched me, only changing when he smoothed back the hair from my face and broke the contact, even as I whimpered for more.

'It is done.'

And so it was.

‡

That was last year, before the brutal cold of my first winter. It's hard to gauge time when all you can go on is the changing of the seasons. At first I had tried to count the nights, until I realised that was pointless. It didn't matter; they were all the same. Clove took us all out to hunt. We killed as a group, with his guidance. We feasted. He took us back to where we slept, and told us what we had done wrong.

Some nights Teal read to us, something that was comforting but Moth didn't like me sharing. I hung around on the outskirts, pretending to be busy, whilst my ears tuned in to the lilt of Teal's voice. Teal didn't mind me listening. On rare nights, Clove took Moth out by himself and those were the best of nights. Teal without Moth was a very different creature.

I had a moment during those first blood-fuelled nights. A moment when I realised there was nothing else for me but this, stretching out into eternity. I'd be forever hovering on the cusp of adulthood, one foot in either camp, straddling the great divide and fucking up the great hereafter. I had Clove, who had gifted me with this—purely for his own agenda, or the agenda of the whole vampire race as he kept telling me. I'd laughed the first time he told me, and then he'd banished me to the back of the cave where we slept, his reprimands ringing in my ears. I needed to know my station. And that was caught between a rock and a hard place, with Clove at one side and Moth and Teal, my adopted brothers, at the other. I sometimes wonder why he did it. What made me so different from any other kid he could have chosen? I'd spent my whole life running, being hunted. But now I was the hunter.

By some strange twist of fate, I had become the thing my family studied, the thing they yearned to be true. Just thinking about the life I had before hurts.

Teal was my only friend; there wasn't a bad bone in his body. He'd been the one to come and sit by me when Clove lifted his ban. He didn't need to speak; his presence was enough. How he ever ended up being a part of this was something I had yet to learn. But Moth protected him fiercely and would growl at me if I even looked in Teal's direction some nights.

Moth hates the fact that I'm stronger than he is. Clove's blood is old and powerful. I'm pure bred, whatever that means. My fangs are longer than Moth and Teal's. Sharper. And I'm faster, too. But I can't control the hunger for blood yet, because the gene in me is so strong. It seems unfair. But what has fairness had to do with any part of my life? The Before, or the Now.

I want to know Moth's story, how he got to be where he is now, his life *before*, but all he does is sneer at me and say, 'The who I was doesn't matter, all there is, is this'. But I can't agree, part of me is still the kid who went looking for the box.

Because I'm unstable, Clove took us far away from The Manor. There were too many temptations in the village for three young vampires learning to hunt. And I was glad to leave, because the thought of seeing any of them again would make me crumble. I didn't want a reminder of what had happened, of my old life.

Still, there was nothing more I wanted to do than to talk to Noah, for him to tell me that it would all be okay like he had when I was a kid. But how stupid was I? Nothing would be okay ever again, and he would hate me, be repelled by me. I couldn't stand the thought of that. Sure he'd seen the others, but it wasn't quite the same as seeing me—undead, with the need for blood branded in my veins.

In the scheme of things, knowing I'll never find love is probably insignificant. Sometimes I wish there had been time to fall for someone, to feel the thrill and ache of something so beautifully painful. To get laid. I'm lonely but I'll never admit it because it's a weakness, and I've learned that showing weakness marks a vampire, makes him an outsider. And I'm making a good enough job of that already.

I'm working on being at one with the night, a shadow of a shadow. Because sometimes I feel like the dark is my only friend.

CHAPTER TWO

This was the moment we had been waiting for.

It was late summer and dusk fell a few minutes earlier each night. The day had been hot, like the days before. A rare English heatwave. I stamped down the unease that crawled around my gut, not wanting to remember what had happened after the last one. A thin film of dust, from the track above the cave where we slept, coated my skin. I wiped my arm over my face. It was dappled in dried blood.

It was, perhaps, too close to the outside world, but a steep drop to the v-shaped valley below stopped any hikers from being too curious, and the mouth of the cave was hidden from view by an overhang of rock.

I was always the last to wake. Moth and Teal stood by the entrance, their instincts trained on something above. As the last drifts of death sleep left me, the smell of blood hit me full force. I scrambled to my feet and joined them. Saliva filled my mouth as salt and heat and blood wafted down from the path above.

Clove flowed down the rock face, a liquid shadow, his feet and hands finding invisible holds, but I knew if I concentrated hard enough I would see them too.

'A single man.'

He told us what we had been longing to hear. I pushed forward and Teal moved aside to give me space. Moth didn't even glance in my direction.

'I believe you're ready for the next step in your education.' Clove's gaze was trained on us, but I knew he was mentally evaluating any change from above.

Me? I was ready to dive in head first and think afterwards. My fangs ached in my jaw.

Clove nodded to Teal, who slipped away in a heartbeat, using the narrow sheep path that clung to the hillside, hidden from anyone above. Moth craned his head out of the entrance until Teal disappeared into the gloom. He was as eager as I was to get going, but the thought of blood was only part of it. He didn't like letting Teal out of his sight.

I climbed up to the track, following Moth, preferring to have him where I could see him. Even after nearly a year, I was sure he would get rid of me if he could. We tolerated each other, that's all I could say.

Twilight had fallen fast and the first few stars already glinted in the navy blue sky. This was moorland country and the landscape was dotted with tors, the granite outcrops from a time long before man. They ranged along the hillside, giant monoliths punctuating the heath and patches of bog. It was wild and desolate terrain. Sometimes it seemed to have no soul, especially when the north wind knifed across the heather. What better place for us to exist?

The day's heat rose from the track, the sandy surface crunching underfoot. The man was nowhere to be seen. A meagre light from a torch beam bounced on the path in the distance, but I didn't need that. I was tuned into his heartbeat.

Moth grabbed my arm. 'We keep to the plan, okay? I don't want you spoiling it for us.'

Us didn't include me. I shrugged his arm off, quickening my pace. This was the first time Clove had allowed us all out together to work as a team. I didn't want to mess it up.

The track curved up ahead at the point where a patch of blackthorn bushes clung to the edge of the cliff. We rounded the bend, keeping to the sparse grass at the edge of the path to hide our footfall. Teal's voice drifted back along the haze of heat. Moth exhaled, a deep release of relief.

Teal sat on the ground, his hands around his ankle as our meal ticket loomed over him. Late thirties, medium build, wide shouldered. He would be strong. But not strong enough. He swung his backpack off his shoulder and unzipped a compartment, producing a bottle of water, offering it to Teal. Teal's eyes flicked towards us and he groaned, easing himself onto his knees as though he was trying to stand.

Moth took up the pace. Teal's groan was all play-acting, but it had triggered something inside him. This wasn't part of the plan. We were supposed to be soundless, invisible, then take our victim down. The element of surprise. Clove had told us there was no point in taking risks, even if the kill looked easy.

Teal took the water bottle and raised it to his lips. The man gazed down at him, and his easy stance told me he didn't feel threatened. Teal played the part of a boy out walking, who had injured his ankle, like a pro. With his beach-blond surfer hair and bright eyes, he looked as if he wouldn't hurt a fly. The man looked around, his gaze towards where we were. His shoulders tensed. Then he pulled something else from his backpack.

I sensed, rather than saw, Moth flinch.

Our quarry's heartbeat quickened, sending his blood raging through his veins. The scent of it clung to the fine hairs in my nostrils, causing the built-up saliva to drool from my lips. Instinct fought with reason in that split second before reaction. I wasn't thinking about being quiet or hiding, I was thinking about that first warm rush of blood against my tongue.

My keen eyes caught a shimmer of metal in an outstretched hand. He knew something was out there. Teal offered him the water bottle back and the man studied it, a surge of salt sweat rising to his skin. Moth flicked out his tongue, tasting it.

Some primal instinct triggered inside our prey. He grabbed Teal by the arm and hauled him roughly to his feet. Sense should have told us Teal was more than capable of bringing him down, but when the blade nicked Teal's wrist, I launched myself forward, covering the remaining distance in a few seconds.

The man stared, his jaw dropping open in horror. The blade dropped to the ground. I hit him, full force, in the chest. A rush of air exploded from his lungs as his body hit the ground with a thud. I straddled him, pinning his shoulders with two hands, making sure he could see my fangs as they glistened with saliva.

I could smell the urine as it soaked into the fibres of his jeans. Teal joined me, his tongue lapping at the wound on his wrist, those blue-green eyes shimmering with anticipation. Moth stood above us. A surge of tension danced along the hunger pangs gnawing in my gut.

I didn't wait for an invitation. Little noises of terror mewled from the man's throat. His eyes were wide, his pupils dilated with shock. I tore open the neck of his shirt, mesmerised by the pulse in his throat.

Moth knelt beside me, his face inches from mine, the same hunger on his tongue. But I'd gotten first blood, that moment where the fangs slice cleanly through the skin and the salt is the first taste to hit, followed by the sweet hot gush of blood. I know I groaned, the pleasure spiralling me off into a warm, dark velvet place.

Then a hand hauled me backwards so quickly that I ended up sprawled on the floor, fresh blood dripping from my fangs.

Clove loomed over me, his face like thunder.

‡

It took me a few seconds to process what had happened.

The taste of blood hummed on my tongue, blurring out my other senses. Behind me, Moth and Teal feasted. The wet sounds of torn tissue. Teal's whimpers of pleasure.

'You were a sitting target, Gabriel.' Clove's eyes bore into my skull. 'If this was a vampire trap, you would be dead. One of you always needs to be vigilant.'

I wanted to say 'why did it have to be me?' but I knew the answer. I might be the youngest, but whatever dark gene ran in my blood, it was stronger than either of my brothers. Clove held me to that fact, something which didn't help my relationship with Moth.

The scent of new blood made my stomach turn over. I went to my knees and licked the remains from my lips. Moth raised his head, the lower half of his face stained red, and smiled. It was a smile of triumph. If it could have talked it would have said, 'fuck you, Gabriel.'

After Teal and Moth had finished, Clove gave me permission to drink. I fell upon the man's corpse even though the blood was starting to congeal. My punishment was the leftovers, like a hyena waiting for a lion to grow tired of its kill. Moth and Teal watched from Clove's side, Teal shifting uncomfortably at my humiliation.

We were all silent as we walked back. Clove had disposed of the body, tossing it over the edge of the cliff as though it meant nothing. The foxes would clear up what we had left. A twinge of remorse flared up in my gut as the body thudded against the rocks below. This man had done nothing wrong. He was simply in the wrong space at the wrong time. I should have felt more but I didn't.

Back in the cave, I sat apart from the others, scratching marks on a rock with a flint-edged stone I'd found. The action helped to stem the sting of my shame. I'd been made an example of because I had broken the rules. It shouldn't have come as a surprise. Moth got the same treatment. Only Teal seemed to get away with it, but then he never tested Clove's patience. Deep down, I knew Clove was right. We *had* been sitting targets, too caught up in the thrall of the kill to take any notice of what was happening around us.

My mind drifted back to the demon. The demon that now wore my mother's skin. I hadn't wanted to believe him when Moth told me. He'd tossed it into conversation like it was no big deal. 'Suck it up, Gabriel.' Those were his words. 'Deal with it, because one night you will have to destroy her.' My mouth filled with bitterness and I spat in the dirt.

Moth looked up and strode across, his form blocking out the view of the stars from the yawn of the cave mouth. He had the uncanny ability to judge just when I was struggling. His words could slice as easily as any knife.

'I'm not in the mood.' I banged the flint so hard against the rock a spark flew between us. Some nights I could tolerate his jibes. This wasn't one of them.

'You're too easy to bruise, Gabriel.'

I glared up at him. 'I am really not looking for a fight tonight, Moth.' But what I saw wasn't antagonism, for once, and it confused me.

'There is no going back, you know. What's in front of us? It's all we have.'

He left before I could answer, the stars swimming into view again.

I wanted to hate him. I wanted to believe there wasn't an ounce of goodness in his worm-ridden soul. But then he would floor me with a comment like that, or I would see him with Teal, and I would wonder about the boy he had once been, underneath that coat of snarkiness he wore. I wanted to get Teal alone, see if I could get him to open up about Moth's history. Maybe if I knew a little bit about it, I could cut him some slack.

Through the darkness, two blue-green eyes pin pointed me like laser beams. It was like looking into the universe and seeing galaxies spinning through time. I didn't know why they shone. But I never got tired of looking at them. It made me realise not everything that is perceived as evil is truly all bad. There are shades of black and white. I'd learned that first a year ago.

A pang of nostalgia twisted in my stomach. Did they think of me still, back at The Manor, or had they all moved on with their lives? As far as they knew, I was officially dead, killed by some freak fallout from the demon. I missed them all terribly. I don't think I'd ever stop missing them. I hadn't asked for the life I'd had back then, but it had worked out pretty much okay. Apart from my final twenty-four hours. But then I hadn't asked for *this* life. Maybe I was destined to be forever at the whim of creatures stronger than me, a marionette dangling whilst they pulled the strings and made me dance. I half laughed, and the sound echoed against the cold walls.

Moth's words came back to me: 'there is no going back.' But I wanted to. To see them all one last time. To say goodbye.

CHAPTER THREE

Noah Isaacs brushed his teeth in the small bathroom adjoining the biggest guest suite at The Manor. Although 'guest suite' wasn't really an appropriate term as he wasn't a guest anymore. Shortly after the night that had changed all of their lives, he had announced to his church committee that he was taking a sabbatical to help an old friend, which wasn't strictly untrue. What he didn't tell them was that the deaths of Beth, Ollie, and Gabe were not the only casualties. His faith had died too. What kind of a God could be so heartless as to stand back and let those horrors unfold? Their losses were a constant dark shadow. Gabe, the darkest of all.

He spat out the toothpaste and rinsed his mouth, putting his brush back into the glass where it rested against the other one.

It was late, well past midnight, but in the next wing a light shone from the window of the research room, as it probably would all night. He sighed. It didn't matter how much he tried, Edward Carver was intent on working himself to the bone in his efforts to try and find a way to beat the demon they all knew would return.

Noah had looked for Gabe's body—half hoping to find him, and half torn apart with fear at what he would do if he did. But there was only a thin trail of blood along the meadow, which ended suddenly in a darker pool. After that, all traces had vanished. Noah couldn't decide if Clove had taken Gabe to soften their loss or just because he could. Some nights, he would walk the boundaries of the house, his senses trained on any dark corner, hoping for the vampire to reappear. Here he was, a man who had been in the service of the Lord, wanting nothing more than to see something undead.

He sighed again and pulled back the crisp white sheet on the bed. Should he pray? It was a hard habit to break, but why pray when nothing was listening?

The house was so quiet. No new students had passed through the doors. Carver hadn't the heart to invite any. Noah suspected he was afraid to put anyone else in danger. The curator blamed himself, as they all did. He had been in charge, he had raged, it had been his responsibility to keep them all safe. Noah had countered that it was as much his fault as Carver's, but it fell on deaf ears. Carver was determined to flay himself with it daily.

Noah climbed into bed, picking up his book, finding the place where his bookmark rested. He read the same lines over and over, but they refused to sink in and interrupt the churning of the darkness in his mind, ebbing and flowing like a sea on the dark side of the moon.

The door swung open, then clicked shut. He looked up and smiled.

'We have to do something, Noah. Ella says he hasn't eaten since breakfast and he missed his appointment with the doctor again.' She tossed her bag onto a chair.

'Did you eat?'

'I grabbed something on the way back from the university. They asked if Carver would be able to present the award this year. I said I would ask.' Her face fell as she spoke, knowing the answer already.

'We'll try and talk some sense into him tomorrow.' He put his book on the night stand and propped himself up on the pillow with one elbow. She was perched on the edge of the bed, scrolling through her phone deftly, the light from the screen bathing her face in a white glow.

Noah pulled back the other side of the sheet, the cotton cool against his fingertips. 'It's late. Come to bed, Olivia.'

‡

Olivia Taverner stared into the darkness, listening to the gentle snores coming from Noah. His hand rested heavily on her hip but she didn't move away. She liked the solid feel of it. It anchored her to the here and now. Anything that did that, she grasped with both hands.

She tried to remember the first time she had pulled him into her bed and couldn't. It had been an organic thing, not planned or dreamt of. The simple pull of two people who were clinging to their sanity by the barest of threads. It wasn't love, or at least not for her, it was comfort. How could anyone who hadn't gone through what they had ever understand? Noah had made her face up to the fact that Ollie was gone. For weeks she had trawled the house and the cellar, sometimes in the dead of night, calling his name, talking to him, begging him to come back one last time. She wasn't ready for never seeing him again. Noah had convinced her, in the gentlest way possible, that she had to let Ollie go.

Noah murmured in his sleep and pulled her closer, his warm body spooning hers. She remembered laughing the first morning after they had fucked, teasing him without really thinking of herself, of the fact that she had probably bought a ticket to hell by sleeping with a man of the cloth. His face had paled, the scar from the crucifix still angry on his brow. She'd stopped mid laugh, her shoulders falling like the sound. That was the first time she'd let him hold her as she sobbed her heart out. They weren't all going to hell. They were already living it.

She missed Gabe too. She saw his face in her nightmares— and Clove, holding Gabe's crumpled, blood-soaked body. The house was so quiet without his footsteps thundering down the stairs or his presence at dinner. Not that they ate together much anymore. Carver frequently missed Ella's call, saying he wasn't hungry, and many nights Olivia ate with Noah in the kitchen. The housekeeper had returned to her duties a little bit after Christmas, much to her sister's dismay. Carver's explanation about the whereabouts of Gabe, Beth and Ollie had been, quite frankly, pathetic. But Ella was loyal. She didn't ask any questions, even if they lingered in her eyes.

Tom had taken to popping in unannounced and per-suading Ella to sit down, after accepting the obligatory cup of tea. How much he had told her Olivia didn't know, but whatever it was, she was grateful for Tom in so many ways. They made an unlikely alliance, the old, gruff farmer and the girl who didn't take any crap.

Olivia's mind swung back to Gabe. He had done nothing to deserve a death like that. A tear rolled down her cheek and soaked into the pillow.

Maybe if she had been quicker getting back to The Manor, it might have made a difference? She screwed her eyes up tightly, her fists mirroring the gesture. If the palm crosses had hit the box sooner, would the demon's power have been weakened enough to give Gabe and Beth a fighting chance? She shivered at the thought of Beth, who hadn't been human when she burst through the glass of the French doors. It was one of those unanswerable questions that refused to lie down, with no logical conclusion.

Noah had his own questions. But he found his solace in the bottom of a glass. She wished she could too, but alcohol depressed her and she couldn't risk going down that road. She had to keep going, for the memory of everyone they had lost. And besides, blotting out the past didn't make it any less painful when it came rushing back to greet you.

She turned over, finding a cool place on the pillow for her face, studying Noah's profile in the close dark. He was a sweet man but he had demons of his own. Maybe she was one of them? She eased forward and kissed his neck behind his ear, trailing more along his jawline. He smelled of sleep but she liked it. He groaned and opened one eye.

'Ssh.' She held one finger in front of her lips, then touched his.

He took the hint.

CHAPTER FOUR

Clove always woke long before Teal and Moth opened their eyes, shortly followed by Gabriel. He was surprised the boy came out of his death sleep so quickly. Most fledglings woke hours after their maker. It had been no whim of fancy that had led him to turn Gabriel. Not in the end. The decision had been made long before then.

He narrowed his eyes, delving back into his memories. If he chose, he could replay them all. Every single minute of every single night for as long as his dark existence. He plucked the moment, experiencing it again in the forefront of his mind. The second Gabriel came to him in his bedroom, the second Clove had touched the mark on his face and felt the warm, racing breath against his wrist. Clove's lips twisted into a grimace. He had been lying to himself then when he'd insisted all humans could be sacrificed. It's why he'd kept Gabriel close through that long night, why he'd refused to let the demon claim him, and why he had taken the limp and bloodied body away from the eyes of the others.

But his decision had not come without peril. He already had two other fledglings, adding one more to the mix only increased the possibility they would be discovered by the ones who hunted newly made vampires. The ones who believed the species should be ruled by those who carried the wisdom of time, or were threatened by the vigour of youth. He was himself pure bred, made by a descendant of a bloodline that went back centuries. There were not many of his kind left, unless they were all in hiding or too bored with any kind of interaction to ever put themselves on the radar. Gabriel now carried his blood, but that wouldn't be enough to save him if their whereabouts were discovered. The boy had not yet learnt the rudiments of his new life, and his lack of control on hunger concerned Clove. But it should have come as no surprise. Pure bred brought with it its own hardships. He would conquer it and be stronger because of his struggle.

Neither Moth nor Teal knew the real reason he had killed Sasha, the young vampire who had been part of his collective fold before Gabriel. Sasha had a rebellious streak a mile wide. Unlike Moth, who had rebelled in a way Clove could control, Sasha had been reckless, often persuading his brothers to venture out when Clove went hunting. It would have been only a matter of time before they would have got themselves noticed. Clove had taken no pleasure in killing Sasha. It was a waste of young blood, but it had been a hard lesson for Moth and Teal. They had looked at him with fear in their eyes for weeks afterwards.

He sighed and gazed out onto the sweeping moorland below. It was a clear night with a thousand stars, away from the smog of manmade light. But they would have to leave. Their kill might be discovered and they had been in this place too long.

Aka Maga's silence disturbed him on another level. He had fully expected the demon to search for them after it had grown accustomed to its new skin. It was waiting. But for what? For him to become complacent? That would not happen. He had learnt his lesson well enough the last time.

But none of them knew why he had devoted his life to keeping them safe, when it would have been so much easier to melt into the night and let them fend for themselves. Moth raged against Gabriel, the two of them butting heads as they vied for their place in this coven of sorts. Both head-strong and proud but limited by true knowledge.

The night would come when he would have to tell them that the one who was truly special was Teal.

‡

The three freshly killed rabbits dropped at their feet told Moth this was yet another moving night.

Teal scooped one from the floor and handed it to him. It was still warm, its neck broken by a flick of Clove's wrist. But after last night and the feast of human blood, it didn't look appetising. And he wasn't really all that hungry. Then he remembered human blood filled the void inside so much better. He let the rabbit dangle from one hand, aware Gabriel was stirring behind him. Moth liked the fact that he and Teal woke up first. It wasn't much, but it was a reminder to their latest brother that he still was pretty much wet behind the ears.

The sting of last night and Gabriel getting the first kill bite irritated him more than it should. But he couldn't deny that seeing him lapping away at what they had left, had been incredibly satisfying.

Clove waited for Gabriel to join them. Moth made sure he didn't even glance in Gabriel's direction. They were stuck with each other, but that didn't mean he had to like him. And he was no Sasha. He tried to put the image to rest of Sasha's scream as Clove grabbed him by the throat. Moth remembered as if it was yesterday how hard the young vampire had tried to fight, and how many nights it had taken for both he and Teal to understand that they weren't next.

'It is time to leave.' Clove interrupted his thoughts.

Moth tensed as Gabriel's shoulder brushed his.

'We're breaking our isolation. There is an acquaintance I need to speak with. We've been solitary for a long time and things have changed.'

No one ever asked why and Clove never offered a reason. Until now.

'What kind of things?' Gabriel blurted out. Moth bristled. Always fucking questions.

Clove held up his hand for silence. 'I'm not going to sugar coat anything. There is discord in our species. I can feel it on the air most nights. I have to find out why, even though it will be challenging for you. We will be visiting a town.'

Moth didn't like to be under scrutiny, but the thought of mingling with so many humans in one place was a definite one up on this hole in the rock in the middle of nowhere. His mouth watered.

Gabriel frowned, a line creasing his brow. Moth wondered how he would cope with so much temptation surrounding him. Clove wouldn't take them into a dangerous situation, but surely his newest fledgling was a ticking time bomb.

Teal had the rabbit up to his mouth, sucking the blood from a small wound in its throat. It was a meagre meal.

'Eat. We leave in minutes.' Clove stood at the mouth of the cave, his profile unmoving in the moonlight.

With a sigh, Moth ripped the belly of his rabbit open, lapping the thick blood from around the organs. Gabriel bent down to pick up the remaining rabbit. Moth spat out a chunk of wet pink tissue. It landed at the side of Gabriel's hand.

Gabriel raised his head and glared, his lips twitching, exposing a slice of white fang.

'You're going to have to control yourself once we're out in the open.' Moth couldn't help a smirk. The rabbit had suddenly developed more taste.

CHAPTER FIVE

The closeness of the small town embraced us, another world of concrete and traffic and chaos.

It had been so long since I had been anywhere with this number of people. Carver didn't like the noise and had only taken me when he had to. I thought back to the last time, a piano board certification in one of the grand old Georgian houses facing the square. But this was a different town.

A fine, warm drizzle whispered into the early evening. Clove fell into step beside me, with Moth and Teal slightly in front. I didn't miss the way Teal's gaze fell longingly on the bookstore windows. He was wearing dark sunglasses, a precaution by Clove. He didn't want any attention coming our way.

A thousand heartbeats sounded in my head and I had to grit my teeth as people swarmed past. A girl about my age, with her head bent towards her phone screen, walked into me. Her eyes darted to mine and she smiled, uttering a 'sorry' as the phone rang. I looked away quickly. Moth turned around and grinned, but it was feral.

Hunting had been meagre as we travelled, but last night we had brought down a young guy on the outskirts of the nearby city where the university stood. He had been drunk.

Too drunk even to scream. I had let Moth deliver the kill bite to try and prove to Clove that I could wait. I don't think he knew that I had driven a fang through my tongue in my struggle.

Now we were a few miles west, in the old town that nestled under the shadow of the city. This was Westport Quay, carved out of the cliff sides and out of a rich smuggling history. A quaint little slice of old England, with a seedier past she kept under wraps.

No one paid us any attention, but Clove kept us off the main streets, negotiating alleyways and cut-throughs with razor-sharp precision. He knew this place well. We all followed with blind trust. He paused as we neared the central part of the old town. The tall, Gothic spires of the cathedral punched into the night above us.

'Keep close and don't acknowledge them.'

Teal's mouth opened in surprise, but Clove had already forged on ahead. I found myself walking by Moth as the path narrowed.

'What did he mean by *them*?' My heart fluttered in my chest.

'I don't know,' Moth answered, for once not goading me.

I trained my senses all around, tuning out the background noise of traffic and people, honing my sight and hearing and smell. Right away, the heady scent of lilies drifted from over the red brick wall that surrounded the cathedral. And then I saw them, rising into the air as they too sensed us, dozens of frail wisps coming together, unmistakably people. Men, women, children. Maybe a hundred translucent forms, their arms outstretched towards us.

Moth's gasp of surprise mirrored mine and, for an instant, I halted in my tracks, unable to stop myself from looking at them. Looking through them.

'Gabriel.' Clove's sharp retort brought me back, and I ran, falling in line with Moth and Teal. I was almost glad they looked as freaked out as I felt.

Clove turned into an alleyway. 'Remember, ignore them.' He paused and added, 'hold hands.'

Teal didn't need to be told again. He was between us and slipped his hands first into Moth's and then mine. I was glad Moth hadn't been in the middle.

The ghosts or spirits or whatever else they were, hovered above us now. I could feel the weight of them even though they looked like they weighed nothing at all. And that smell. I shuddered. Funeral flowers.

Keeping Clove only a few steps in front, we walked together with hands clasped. This was the first time I'd had any real contact with another person since the night Clove made me. There were the people we killed and fed upon, but I barely felt them. This, this was different. Teal glanced towards me and smiled. Even behind his sunglasses, I swore I could almost see those beautiful eyes glinting. He might not be a very good example of a vampire in cunning, but he had won the lottery in a physical sense.

Without warning, a form dropped onto the path right in front of us, its mouth open in a silent wail. Despair flowed from it in waves. Teal hesitated and I squeezed his hand, gritting my teeth and forcing my feet forward. We walked right through it and a chill ran along my bones. I glanced over my shoulder. It had disappeared, the others with it, leaving only the cloying smell.

Clove waited under the shadow of an old gas lamp, its bright flame dancing behind the dirty glass.

'Spirits of the dead always congregate in places such as this.' Clove gestured to the brooding mass of the cathedral. 'They sense us as we sense them. But never try to engage one. They will steal your sanity.'

I swallowed a lump in my throat, hoping to see a slight twitch of a lip as he teased us. But he was deadly serious.

'But why don't they go into the light?' I was too freaked out to care if Moth glared at me for all of my questions.

'What makes you think that there *is* any light, Gabriel?'

The chill in my bones deepened. I knew there were vampires. I knew there were demons. I knew there were ghosts. But each one seemed to come with its own rule book.

At the end of the alleyway, where it widened onto the frontage of the cathedral with its vast wooden doors, people were teeming, thrust up against each other as they pushed past, never knowing this increased the heat, increased my need. I groaned softly and Teal tightened his grip on my hand.

Golden light streamed from the doorway, spilling out into the night.

Clove stopped and gestured for Moth to join him, then turned to me. 'At the other side of the cathedral, you will find a door. It will be open. It always is when they hold a service. I want you both to go in and follow the steps to your left. They will lead you down into the crypt.' It took a moment for me to realise he meant for Teal and I to go off alone. It dawned on Moth at the same time and his eyes narrowed. 'Don't be concerned. It is off limits for human use. Foundation issues. But it is safe. Wait for me there.'

'Wouldn't it be better if we all stayed together?' This time it was Moth with a question.

'Not this time, Moth. I need your presence with me.' Clove pressed his hand against Moth's shoulder and, in a moment, they had disappeared into the crowd.

'Let's get out of here,' I whispered to Teal, making my way through the throng towards the other side of the cathedral. I was still holding his hand.

‡

Moth quickened his step to keep up with Clove. The master vampire strode ahead, gaps opening in the crowd as he passed. Clove carried himself with purpose. More than a few people stared and visibly paled.

The drizzle had cleared to leave a sultry evening. All around, people were baring flesh as an invitation to bare more. Temptation met him at every corner. Their heartbeats and scent sung to him like birds.

Moth was confused. On one hand, he was happy Clove had picked him. But on the other, it left Teal alone with Gabriel. And he didn't like that. He hadn't missed the glance Teal had given Gabriel, or the way he hadn't balked at holding hands. Teal was his to protect. Something that could only be called jealousy ran alongside his happiness, turning it into a bitter void.

'Gabriel is not your enemy. We will return soon.' Moth didn't know whether Clove had read his mind or simply knew him well enough to know where his thoughts were dwelling.

'Why couldn't they come with us?' Moth tried a different version of the question he had asked only minutes before.

Clove paused at the side of a set of rusted iron railings standing on a low wall. He clasped Moth on the shoulder. 'Don't speak unless you are spoken to, and then only proceed with caution. Do not think about Teal or Gabriel. The inhabitants of this house will try and catch you unawares, but keep your mind shield locked tight.'

Moth opened his mouth to answer, but Clove had already disappeared down the stone steps leading to a basement. A weather-worn door next to a filthy window set behind bars met him. Moth wrinkled his nose. The doorway smelled of stale vomit and piss. Before Clove could knock, the door opened. It was pitch black inside and a flutter of fear danced across Moth's skin.

The figure behind the door was a young girl about Moth's age. She kept her head bowed and her long, black hair fell over her face in matted hunks. She was vampire. Moth registered the darkness in her, then withdrew his probing and slid his mental gate into place. It didn't come easy to him, but he could manage it as long as he concentrated and didn't let his mind wander.

The girl led them through a narrow corridor, faded wallpaper hanging from the walls in mouldy ribbons. It was a foul place, imbued with the scent of death. Moth shivered. He was following Clove so closely that he might as well have been a shadow. Up ahead, a light pressed out through a crack under a door. The girl pointed at the door then melted almost apologetically into the gloom.

Moth's heart began a rapid dance, and he swallowed as if the act of doing so might steady the beat. Clove stopped and Moth saw his shoulders drop a couple of inches. He raised his fist and banged on the door. One loud rap that echoed down the corridor they had just come from.

The door swung open and Moth was met by a blinding light.

CHAPTER SIX

He hadn't changed in over a hundred years. The figure sat at the far end of the room, a canopy of worn red velvet above his head. It shielded him from the glare of the photographer's lamp, which bathed the rest of the room in a harsh white glow. Emron D'Grey had never liked making unannounced guests feel welcome.

Clove sensed Moth shrink back against the glare. He knew it would be pricking the light-sensitive cornea at the back of a vampire's eyes. It was meant to simulate daylight. And the fact that D'Grey was always in control.

'My old friend, come closer!' The figure stood and the tails of a ringmaster's coat trailed from the chair. 'Clove, you old dog. Nice of you to call.' He opened his arms as if he were conducting a choir.

'Master D'Grey.' Clove strode forward, letting the man clasp him in a bear hug. It was like being caught in a vice. Waves of cloying incense assaulted his sense of smell and Clove lowered his breathing rate.

'And who do we have here?' D'Grey's attention swept to Moth, who was trying to be as inconspicuous as he could, despite being caught in the searchlight. 'I heard you had been fucking around, Clove.' D'Grey's laugh was like the bark of a fox.

'This is Moth.' Clove released himself from the grasp and beckoned the young vampire forward. 'He is not of my blood.'

'A pity. You have such fine blood, if I recall.' D'Grey winked at him. Clove swallowed down the taste of revulsion.

D'Grey's gaze caught Moth in a stare that had weakened far stronger vampires. Clove gritted his teeth and hoped Moth had taken his instruction to heart.

D'Grey pushed his face right in front of Moth's. Then, with a quicksilver movement, he raised Moth's upper lip as if he was ageing a horse. 'Ha. I see you speak the truth. Not much in the slicing department there. But he has uniquely pretty eyes for one not pure. Odd, but pretty. Does he warm your bed well?'

Clove's mouth curved into what he hoped would pass for a smile. 'I wouldn't know. I don't indulge now. As you undoubtedly know.'

'You're missing death's greatest pleasure, spice master. Apart from the blood. Combine them both and it's well worth the price of selling your soul.' He licked his lips and grinned, showing the curve of an impressive fang. 'If you ever want to loan your Moth out, I'd be pleased to pin him to my bed.'

'I thank you for your interest.' Clove bowed his head a fraction.

'Oh, you're bored of the playing. Such a shame.' D'Grey's eyes narrowed and he sighed like a petulant child. 'I assume your presence means you want to know the latest news on the vampire grape vine?'

Clove inclined his head towards the seating under the canopy. 'May we?'

'Of course, my old friend. Get comfortable. Your boy can sit at your feet. But first, refreshments, yes?'

D'Grey clapped his hands and two figures appeared from the shadows in an instant. Two young vampires, a girl with skin the colour of soft caramel and a boy, his long blond hair caught in dreadlocks. They were both naked, their flesh covered in bite marks. Clove knew D'Grey's preferences. He had always kept a small harem of freshly made fledglings to feast on. Their skin healed slowly; he liked to see the marks he had made.

Moth sat at Clove's feet, unmoving and no doubt terrified. Afterwards he would be owed an explanation. A vibration played along Clove's finely tuned senses, an insect on his web. He caught it and silenced it in a split second. *Not now.*

The young girl knelt at his feet, brushing against Moth. Her eyes stared at the floor as she offered Clove both wrists, her fingers curled into her palms. D'Grey always played this game of cat and mouse. If you didn't follow the rules, you would leave empty handed. Or not leave at all.

Clove gripped one of the girl's wrists. A blue vein throbbed just under the surface and his mouth watered despite his revulsion at the circumstances. He pulled her onto his lap, spinning her around as if she were a doll, then swept back her hair. She arched her neck like a broken flower. His fangs pierced her skin and she gasped, her blood sweet and tinged with opium.

Over her shoulder, D'Grey feasted on the boy, licking his skin, the crook of an elbow, the soft flesh at the base of a thumb, before settling for the inside of a thigh. The boy tensed in pain and whimpered.

Moth sat like a statue. But Clove knew he was imagining himself caught in that grip.

CHAPTER SEVEN

Stone cold. You never really think of it as literal until you're surrounded by it, or next to a vampire who hasn't fed.

We'd gone deep into the crypt, which ran in a north-south direction, the arched brick roof gradually dipping lower and lower. Dim safety lighting made the journey a little less foreboding. But it wasn't the dark I was scared of.

What would I do if we came across anyone down here?

Teal had let me lead, trusting me to pick a spot that I thought looked safe. It amazed me how he gave me his faith. Or maybe it was because he was the polar opposite of Moth that I felt it so much. I paused as the crypt branched off in two directions, each disappearing into the gloom. Under the guard of the intersection sat a huge white tomb, the effigy of a knight carved from marble on the top. The knight's features had blurred with time, but his bones were still remembered. I shivered and Teal pulled me down to the shelter of the tombside. Behind it, a set of well-worn steps led up to a thin door and for a moment, I was back at The Manor. I swept the thought away.

'Do you think Clove and Moth will be okay?' Teal's voice was a whisper, but it seemed to echo in the stillness. Water dripped from the curved roof of an alcove.

'They'll be fine.' I raised a smile I didn't quite feel, and wondered why I'd lied. Then it hit me: I wanted to protect him, just as Moth did. There was something about Teal that just made you want to keep him safe.

'He doesn't mean to be so...' Teal paused and pursed his lips. '...difficult, you know.'

'Clove or Moth?' I laughed, but knew immediately who the 'he' was.

Up above, a church organ stuttered into life and we both looked up as one, listening as the sound of singing followed.

'It's beautiful.' Teal's eyes glowed softly.

I stopped myself from gaping by continuing the conversation. 'I don't know what I did to make Moth hate me so much.' I tried to sound nonchalant.

'Oh, he doesn't hate you.' Teal turned his still-rapt expression towards me. 'I think he's just scared of making another attachment.' The sound from above reached a soaring crescendo as the organ boomed out a final verse. Teal waited until it had finished, lost in the grace of it all. I don't know how he did it. Finding light in darkness. That was pure magic.

'He's lost a lot of people. And he blames himself for most of it. He was devastated when we lost Sasha.'

I'd heard the name dropped into hushed conversations. I grabbed the opportunity to ask.

'What happened to Sasha, anyway?'

'Clove killed him. For breaking the rules.' Teal clasped his hands together and raised them to his mouth. He stared out at a space on the dusty floor.

'Jesus.' Whatever I'd expected, it wasn't that.

The slow dripping of the water ceased. The sound from above gone. Nothing moved, not even the air around us.

And that's when I felt it. A shift in the atmosphere at the entrance to the crypt. A split second later, Teal grasped it too, and his wide-eyed look of fear pierced through me like an arrow. I held one finger to my lips and concentrated, quietly drawing my mental shield around me like a cloak. All of those hours with Clove demanding that I try again, suddenly slipped into place.

The safety lighting died.

I peered around the side of the tomb, the stone like ice against my cheek. In the depth of the shadows, the barest flicker of movement. I froze in place. Teal glued himself to my side and I reached back to touch his arm. I hadn't taken my eyes off the spot where I'd seen the movement, and it shimmered again, this time halfway down the crypt. I wasn't stupid. This wasn't a fight I could win.

I grabbed Teal's wrist and tensed, hoping it would give him a signal. Out of the corner of my eye, the light changed at the side of one of the stone pillars. I was fast. This was time to see if I was fast enough.

Leaping up with Teal at my side, I sprinted up the stone steps and barged, full force, against the door. It shattered, splinters of old wood hitting me in the face, and I put my other arm up to shield Teal. I didn't know what was behind it, but I'd take my chance.

CHAPTER EIGHT

Edward Carver was alone at The Manor. Although that wasn't strictly true, as Ella had gone to bed and was sleeping soundly. Light snores drifted from her bedroom as he went past. He wouldn't see her until the morning, and that was good. Shame stabbed his conscience. They had nearly lost her a year ago and here he was, quite happy he didn't have to make small talk. He must be a terrible man. But then, he knew he was. When it had come down to the wire, he had failed. The weight of that failure dragged him along, through every day and every night. It shackled him like a tombstone. But he wasn't the one who was dead.

He hitched up his trousers. The belt was on the tightest hole and he sighed. He knew he'd lost a lot of weight but he had no appetite—at least, not for food. If he was forced to share with the others, he made what he hoped was the right conversation as he pushed the food around his plate. Ella fussed over him like the mother hen she was, but he didn't deserve any fuss.

The house was deathly quiet, as though it, too, was mourning. Only the *tick tock* of the great clock marking the passing of time. He checked his watch as he passed by and sighed again. It was losing time. He stopped the pendulum and turned the regulator nut, then moved the hands forward a couple of minutes, and swung the pendulum back into action. Lost time. The story of his life since that night.

Part of him was glad Noah and Olivia were gone, too. He knew they worried about him and that only increased the guilt. They both had enough to deal with. It was Olivia's birthday weekend, the first since Ollie had gone, and Noah had whisked her away, no doubt to try and take her mind from the loss of her twin, and the other birthday that was sure to be on her mind. They had tagged the trip onto a few professional engagements in the area, or rather Noah had. That way Olivia couldn't really refuse. Carver knew they were sleeping together, and it should have bothered him. But who was he to judge where people found their solace?

A sudden pain flared in his stomach and he winced. He should go get it checked out, but it was probably only years of drinking neat whiskey. And he didn't want to go down into the village. People asked questions and he couldn't deal with those. Not when he had more important things to do. Maybe just one drink would be okay? It would settle his nerves and he had a long night ahead.

Over the last week, he had followed numerous bread-crumb trails in his attempt to find out more about what had happened a year ago. And now, finally, one of those trails had borne fruit. But it wasn't about the demon. It was about the vampires.

Once downstairs, he hovered in the entrance to different rooms—the kitchen, the parlour, the White Room. Too many ghosts in all of them. They pressed against him, their silence its own accusation. He went into the parlour long enough to pour himself a stiff measure of whiskey. Then he retraced his steps and disappeared behind the door marked 'research'. It had a more professional decor, with its clean lines and muted colouring, designed to instil a work ethic in the many students who had passed through. But none had, not for a year. He couldn't possibly risk any more young lives. His heart didn't want to teach. It wanted knowledge.

The laptop whirred into life from its sleep mode, the pages from yesterday still in the browser. He took a sip from his glass. The amber liquid burned as it hit his throat and he slid a finger under his collar. It was still a surprise to find it open. He hadn't worn a tie since…he frowned, dark thoughts hovering.

He clicked into a page from an undated early paranormal study book. The text was dry and written by a mind afraid of being judged with the words it had penned. But back then, you were either a devil worshipper or one card from crazy, and both could get you locked away. He opened the book by his side and prepared for a long night of cross-reference.

If his mind was occupied, it couldn't go back to that night. It couldn't relive the mistakes he had made.

CHAPTER NINE

Moth's hunger raged in his belly like a living thing, the scent of fresh blood cramping his stomach. But he kept his eyes fixed on a spot on the floor, a knot in the wooden boards criss-crossing the room. He counted to a hundred, then back again, curled up at Clove's feet like a lap dog.

At any other time, he would have been humiliated, but right now all he felt was terror. It didn't mix nicely with his need for blood. He wanted to be anywhere else but here. Even with Gabriel. As soon as the thought hit his mind, he quenched it, darting his gaze in D'Grey's direction, but the vampire was too involved in lapping a thin trail of blood as it ran down the boy's inner thigh.

If these were the kind of activities other vampires got up to, Moth didn't want to know. All of a sudden, the cloistered upbringing Clove had provided him seemed to be the most comfortable place on earth. He didn't know much about his species. His maker had literally grabbed him off the street one night. A night when Moth should have been at home. A night he had slipped out, instead, for fun. Fun had left him for dead in an abandoned warehouse, bloody and stinking and desperate. *Don't think. Don't think.* A small voice in his head floated over his thoughts. He buried them.

'Enough.' Clove pushed the girl away and she padded across the floor, smudges of blood marking her breasts and neck. She kept to the edges of the room, avoiding the harsh glare from the lamp.

'Oh, spice master. I was just getting started.' D'Grey pouted like a small child, his lips pulling his skin tight against his cheekbones.

Moth shivered and Clove pressed his knee against Moth's shoulder gently. The naked boy slinked off into the shadows, bent over in pain.

'Does your pup stay?'

Moth found himself under scrutiny again.

'Yes. I am instructing him. He can be trusted. And if he betrays me he knows the consequences well.' Clove's voice was steady and measured, as if he were tasting each syllable before it fell from his tongue.

D'Grey made a small sound, somewhere between a sigh and a growl. Moth stiffened, his muscles taut for flight.

'I assume you've picked up that there is restlessness? Of course you have. That is why you are here. The spice master doesn't make social calls, after all.' Moth caught the trace of bitterness in his tone. 'Apparently, there is a need to track down any vampire which carries the mutation. Frankly, I didn't think any existed anymore after the last cleanse, but who are we to question the rules, my old friend?'

Clove was silent and Moth half wished he could see his expression. This was a game. But the vampire in the ring-master's coat was the beast, not the trainer.

'So,' Moth heard the sandpaper sound of skin against skin as D'Grey rubbed his palms together. 'The Hunters are out in most vampire-populated places on the globe, working their way through clusters. They are using their search to weed out any weak strains of blood and eliminate them, which I'm all for. Far too many runts roaming the streets, creating mayhem and spawning their own bastards. Not that I'm against a little mayhem.' He laughed lazily.

'Ah.' Clove finally spoke up. 'I see now why the air has been charged with discontent. Vampire blood spilled, runt or not, is always felt.'

'It has been quite ruthless, I have heard. All since a new vampire started poking around in the soft belly of the council.'

'A new vampire?'

'So many questions. Do you know more than you are letting on, spice master?' D'Grey clucked his tongue against the roof of his mouth. Moth glanced up.

'Only curious.' Clove inclined his head slightly, his hands clasped as if in prayer. 'I have been away for a long time, and, as you well know, an informed vampire is a vampire who survives. Your ear to the ground has always been'—Clove paused, and Moth held his breath—'exemplary.'

Moth knew he was party to what he had only heard about in whispers: A rally between two masters, where words replaced weapons and were sharper than swords.

'Touché. All I know is this infiltrator has raised many issues long buried. I have no idea if there is an ulterior motive behind the action.'

If Moth had to guess, he would have said D'Grey was lying, but it was only a feeling. The expression on his face hadn't changed, the tone of his voice didn't falter. D'Grey's pale eyes wheeled to Moth's face, fixing him with a predator's stare.

'I believe your boy needs to feed, spice master. Either that or he is up past his bedtime.'

Moth withered like a plant left out in the sun. Clove hauled him to his feet.

'Yes, indeed. And we don't want to take up more of your valuable time. You have been gracious in sharing with us.'

Moth stayed rooted to the spot whilst Clove and D'Grey embraced, stiffly, cautiously, like a lion would with a tiger.

Clove strode towards the door, passing through the searchlight as though it was a candle flicker. Moth followed on legs that couldn't get to the door quickly enough.

‡

Clove and Moth left the basement as a fine drizzle swept in from the south. Clove could taste autumn on his lips.

Moth stayed silent, which he was grateful for. He needed to collect his thoughts. Emron D'Grey was not a friend, but the type of acquaintance you kept close, always aware he might strike and bite you if his venomous feathers were ruffled. Taking Moth there had been a risk, but Clove had to be seen with a fledgling. News was already out that he travelled with at least one, and the more he tried to keep to the shadows, the more others would seek him out.

Clove stopped and probed the darkness. They hadn't been followed, but that didn't mean they were safe. This was not their territory. Vampires, like wolves, guard their space, sometimes to the death.

The crowds had thinned. People cloistered in restaurants or bars or simply stood in groups, enjoying the last of the late evening's warmth before autumn danced in. Even the light drizzle did not seem to faze them.

He glanced at Moth, who walked close to his side, his head bowed and his hands thrust into his jacket pockets. It had been a baptism of fire for him, and Clove regretted not preparing him more fully, but really how could one prepare for a force like D'Grey? Clove had kept his fledglings away from any scrutiny for a reason, but it hadn't made them worldly wise to the politics of the race they had been drawn into. And D'Grey had confirmed what he had feared: The hunters were out, and they carried no compassion. Still, Moth deserved an explanation—even if the finer details were left unsaid. If Gabriel had been here, the questions would have been relentless. A twinge of unease stirred in his gut. Leaving Gabriel and Teal had been a huge risk, but taking them had not been an option.

'I apologise for what went on back there. I know it wasn't fair not to warn you. Ask what you need to know.'

Moth stared up at him with wide, confused eyes. For a killer, there was still some innocence there.

'All that about hunters and mutations and cleansing.' Moth's words came out quickly, fuelled by fear. 'Are we all in danger? I mean, me and Teal and Gabriel?' He paused and glanced over his shoulder. 'And who is D'Grey, some kind of authority?'

Clove half smiled. 'D'Grey would like to think that he *is* The Authority, but he is self-made. And dangerous. Moth, don't ever underestimate him. He has many ears to the ground and many followers who fall over themselves to carry juicy little snippets of information his way. And he doesn't always tell the absolute truth, as you picked up

45

on.' Moth lowered his eyes as he always did when faced with heightened self-consciousness. 'You did well to sense it, but not to show you knew. Lies and truths. Power and corruption. These are not strictly human things. Sadly.'

He watched as Moth absorbed the information. The young vampire's mouth twisted into a knot of wondering.

'I will not lie. You asked if you are in danger, and it could be true. Your maker was weak. Your powers are limited. Although the perception you showed back there surprised me. We need to hone that.' He smiled, and this time it was genuine. It was hard for him, this nurturing, walking the fine line between encouragement and discipline. 'Gabriel is safe. You know he has my blood and is pure bred.'

Moth's lips set into a hard line and a dark shadow passed across his eyes. 'What about Teal?'

Clove wanted to gloss over his question, wanted to try to keep the circumstances secret for a little longer. But secrets had a habit of coming back to burn you. He slipped his arm around Moth's shoulders, the fragility of the bones apparent, despite the vampire spirit.

'Teal is who they are looking for, Moth. He has the mutation.'

CHAPTER TEN

We fell through the old door together, the noise clattering in my ears, and my senses spiralling into overdrive at what we might find at the other side. I prayed there was another exit close by so we wouldn't have to push our way through a throng of people, whose attention was sure to swivel to us straight away. Teal no longer had mats in his hair, but we still looked half wild and socially unacceptable.

The unforgiving stone floor jarred my knees, but I was on my feet again in an instant, Teal's fingers clinging to mine. I didn't risk looking back. We were in some kind of ante corridor with small, arched windows lining one wall. The soft glow of floor lighting stretched up ahead to a set of larger double doors. From behind those doors came applause, its echo bouncing down towards us like a rubber ball.

Teal suddenly jerked backwards, and I spun to see an arm reaching through where the door had been, grasping his ankle. I didn't stop to think. I grabbed the edge of a console table set against the wall and sent it crashing behind Teal. The full force of it landed on the outstretched limb. Bones splintered, followed by a scream of rage. Teal's face was paler than any vampire's should ever be.

The applause rose again and Teal hesitated.

Trust me, I mouthed at the same time as I set off at a run. He was my shadow and a strange thrill passed through me. God, please make those doors be open. If they weren't, we'd have to break through and that didn't bear thinking about. My feet skidded on the mosaic edging as we came to a halt, and I grabbed for the iron ring handle. I pulled and it gave with a soft creak. The smell of beeswax and old paper hit me right between the eyes. And the smell of blood, ripe and hot and racing. Teal groaned and I pressed close to him, only then daring to look back down the corridor. It was empty.

The vast stretch of the cathedral yawned open in front of us. Nearly every seat was full. At the far end, a women's voice rang out, amplified by a microphone. She was nervous. If I concentrated hard, I could pick up her racing heartbeat. A large photograph of a man stood at the end of the aisle, distinguished looking, glasses, thinning hair.

'It's a memorial service,' I whispered to Teal. 'Must have been someone very popular. The place is packed.'

It was unbearably hot and the air too full of tempting scents. A few people fanned themselves with their programmes, and somewhere further down a baby cried.

No one had paid us much attention as we entered. Teal stayed close to my side, his fingers twirling a lock of hair. I stopped at the base of one of the wide stone pillars, glad to be partly shielded from any prying eyes.

'Who were those vampires?' Teal's eyes were wide and bright. Somewhere along the line he had lost his sunglasses.

I shook my head. 'I've no idea. But they came out of nowhere.'

'Clove said we'd be safe here.'

My heart broke a little bit for him. He sounded like a child who had been let down by someone he trusted.

'He wouldn't have knowingly sent us in somewhere dangerous, would he?' I kept my tone light, despite my nerves. 'Come on, the main doors are over there. We can sneak out and keep watch for Clove and Moth.'

We crept behind the back row pews and a small child turned to look at us. She had blond hair that was doing its best to escape the ribbon tying it back. She regarded us solemnly. In her hand was a plastic dinosaur.

'Rawrr!' Her voice was shrill for such a little kid.

The woman at her side shushed her as everyone rose in a rustle of clothes to sing another hymn.

'Look at that boy's eyes, Mummy. They're all shiny.'

Out of the mouths of babes.

'Don't be rude, Alicia.' The woman took her hand and thrust the hymn sheet under the child's nose. She looked back forlornly, the dinosaur abandoned on the back of the pew. At least she hadn't screamed. We didn't look exactly inviting.

A security guard stood by the huge entrance doors. He was stocky and sweating and quite obviously bored out of his skull. His finger kept running under the collar of his white shirt and a sheen of sweat coated his face. He turned to look at us as we drew close.

'Keep your head down,' I hissed at Teal.

With one arm slung around his shoulder, I tried to fake a friendly smile. This was the first time I'd had contact with anyone human that didn't end up as a meal.

'It's too fucking hot in here.' I attempted to swagger, hoping he would be glad to see the back of us.

For a long time, he looked us up and down, tapping his fingers against the walkie talkie strapped to his waist. Just as I was sure that he was going to stop us, he swung open one of the doors. The air that drifted in was cool and smelled of salt.

'Stupid night to have a service,' he said. A trickle of sweat ran down behind his ear. 'You get your mate outside. I don't want him throwing up in here.'

The walkie-talkie crackled and a tinny voice sounded out. He gestured to the door with an impatient wave of his hand then walked to the side of the other pillar to answer.

Relief flooded into my limbs. But it soon turned to ice.

Beyond the doors, beside the railings that surrounded the park, was another vampire. His eyes met mine and drilled into my thoughts. I slammed down my mental shield, but could still feel the aftermath of the probing.

Teal and I turned on the spot and slid back into the heat and the humanity of the cathedral. We had no choice but to wait it out and hope this service droned on for hours. The vampire outside wouldn't come in for us, I knew that. But at some point we had to leave, and I was kidding myself if I thought he would give up and walk away. I needed Clove, but I wasn't skilled enough to call him without breaking my shield.

'Did he try and get into your head?' Teal kept looking back to the door, but he didn't appear under any kind of assault.

'I don't ever feel other vampires like that.' He smiled, but there was sadness in his eyes. 'I guess it's just another one of my failings.'

'Don't knock it.' My head ached, as though someone was tightening a metal band around it. 'Right now, that's no weakness.'

I knew, now, why Clove had kept us all hidden away for months. We wouldn't have lasted long if we'd been thrown into this any earlier. I didn't know *why* we were being hunted; we weren't much of a threat to any other night walker.

Teal closed his eyes as we stood in the shadow of the pillar. The stifling air was full of the scent of blood and saliva built in my mouth. I had to keep swallowing. Last night's kill was a distant memory, and my focus always drifted when hunger opened its jaws.

During those first few months when everything hurt, when the darkness consisted of one long craving for blood, I'd kept myself sane by imagining how I could get away. Anything had to be better than this existence. Even death. But maybe I had been kidding myself. I'd been glad enough to take a second chance.

How easy would it be to slip away now? Teal couldn't stop me. I could be miles away by the time Clove got back. And I wouldn't have to put up with Moth's sneering and contempt ever again.

The hymn finished and a young woman began to play a haunting melody on a violin. Teal's mouth fell slightly open and his features relaxed. Despite the hole we had found ourselves in, he had discovered beauty.

I couldn't leave him. But could I ask him to come with me?

CHAPTER ELEVEN

Moth felt as if someone had sucked all the bones out of his body.

Clove's bombshell had rocked him to the core, but he didn't get a chance to ask any more questions. As they rounded the corner, two streets back from the cathedral, Clove told him to be on guard. No talking. No thinking beyond the scope of his brain's perimeter. He wasn't sure how good he'd be at that last one, but after the visit to D'Grey he was wise enough to realise that events might be about to go to shit fast. Just like the night when Gabriel had joined their family. He hunched his shoulders and quickened his pace to keep up with Clove.

Trouble followed Gabriel around. That fact wasn't up for debate, and even though he knew leaving Teal and Gabriel back at the cathedral had been the right call for Clove to make, something unpleasant prickled along the lines of his conscience: Jealousy. He wasn't proud of it, but it was part of his make up so he was damned if he was going to apologise for it. Teal was his to protect. He couldn't fail him. Moth had failed far too many people in his life.

Still, it would take a fool not to notice that Gabriel and Teal enjoyed each other's company. The nights Clove picked

Moth to go on a solo hunt should have made him feel important, but there was always that thought, that worry. What if
Teal confided something to Gabriel that Moth didn't know
about? They had both come from fine things. Gabriel understood Teal's eye for beauty, they had read the same books,
moved in the same upper-class circle of privilege. Moth was
the kid who fell off the radar. The one whose absence from
class made teachers breathe a sigh of relief. The small child
who stole food from shops in order to put a meal before
his mother.

Dark thoughts matched his mood, but helped him keep
the news about Teal buried. Just about.

He slowed as the side door to the crypt appeared, but
Clove swept right by without giving it a second glance. The
master vampire's face showed no emotion. It was set in stone.

The area in front of the cathedral was quieter than earlier.
A man sat on the steps leading to the door with a guitar
on his lap. A small dog sat at his side. It wore a red spotted neckerchief and slunk back against the man's body as
Clove and Moth drew closer. Two young women, dressed
in summer white with bad fake tans, looked Clove up and
down as he passed. One took her friend's arm and pulled
her towards the gate to the park.

From inside the cathedral came the strain of a single
violin.

'What's wrong?' Moth risked a question. He dug his fingernails into his palms.

'Another vampire is close. And not the kind you want
to run into.'

Moth bit his tongue before his lips could say what he
was thinking: he had hoped never to meet another vampire,

because they were all pretty fucking scary. He had learnt tonight that he and Teal and Gabriel were tiny, insignificant wheels in the vampire machine.

'What did you mean about the—' Clove cut him off with a single look.

'Not here. Not now. And not a word to the others until I say so.'

Moth reeled. How was he supposed to act as if his world hadn't caved in?

'Come. We will collect your brothers and find somewhere away from prying senses.'

Moth followed Clove back to the side door. His nerves were jumpy, rubbed raw by the events of the night.

As they went down into the crypt, the air was cooler. Moth tasted it on his tongue. Stone and cold and age. He was grateful for the anchor.

Clove stopped at the far end of the long chamber. His fingers swept over the edge of a large white tomb. Moth glanced around. Teal and Gabriel were doing a damn good job of hiding away. Then his eyes fell upon the smashed door, the splinters of wood littering the steps, and his heart dropped into his stomach.

‡

Even though the strains of the violin had finished a few minutes ago, I swore Teal could still hear them. His face was upturned, his lips slightly parted, studying the vast arched ceiling of the cathedral with its theatre of angels and gargoyles. Good versus evil, light against the dark. This was the wheel the whole world turned on, my old world and the new.

Should I ask him now about running with me? I wondered how I'd feel if he said no. I'd have to do it then, with or without him, because if Clove ever found out...I shivered, the image of Sasha in my head. Not that I thought Teal would tell, but Clove had an unnerving knack of knowing without asking.

The woman at the front of the cathedral stopped talking, and a burst of applause began, slow at first, but soon everyone picked up on the energy. People started shuffling, some looked around sheepishly, as if they didn't want to be the first person on their row to make a move.

Teal lowered his head, his hair hiding his face, and stared at the embroidery on a purple hassock on the back of a pew.

We had two choices: Stay until everyone had gone, and hide, or mingle in the crowd as it left. I chose the latter; even in here, we were prey. I didn't like the feel of that on my tongue. But as the congregation stirred and went about gathering their belongings, and offering sympathetic handshakes to the family, the air became charged with the vibration of heartbeats and the salt-copper tang of blood.

We'd held it together pretty well so far, but this was raising the temptation. Maybe we could slip out and follow someone down the alley that ran past the graveyard? But I knew we couldn't pull off a public kill, and there was a chance we'd meet up with the ghosts again. I chewed my bottom lip in frustration.

People began filing past, most too caught up in their own bubble, but a few glanced our way. Clove had made sure we all found cleanish clothes before we got here, and Teal's hair was no longer filled with bits from where he had slept. But still, I knew we looked different, probably nothing anyone could put a finger on, but enough to warrant attention. I wished I'd picked up a phone somewhere. At least then I'd fit right in.

I turned my back to the throng and leant against the pillar, keeping Teal at my side. Bored nonchalance was the vibe I was going for.

Over the hum of conversation, a man's laugh rang out. People turned to stare. Shock paralysed my limbs as Teal spun around to look over my shoulder. I knew that sound.

'What else could I say when she asked me if I'd known him well?'

'Maybe saying you remembered the scandal about his mistress wasn't the best thing to say to his wife.' The male voice shook with suppressed laughter.

'Ex-wife.'

It was a perfect comeback. And a voice I had heard frequently.

Teal put his hand on my shoulder. I concentrated on the weight of it over the sound of conversation between Noah and Olivia.

As the last few people trickled through the door, I risked a glance back. How many nights had I wished to see them again? And now that I had the chance, I found myself rooted to the spot and struck dumb. I swiped at the corner of my eyes with my thumb, tried to swallow the choking sadness.

'Come on.' Teal tugged at my sleeve and dragged me over to the doorway. In the shock, I'd forgotten about my plan, and this time Teal took the initiative.

I scanned for any signs of the vampire, but he had either moved or was too clever for my probing. Both possibilities scared me.

Something growled at my ankle, and I looked down to see a dog with a red spotted neckerchief. Its hackles were raised.

'Gabe!' The familiar voice sliced through me like a spear. Only my name, but that one word filled with shock and hope and longing.

A group of people swarmed in front of us, led by a tour guide with a clipboard and a pink umbrella—despite the fact it wasn't now raining. He droned on about the history of the cathedral door, and I tuned in as my feet remained glued to the concrete.

A firm hand grabbed me by the arm. I looked up at my maker. Saw him through a haze of unshed tears.

I thought I heard my name again as Clove ushered us down into the evening bar crowd, away from Noah and Olivia. But part of the old Gabriel Davenport stayed there.

CHAPTER TWELVE

Noah Isaacs sat at the bar in the crowded restaurant. All around him, people were talking and laughing, but he barely heard them. He picked at the damp label on his bottle of beer. At his side was an empty bar stool people kept trying to sneak away without asking.

The occupant of the seat had gone to wheedle a table, even though the woman at the door had told them there wouldn't be one for hours. He had no doubt she would accomplish her mission. Olivia Taverner was a force of nature, and unlike any other woman he had ever met. It had been hard for him to accept that the same young girl who had arrived at The Manor five years ago, was now the woman who shared his bed. She didn't ask any more from him than that, and he partly wondered if she was using him as the only port in the storm of her grief-fuelled memories. But wasn't he doing the same? It was possible what they were doing was wrong in so many ways, but life was short. He sighed, pressing his lips together in a thin line as his nails scratched away at the label.

For once, his relationship with Olivia wasn't at the fore-front of his mind. He tried to recall every detail of the boy outside the cathedral, but it had only been a fleeting glimpse before that bloody tour guide with the pink umbrella had interrupted his view. Same height, same build, dark hair. Like seventy percent of the boys in this town. But there was something about the set of his shoulders, the way one hunched up a little more than the other. Gabe had done that when he was chewing over something. And the boy he was with—blond hair, like Teal. True, it looked a bit tidier but maybe…

A hand sneaked out from behind him and grabbed the edge of the stool. Noah planted his own on top of it and wheeled around. The man took one look at Noah's face, and muttered some kind of an apology. Somewhere amidst the minefield of the past year, Noah had grown a pair of balls. Being with Olivia had more benefits than simple sex.

The common sense part of his brain told him he had been seeing things. It was only a boy who looked similar to Gabe. He had seen how badly injured Gabe had been—there was no way he could have survived those injuries and that blood loss. Unless…he shivered. No, surely not that.

A hand touched his shoulder and light fingers walked across his back. Olivia perched herself back onto her seat, pulling her hair over one shoulder.

'Table for two in half an hour.' With any other person, it would have held a ring of triumph, but with Olivia it was simply a matter-of-fact comment.

'Show off.' Noah grinned.

'Please remind me to tell Carver that he owes us two hours of our lives. That service had to be the most boring thing I've sat through in a long time. No wonder he didn't want to come himself.'

But they both knew the real reason was because Edward Carver rarely left the confines of The Manor anymore. He had made it his own personal prison, hell bent on finding anything that could help him figure out a way to kill the demon that had taken so much from all of them. There had been nothing to suggest it would return, but if it did, he was going to make sure it didn't leave again.

Noah took a long sip of his beer. It was cold, slipping down his throat in a welcome stream. 'We couldn't really decline, not with Carver working with Rice on their research paper. It would have looked odd if no one had turned up.'

'We're getting really good at playing proxy, Noah. But you know, at some point, people are going to start asking questions.' She caught the bartender's eye with a flick of her wrist, the chain of her silver bracelet catching the light from above. The bartender sidled over and gave her his full attention. And a come-on look. She pointed to her empty bottle and held up two fingers, then linked her arm through Noah's.

The bartender's eyes flicked across and immediately dropped. Noah's scar had faded, but it was still evident. It made him uncomfortable when people noticed it, and he had to fight the childish need to try and explain it away.

Olivia's hand settled into his. She knew him better than anyone ever had. Even Gabe.

'Talk.' She slid the new bottle of beer over to him, ignoring the sidelong glance from the bartender.

'That boy. I'm sure it was Gabe. I know you think I'm crazy. *I* think I'm crazy. What if it was our only chance to find him?'

‡

Olivia listened as Noah talked, letting him unburden himself as he had done for her through all those dark months. She watched the way his Adam's apple moved in his throat as he sipped his beer, the way he tugged at his hair to make sure it was half covering his forehead. Five years ago, she had thought age brought reassurance, that somehow time gave you clarity and knowledge, but now she knew years only gave you more fucked-up baggage.

'You think I'm insane, don't you?' He downed the contents of the bottle like a pro.

'Not insane, no.' She contemplated whether this was the time for support or tough love. 'Remember what it was like those first few months?' He glanced at her and nodded, his eyes clouding with pain. 'You were the one who told me we can't bring back the past, no matter how much we want to. You know how much I longed to see Ollie again, but you made me understand that no matter how much I wished for it, I couldn't have it.' She played with the single charm on her bracelet, two hands linked in unity. Noah had bought it for her. 'I just think you're hurting, and you thought you saw Gabe.'

He pursed his lips and raised his hand to the bartender.

Olivia made a split-second decision. This was not the night for getting drunk in order to forget. She slid off the bar stool and grabbed her bag with one hand, and his arm with the other. He gave her a confused smile.

'Come on. We have somewhere to be.'

He followed her without questioning as the maître d approached them with a menu as thick as a book. Olivia had lost her appetite anyway.

They retraced their steps back to the cathedral. Hidden spotlights lit the stone carvings from below, giving them an air of weary benevolence. The main door stood open and a light came from within. A gargoyle poked its tongue in a hideous grin from above the apex of the arch surrounding the door.

Noah planted himself on the spot he thought he had seen Gabe and turned his attention to the occupants of the square. Olivia saw his eyes flicking from person to person in a frantic optimism.

It was a Friday night and the students of the nearby city had emerged. All week, they kept to the cheaper drinking dens of the university, but the weekend was their time to cut loose. It was some kind of party night and most were wearing fancy dress—an angel with a devil's pitchfork ran past giggling, hotly pursued by Kylo Ren. Olivia watched them in their high spirits, a pang of jealousy catching her unawares at the simple ebb of their lives.

She didn't need to convince Noah about Gabe. He would come to his senses. But she knew that faint flicker of hope. It was imbedded, just under the skin, an itch that never quite went away. She walked by his side as he wandered to the black iron railings and scanned the square of park garden.

A sudden wind blew up, scattering the first few dry leaves of autumn. She caught the tang of salt air from the estuary. It was easy to forget this town had sprung from a tiny fishing port.

The tour guide with the pink umbrella hustled his next group to the cathedral steps. His voice droned on in a bored monotone, whilst his group pointed camera phones at the grand facade of the cathedral. Olivia wondered how many times he had done this. He was like a clockwork figure from some eternal nursery, all wound up and bleating the same dialogue time after time. He ushered them inside, pink umbrella disappearing amidst the bobbing heads.

A slow shiver ran down her spine and she turned, her heartrate hastening. She hadn't felt that instinct in a long time. It was possible Noah's edginess was rubbing off on her.

On the exact spot where Noah thought he had seen Gabe, stood a man. Olivia watched him from the corner of her eye, aware that her mouth had lost its moisture. He fixed her with a heavy stare, and she grabbed Noah's arm, squeezing it with fingers that felt too stiff.

She could feel the weight of scrutiny as though it was physically pushing against her thoughts. Noah responded to her urgency. His eyes fell on the figure over her shoulder, and his jaw tightened.

The man in the ringmaster's coat nodded once in their direction before following the tour group. Olivia had a sudden thought that his manner of dress didn't seem like it was simply for fun.

CHAPTER THIRTEEN

Emron D'Grey was a scheming, manipulative creature. And he was proud of every last negative molecule.

He was considered one of the original pure breds, along with Clove and a handful of others scattered across the globe. D'Grey didn't see the point of existing if he couldn't rule from the shadows, watching and twisting the information he received to his own ends. He had no doubt he had a little bit of crazy in his veins too. They all had, the ones who had survived the passing of time. He cracked his knuckles in the foyer of the cathedral, watching the tour group going about their business. But he hadn't come for them.

Two hunters had arrived shortly after Clove and his whelp had left. Their news made an already interesting night turn into one of possible epic proportions. Other masters might not have put it together—Clove's sudden appearance, and the discovery of two other fledglings, but D'Grey had a knack for taking unmarked puzzle pieces and fitting them into a whole without the aid of a picture. Clove had been silent for at least a decade, and there were rumours of new fledglings, powerful fledglings. D'Grey meant to stamp on them before their wings dried out too much.

The vampire world had been quiet for far too long, but he knew everything was cyclical. And this turn of events excited him to a point where his imagination began to whirl, conjuring up the most exciting games and twists.

The spice master had been keeping things very close to his chest, only saying what he needed to glean the information D'Grey knew. There was a certain etiquette amongst their set that could not be broken if rules were adhered to. And as much as he had wanted to pick around in the mind of the scrap at Clove's feet, that was not permitted. It hadn't stopped him having a swift sweep over the surface though, just so the bastard knew his place. Clove had trained him well, something which both irked and excited him. Why would the spice master bother if he didn't have things to hide?

D'Grey chuckled and clasped his hands together in front of his worn embroidered waistcoat. His thumbs circled each other like the coils of a serpent.

He missed the theatricals of the old nights, the gas-lit streets of old London where he could kill at will, and leave the corpse in full view before tidying himself up and retiring to a gentleman's club. The card games grew boring after a while, as he could tell from an opponent's eyes what hand he held. But what he really enjoyed were the shadowed back rooms where a gentleman could indulge in any manner of dark perversions. And Emron D'Grey had many.

Moth made the buds of those perversions water. So unspoilt in an ironic kind of way. Such a waste of young flesh. It had a fluidity to it, a softness as the muscles arched in agony or orgasm, something that was lost as the years hardened the vessel and the mind. And if the two other fledglings were Clove's too? Oh yes, it was very sweet to contemplate. He moved a hassock out of the way with the toe of his boot, and strode down the stone corridor towards the remains of a wooden door. His footsteps rang out in the darkness.

A thought gnawed away in the pit of his mind. If Clove was travelling with three fledglings, by the law of averages it had to mean one was pure bred. And the spice master had never sired before, not to D'Grey's vast and detailed knowledge. That could only mean that this one was special. He ground his back teeth together as he stopped at what was left of the door. He moved a few splinters with his foot, then jumped down into the crypt. His nose wrinkled at the dusty smell of time. As much as he enjoyed the theatricals, the thought of spending any time holed up in a place like this repulsed him. He had earned his luxuries.

His eyes fell on the tomb, and on the scuff marks in the dust at its base. He bent down and fingered the fine sand, rubbing it between his thumb and forefinger. Oh Clove, who were you hiding and why?

The call might be out for cleansing the night of the runts, and the search for mutations, but he had a feeling Clove carried his own secrets. And Emron D'Grey meant to find out why.

‡

At the same time as Emron D'Grey's curiosity became more than simply a passing fancy, Clove took his fledglings down into the bowels of the town.

The sewer grating proved no match for his strength, and he knew that deep underneath the ground, any vibrations they might send out would be muffled and difficult to pin-point. He had no doubt D'Grey would put out his feelers as soon as he decided that Clove had been granted time enough to clear D'Grey's territory. It was not etiquette to trail a fellow vampire from a meeting place, but there was nothing set in stone that said he couldn't be tracked in the aftermath. Clove was not on his home ground and he knew that was a disadvantage.

None of his wards had said a word as he led them away from the main throng of the streets. They were all deep within their own thoughts. Subdued. A wave of empathy arose for how the night had treated them so far. For so long, he had kept them hidden. For their own sake, but that made it even harder for them to accept what they had seen.

He motioned for Teal and Gabriel to climb down the metal ladder first, waiting until he could hear their footsteps splashing in the water below.

'Not a word.' He pressed his forefinger against Moth's lips before letting him join his brothers.

With a final scan of the empty street, Clove pulled the grating back into place with a heavy clunk. The echo followed him down into the brick-lined, foul-smelling tunnel. Teal had clambered onto a ledge running along the edge of the sewer, hunched underneath the curving wall. Moth and Gabriel stood, ankle deep in water, on either side of him. The darkness covered them like a black fog. Sight down here was mainly a redundant thing. The only brightness came from the soft glow within Teal's eyes.

A rat scurried by, its whiskers twitching as it passed them. Gabriel shivered, his lips twisting in distaste. Sometimes Clove forgot how new he was to this life. The things the others took for granted were things Gabriel had never encountered. If it had been any other time, he might have been a little gentler with his first born, but the unease on the vampire mental grapevine, the Bloodvyne, had begun its whispering not long after Gabriel's making. And then there was always the threat of the demon. Clove didn't like the fact it had dropped off the radar completely.

He led them a few hundred yards down the sewer, stopping occasionally to feel the bricks and gauge his bearings. This place was an old friend. It had saved his life countless times, and up until now he had kept it secret.

'In here.' He paused at a small door set into the brickwork. Time had softened its edges with a moist moss, like fur. It was soft to his fingers as he pressed against it, finding the give in the top left hand corner. It opened into a small chamber. A few dusty metal drums lay upended at one side. A rumpled tarpaulin sat in a heap in the middle of the floor. Exactly as he had left it last time.

He waited until they were all inside and closed the door. Immediately the rush of the water hushed. He reached into one of the drums and brought out an old hurricane lamp. Its rim was cracked. Inside the lamp, and protected by a wad of waxed cloth, was an aged box of matches. Taking one in his fingers, he struck it, the intensity of the flare casting the faces of his fledglings into life. The trust they had in him now surpassed his expectations. He lit the cotton wick and waited until the flame had steadied, adjusting the airflow through the bottom vent.

Clove placed the lamp on the floor and knelt beside it. One by one, they joined him—Teal first, followed by Moth and Gabriel, each taking his place at either side of Teal. They sat in the dust, their legs crossed like children, and with uncertainty in their eyes. Something touched him deep inside, in the place where his heart once had been. Moth and Gabriel might resent each other, but they were naturally gravitating towards becoming Teal's protectors. And Teal would need every ounce of care they could give.

'You all need to put aside any differences and work together. There is danger here, old grudges dredged up and reignited. It will be easier for you because you are all young. As time passes and your instincts become honed, you will undoubtedly drift apart. Your bonds will melt away like snow. Vampires are lone creatures and do not hunt in packs. Who was once the wolf cub you tumbled with, will become your adversary.'

He did not add that he knew this first hand.

CHAPTER FOURTEEN

We had followed Clove without question.

On one hand, I was grateful to see him, because Teal and I were way out of our depths.

But on the other, he had stopped me from making contact with Noah and Olivia. I wondered if I would have had the courage to catch Noah's eye. Whether I could have stood if he'd recoiled from me in horror. After all, I was a killer now. I had to be to survive, but what did that say about my morality?

Even Moth was silent as we walked, his hands thrust into his jacket pockets, head down. Something had happened when he was with Clove, something that had made him retreat into himself. He looked younger when he wasn't sneering and casting black looks in my direction. I remembered Teal saying Moth had lost a lot of people. He wasn't that much different from me on the inside.

Going down into the sewer had freaked me out. The stench was only part of it. Being enclosed in the tunnel with its thousands of bricks made it hard to breathe. My heart was thudding so hard I could feel it in my throat. I knew if we got trapped down here I wouldn't die; I would slowly go insane, but remain fully conscious. I wondered if there were any vampires entombed around us, unable to move but aware of our every action.

I was almost glad when we followed Clove into the chamber. At least I could pretend we weren't thirty feet underground. I'd never seen Moth so subdued, and it scared me. The sudden glow of the lamp wick was about the most welcome thing I had seen all night. Clove's features flared into view, then his eyes settled on all of us as we sat on the floor. I held my breath as he began to talk, hyper aware Moth had slid his arm around Teal's shoulder. A sharp pang rolled through me. I was always going to be the one on the outside.

'Tonight I took Moth to the house of an old acquaintance, Emron D'Grey. I would not have brought you into public view without reason. He told me what I had feared: A cleansing has begun.'

No one spoke as Clove paused and listened, his attention caught by some tiny flicker of movement none of us had heard.

'A cleansing is a purging of weak vampires. There hasn't been one for over a hundred years. Hunters are out scouring the world for vampires, especially fledglings.'

A rush of air left my lungs and Moth's face turned to mine. Flickers of shadows played across his profile. Something dark lay hidden in his eyes.

'Gabe and I were chased by two vampires when we were hiding in the crypt.' Teal's quiet voice bled from the shadows. 'His quick thinking saved us both.' He gifted me with the sort of smile people write poetry about.

'I felt the disturbance.' Clove's brows knitted together for a few seconds.

'What happens when they catch a weak fledgling?' There was the tiniest hint of a tremor in Teal's voice. He knew, as we all did, that he would be at the top of their list.

'They are examined, tested. And if they are found lacking, they are taken to a holding ground.' Clove stopped. We all wanted to know what else. But no one asked. 'Depending on where the holding ground is, they are either left in a place where there is no shelter or they are burnt alive. It is the only way to kill the spirit inside that makes us night walkers.'

A lump formed in my throat as Clove spoke. The thought of Teal going through that was too horrific to even think about.

'There must be a way to stop it.' The words blurted out of my mouth, falling on top of one another in their haste to be heard.

'There's only one way. And that is to appeal to the ruling body, stating your case as to why a vampire should be spared.'

'We can do that, right?' I grasped at the straw. 'I mean they'll listen to you. You're a master. Your word must count for something.' I waited for Moth to back me up.

'My word will mean nothing. I cannot appeal, not in this case. It is… complicated.'

I waited for him to continue as the stark reality of his words sunk in. No matter what way I looked at it, he was saying Teal wasn't worth saving.

‡

Clove's resolve faltered for the first time in decades.

The look in Gabriel's eyes alone was seared into his mind. Without speaking the words, he had more or less told them he could help, but wasn't prepared to. What he couldn't tell them was that if he brought the three of them before the ruling body, it was probable only Gabriel would be spared. Moth might be walking a fine tightrope. If they decided his strength of character meant nothing, they would take him to destroy. But Teal would suffer more. Clove had heard about certain things the ruling body did, and death was by far the kindest action.

The mutation running in Teal's blood was a rarity. Most vampires who carried it died within weeks. It took over their nervous systems, leaving them unable to function. But Teal had somehow managed to survive this. Vampire genetics had skipped a few generations and made something out of nothing. Clove had sensed there was something special about him after only a few weeks. The glow in his eyes wasn't a permanent fixture back then, more of a shine that ebbed and flowed depending on how Teal was feeling. Clove had studied him, looking for signs of problems, expecting the worst. But with each new night, it became apparent that whatever anomaly flowed in his veins, it was quite happy to co-exist.

It was why he kept Teal and Moth hidden away. Away from prying eyes and mouths that might whisper, and send the presence of a mutation tip-toeing along the wires.

'How can it be complicated?' Moth's voice, sharpened with pain, brought Clove back into the present.

'Enough for now, Moth. It has been a trying evening for all of us.' Clove pushed the hurricane lamp towards them. 'I'm going out to hunt, but I can't risk taking you with me tonight.

I will bring a kill back. But it is of vital importance you stay here. Do you understand?' He stood, and his shadow grew ominous against the back wall of the chamber.

One by one, they nodded. Moth's and Gabriel's eyes were full of questions he couldn't answer. For their own sake. Part of him wanted to hover outside in the soft rush of water from the sewer and eavesdrop. Their conversation would be interesting. But he knew he had to bring them blood. A hungry vampire cannot focus and that could prove fatal.

He climbed down into the sewer, a line of rats scurrying away from him into a gutter.

His thoughts came with their own dark shadows. How had the news of Teal leaked out? Clove had been extremely careful, and he couldn't recall running into another vampire when Teal had been present. Over the last year, their only interactions had been with the people in The Manor. And the demon.

He remembered Beth as she fell through the door, the madness in her eyes more alive than she was. A renegade made unintentionally by Moth and Teal. The demon had cracked her wide open, scattering the atoms that made her into millions of pieces, before regrouping her body into something incomprehensible. Then she was simply gone. At the time, his attention had been on Gabriel, dying in his arms. Clove rebuked himself for not taking more notice.

The metal ladder loomed in front of him. Clove climbed it with ease, his long limbs taking the rungs three at a time. He paused at the top and scanned for any sign of movement on the street above. The soft padding of feet nearby: Animal. The clunk of the grate lid against the tarmacadam sent the stray dog hurtling into the distance. Nothing moved. There was only the faint hum of traffic noise from far away. Up above, a blinking white light signalled a plane on its journey. Normal human distractions. He replaced the grate and pulled the collar of his coat against his neck, despite the warmth of the evening.

Clove walked quickly, putting distance between himself and where he had left his fledglings. This had not been his intention when he left them. He'd wanted to make his kill and return. But he was not the only vampire out hunting.

He didn't make for the centre of the town, keeping instead to the outskirts, past the wired-in enclosures where the containers for the docks loomed like metal monsters. The tang of the sea swept in on an incoming breeze and for an instant, he was the child on a moving deck, hardly tall enough to see the land approaching. The land, which would give him life, and then death.

The hunters stepped out in front of him as he knew they would. Fools if they thought otherwise. But he did not run. This would imply a criminality of some kind.

He studied them as he would a crushed insect. 'Gentlemen.' His arms opened in a gesture of greeting.

They didn't reply and he hadn't expected them to. With the precision of a surgeon, he slid down his mental shield and locked it into position. It was a safety device he used on only the rarest of occasions. Because with it shut tight he couldn't detect any disturbances from his fledglings.

They were, for now, entirely on their own.

CHAPTER FIFTEEN

The silence since Clove had left was deafening.

None of them knew what to say. But it was Teal who finally spoke.

His eyes stayed fixed on the flame behind the dusty glass of the lamp. 'It's okay. I can't expect Clove to risk himself for me.'

A rage built up inside Moth, a churning volcano of feeling he'd kept locked up all night. 'The hell he can! It's not like he'd be putting himself in danger.' Right at that moment he wanted to kill something, to feel flesh giving way under his fangs, to shake the life out of something insignificant. He slid his arm around Teal's shoulders. Teal was trembling despite his brave words.

'I don't understand either.' Gabriel picked at the floor with his fingers, leaving a fine trail in the dust.

'There's nothing to understand, Gabriel.' Moth's eyes found an outlet for his rage, and Gabriel stopped dead in his tracks, his finger poised above the floor. 'Of course, *you'll* be fine, being pure bred. They'll probably hold a fucking party for Clove's chosen one.'

Gabriel recoiled at the bitterness in the accusation.

Teal spun around onto his knees, forcing Moth to lift his supportive arm. It was the first time Teal had ever moved out of his comfort, and Moth felt it like a blow.

'Gabe can't help his making or his bloodline. He didn't ask for this. None of us did. I've been on borrowed time since the night I was brought over, and you both know that.' There was nothing in Teal's voice but calm resignation.

Moth's anger twisted itself into a confusing maelstrom of feeling. Indignation and sorrow, and a protective ache for the unfairness of it all.

'What else happened tonight? When you were with Clove?' The questions, of course, came from Gabriel.

His new brother sat with his head in his hands, a picture of dejection, and Moth felt a small satisfaction in that. He wondered how much he should say. Even now it all seemed farfetched, like the contents of a weird dream. He wanted to tell Gabriel to fuck off, wanted to share only with Teal, but that wasn't on the cards.

'I'm not sure you really want to know.' Moth paused and steadied his voice. 'You know the talk about crazy vampires? Well, this guy, Emron D'Grey, was so far on the edge of crazy he wrote the book. But not *just* crazy. Devious and crazy. Clove was his equal. From what I could tell, they had history. Clove made me shut down my shields so my mind couldn't be read, but D'Grey's touch kept picking away...'

Teal reached across and touched Moth's arm. Gabriel sat, occasionally glancing up, listening with troubled eyes.

'There was this fucking scary ritual thing where they both drank from two other fledglings. Then D'Grey told Clove about the cleansing and about the hunters looking for weak vampires and mutations.' He forced the last word out. It hung like poison on his lips.

'That's why he couldn't take me then, because I'm weak.' Teal's voice was barely a whisper. 'But the hunters know Gabe and I are out there. They won't stop looking.'

Moth didn't want to add that Clove had said he, too, might not be safe. He wanted nothing more than to be back in the middle of nowhere. At least there, they were the predators.

He caught Gabriel looking at him over Teal's shoulder. It was obvious he had taken the hint. Clove might call them all brothers, but as far as Moth was concerned, Gabriel was a bastard in more ways than one. And if he thought he could replace Sasha, he was fucking deluded. But… he had saved Teal's life tonight.

'Thanks for helping Teal out earlier.' The words stuck in his throat.

Gabriel looked up in surprise, his eyes widening slightly. He shrugged. 'It's okay. I didn't know who they were or what they wanted, but I wasn't hanging around to find out.'

Moth wondered if Gabriel would have been as quick to act if it had been him in Teal's place.

Teal pulled a thin volume of poetry from the inside of his jacket and started to read, his quiet voice an instant calm. In the flickering light, Moth tuned into Gabriel's measured breathing. Moth didn't care much for fancy words, but from Teal, they took on meaning, and anything that helped pass the hours was a plus. He sat back against the wall, his head bowed, and closed his eyes. The weight of the awful secret he carried clawed its way into his brain.

'Clove is taking a really long time.' Teal glanced at the door, as though the act of doing so might bring their mentor home.

Moth wearily raised his head. 'He'll be back soon—don't worry. Are you hungry?' Moth put an edge of bravado on his words, but Clove was taking longer than usual, or maybe it was because the situation they were in wasn't comfortable. If Teal was hungry, Gabriel must be too. But he was doing a good job of hiding it.

They listened for any signs of Clove approaching. Sewer life went on behind the door, the gush of water, the nauseating stench filtering through any tiny crack, the *scritch scratch* of rodent feet. Gabriel had his knees pulled into his chest, his hands clasped tightly around them. Teal rocked slowly from side to side, his default when the thirst crawled into his throat.

'Something's wrong. My head is woozy. It must be close to dawn.' Gabriel's voice interrupted the passing of time. And as much as Moth wanted to shoot him down in flames, he knew Gabriel was right.

CHAPTER SIXTEEN

Olivia stared up at the ceiling, listening to the whirr of the fan blades as they sliced through the darkness. The night was blanketed in sticky heat, desperate for a storm to clear the air. Her thoughts raced back to almost a year ago. That night. That storm. There was no way she could sleep.

Noah lay beside her on his back, snoring softly. It had taken him a while to settle, and even now he muttered in his sleep, his hands reaching up to cover his face. He had made small talk all evening, and she ached for his turmoil. Some days they got through without crumbling, but this sighting of the boy who looked like Gabe had thrown Noah back into a cycle of self-deprecation and false humour.

The odd man in the fancy dress picked away at her instinctive shield. As much as she tried to reason with herself that he was only part of the weird student horde, she couldn't shift the way his eyes had seemed to look right through her.

Olivia slipped out of bed, gathering her clothes from the chair, and crept into the bathroom to get dressed. The stifling air of the tiny, windowless room clung to her skin. She didn't leave Noah a note. They didn't have that kind of relationship. Or maybe she had decided they didn't.

It was a little after 3 a.m. when she stepped out onto the street. Their hotel, an old Georgian town house with an impressive pillared entrance, stood only a few streets back from the cathedral, in the old part of town. This whole area had once been part of the thriving community that made up the small port. Even now, a tall ship sat at the dock, its masts trimmed with garlands, waiting for the next tourist band to grace her decks. Olivia had refused Noah's offer to go to look around. She found it slightly off putting that a once-great ship was now reduced to this, the property of a commercial business.

She didn't have a plan as to where she was heading, but she wasn't surprised when she found herself standing by the old town map, staring at the cathedral again. Her thoughts seeped out like ink on damp parchment, creeping into places she didn't want them to go. What if Noah had been right? Logic steeled her. It was impossible that Gabe could have survived his injuries.

The imposing frontage of the cathedral loomed, and as her eyes travelled to the uppermost spire, the sensation of falling backwards flooded through her, as though the whole building would come crashing down, swallowing her life in a stone kiss. She stepped back and grabbed one of the iron railings surrounding the deserted park. The disorientation rose in waves, and her breath came heavy and fast as the darkness pressed in all around her.

Slowly, the dizziness passed. She crossed the narrow, cobbled street, which ran adjacent to the square. A row of upmarket shops stood in a quaint huddle. Each of the shop fronts was painted a different pastel colour, and they all had the town's ancient shield hanging from a pole over the door.

She walked past two, a florist with empty containers in the window, soon to be filled with fresh flowers from the early morning market, and a furniture shop with shabby-chic French-style dressers and tables.

She remembered the dresser in Tom and Betty's kitchen on the night Tom had, quite literally, pulled her out of the hole she had fallen into. Tom, who with his unflappable kindness edged with a gruff cover, had been such a support. Their relationship since had been tight. He dropped by whenever he felt like it, more so since losing Betty. Olivia had sat by him at the funeral. Noah, despite his sabbatical, had insisted that he officiate. Tom had stared straight ahead, his tanned neck ringed by a collar and tie, which looked as startled as he did about the circumstances. She had put her arm around him, the heat rising from his neck. Her heart had ached as he dabbed at his eyes with a crumpled handkerchief.

She stared into the black mirror of the shop window, seeing nothing but her thoughts.

A movement caught her eye. In the square, a figure moved easily across the grass.

She froze in place, her breath halting in her throat. It was a tall figure. No, not just one. Behind came two others, as one with the night as the first. She knew this first form; it was etched into her memory. How could anyone forget?

It was Clove. She wanted to stuff her fist against her mouth to stop any sound escaping, but she didn't dare move.

The figures glided through the park as if they were on ice. Clove's eyes were focused on the path in front of him, as though he was wearing blinkers. He hadn't seen her. They passed through the gate a few feet from where she had held onto the railing. As they crossed the street with the two other figures still flanking Clove, his head turned slightly. The wind whipped his long black hair into a frenzy, and he slowly raised a hand to smooth it back into place. But he didn't just do that. He took the weight of it in one hand and pulled it over one shoulder. Exactly as she did. Olivia's heart fell into her stomach.

The figures disappeared into the shadows of the balconied old townhouses across the street.

She couldn't discount the feeling now. Her instincts had been spot on.

Clove *had* seen her. But something was wrong.

CHAPTER SEVENTEEN

Being woken by Moth shaking me roughly wasn't on my list of how to start a night off right.

I was drifting in that grey space between my death sleep and opening my eyes. I knew because my head felt like a lead weight and my body refused to listen to any signals my brain might be sending. If this was his way of trying to get back at me, it didn't bode well for the rest of the night. I managed to raise one arm and push his hand away from my face. But one look at the expression in his eyes drilled through the fog in my head. It was panic. And Moth didn't do panic.

I glanced around, looking for Clove, but he wasn't here. Moth pulled me from the floor, his hand catching my arm, trying to drag me towards Teal. It was only then I realised Teal wasn't moving.

'I can't wake him, Gabriel.' Those words brought me to my senses like a slap in the face.

'What?' Surely I hadn't heard him right. A vague thought flitted through my head that maybe this was all a game. But Teal wasn't cruel.

I crawled across to his prone body and grabbed his hand. It felt like stone. My heart rate spiked as I rolled him onto his back. 'Is he breathing yet?'

'I don't know. I couldn't tell.'

I pressed my fingertips to Teal's lips. *A sleeping vampire's body is in suspension, movement only present near waking.* I tried to remember all of the things Clove had told me. I listened as Moth hovered above me, his fingers raking through his hair. Finally, a whisper of breath, the slightest of movements.

I turned to Moth, relaxing my shoulders, letting my own breath leave my body in a long, drawn-out gasp. Moth threw himself down beside me, and gently eased Teal's head onto his lap.

An ache I'd buried in the shock of seeing Teal gnawed away at my stomach. I was hungry, really hungry. Clove wasn't back and Teal, for some reason, remained in his death sleep. I tried to ignore the knot of unease forming in my gut.

'Maybe it's because he didn't feed?' I offered what I hoped was a logical explanation.

Moth slowly raised his head, his bi-coloured eyes heavy with worry. He gently smoothed the hair away from Teal's face.

'There's been nights he didn't feed before, and they didn't affect him like this…and where the fuck is Clove?'

I shook my head then crawled across to the door. Carefully, I scanned for any sign of threat. We couldn't just sit here and wait, but Clove had forbidden us to leave. And I knew the penalty for disobeying the rules.

'One of us has to go out.' There was no other choice.

'No.' Moth's reply hit me right between the shoulder blades and I wheeled around.

'I can't do anything for Teal here. I'd be more use with you. We can find a quick kill and bring it back, see if we can get Teal to drink.'

His words surprised me, but they made sense. Still, I wasn't sure—given our history—how good we'd be, acting as a team under this insane amount of pressure. He must have seen the doubt in my eyes.

'Or I can stay here, and let you go out by yourself and fuck it all up.'

There it was, the old Moth, ready to go for my jugular given half the chance.

I made my decision and opened the door, sliding down into the rush of black water below. I waited to see if he would follow me, but he didn't. Part of me wished I'd given him a chance. He had offered, and I'd been the one to mess it up this time.

My vision was better than it had been last night, even with the pangs of hunger rolling around my stomach. My senses had become accustomed to the dark just as creatures do that live underground, but the solidity of the tunnel still hung heavy around my shoulders. I wondered which way to go. We had come in from upstream, so this was the logical direction, but something made me turn left and head in the direction of the water.

I recalled all of my lessons with Clove, as concern for Teal nipped away at my thoughts. How fresh blood, or the lack of it, affected us physically. How surprised I'd been to discover that my heart still continued to beat. The shocked wonder when Clove told me how that changed when we were in our death sleep and that I would learn to control it as I aged.

I tried to shake the feeling that something awful had happened to him. If he didn't return, the chances of us all ever leaving this town looked very slim indeed. Up ahead, at the junction of the main tunnel and a tributary, something caught my eye. Its pale form bobbed about in the current. As I splashed through the water towards it, the stench of the sewer grew. I think I knew what it was before I got there.

I put my hand over my mouth as I looked down on the bloated body of a naked man. His eyes bulged and his tongue lolled, hideously. The skin on his head and neck was greyish green. The putrefied body mocked me with its lifeless eyes. *This is what death looks like. This should be you.* I gagged and spat out a mouthful of fluid. It did nothing to dispel the feeling of dread crawling across my skin. I hurried past. Death shouldn't bother me, but presented like this, it still freaked me out.

I needed a plan. I couldn't simply wander about and hope I found an easy kill. This was early evening, a dangerous time for a fledgling to hunt. But I didn't have a choice. At the back of my mind, a dark thought niggled away. If Clove came back and found me gone, would Moth explain and give me a chance?

Behind me, something moved through the tunnel. I paused, stock still, as the water lapped around my ankles. What if the hunters had heard me, or had been waiting for one of us to emerge? I wasn't far from the door that hid Moth and Teal. I set off again knowing I was making far too much noise, but I had to lead whatever or whoever it was away from that door. I'd have to take the chance Clove had been right in saying that because of my bloodline I would be okay.

The brick walls, slick with water, seemed never ending, the incessant darkness cloying and nauseating. A panic welled up and swarmed through my veins, the sting of it numbing my reasoning. Up ahead, a gleam of metal caught my eye and I ran for it, catching the cold steel in my fingers and clambering up. My feet fumbled for grip and I slipped, one foot dangling. Something grabbed my ankle and terror rose into my throat. I glanced down, my fear manifesting the thought of the bloated corpse hanging on with a dead-man grin.

But the eyes looking back at me were bicoloured, and the most welcome sight I could have hoped for.

CHAPTER EIGHTEEN

Noah awoke to find Olivia sitting on the edge of the bed, holding two large coffee shop containers. She thrust one at him before his eyes were truly open.

One look at her face and Noah's heart missed a beat. Dark shadows pooled under her eyes, and the slight frown lines on her brow seemed to have deepened. Is this where she told him it wasn't working for her? He sat up in bed and a muscle in his lower back complained. Their room was on the ground level and faced a small swimming pool. Outside, someone jumped in with a loud splash. A chitter of birdsong came through the window. He looked down at his coffee cup, at the small stream of steam escaping from the vent hole, and tried to prepare himself.

'I saw Clove. In the park by the cathedral.' Olivia's voice was quiet but resolute. Those were definitely not the words he was expecting to hear, and a surge of relief tightened his grip on the cup. The heat seeped into his fingers. The last remnants of sleep fell away into a void.

'Tell me.' It was pointless to ask the usual response of 'are you sure?' If she wasn't sure, she wouldn't have mentioned anything. He listened as she recalled the last few hours, ending with her wandering of the streets until dawn broke.

'The other two...' Noah paused as he almost said *people*. '...vampires with him. Definitely not Moth or Teal.' Just speaking their names brought back the sheer hell of that night. He touched the scar on his brow.

'Definitely not. And the way they were walking behind him was odd, not in a subservient way, more like they were taking him somewhere.'

The thought of Clove going anywhere against his will didn't seem possible.

'And he saw me, but didn't want to make it obvious.'

Noah tried to take a sip of coffee but it burned his tongue. She was doing it now, pulling her hair over her shoulder, her fingers coiling around the tail she had made.

Outside, the occupant of the pool climbed out, then the sound of bare, wet feet slapping against the ground going past their door.

'I'll ring Carver and tell him we can't come back today,' Noah voiced both of their thoughts. 'I'll make up some excuse. God knows I can't tell him the truth, not with how he is right now. And we don't even know if we have something here anyway.'

'Bullshit, Noah!' Olivia exploded like a firecracker, a stream of coffee leaping up from the cup to cover the crumpled sheets. 'You know as well as I do that seeing Clove anywhere, especially with the fact that you thought you saw Gabe earlier, means something.'

Last night, she had been the one gently trying to persuade him he was clutching at straws, but two sightings couldn't be just coincidence. Could it? He set down his cup on the night stand and took her hand in his, pulling her down beside him. She slid her arm around his waist, her head resting on his chest. No one spoke. He watched the slow rise and fall of her hair as he breathed.

After a few minutes, she turned to look at his face. 'Tonight we go back to the cathedral at the same time as we were there last night. It's the only starting point we have.'

The professional side of her brain was already making plans. Noah smiled and a low laugh rumbled in his chest. He wondered if this was the sound of insanity. Hope and fear swirled together in his stomach, mixing with the waves of relief. He felt light headed and slightly drunk.

'What?'

'I thought you were going to dump me.'

Her brow wrinkled and she pursed her lips. Her thinking expression.

'If I was going to dump you, I wouldn't have brought you coffee, Noah Isaacs.'

'You need to sleep.' It was the only answer he could come up with and it was lame, but the truth. The evening and the cover of darkness seemed as distant as starlight.

'I will soon.' Her fingers trailed down and ran circles around the hair surrounding his navel. He shivered.

Shafts of early morning sun pierced the slats of the window shutters. The beams hit the bed with arrows of gold and shadow. Light and darkness and the Neverworld in between. Gabriel. Noah's heart twisted.

But sleep was apparently not on Olivia's mind. Her head disappeared under the sheet and he arched, a low gasp torn from his throat, chasing the thought of Gabriel into the shadows.

CHAPTER NINETEEN

Moth reluctantly followed Gabriel up the steep ladder to the surface. He wanted to be back in the chamber, with Teal. The aftermath of panic still lodged inside his throat like a stone. A slow rage bubbled underneath at being forced to go along with Gabriel as a sidekick. But he begrudgingly had to admit his newest brother had balls to go off by himself.

Gabriel paused with his palms pressed underneath the circular grating. A few seconds later, a car rumbled past then disappeared into the distance.

The street was mercifully quiet and they both slipped out. The noise of the grating settling back into place sounded like the sealing of a tomb. Gabriel caught his eye and grimaced. Their thoughts were both on Teal.

'If this is where you ask me if I have a plan…' Gabriel's voice tailed off. 'I don't.'

Moth looked away. Part of him wanted to come back with a snarky comment, but that wasn't going to help either of them.

A truck turned onto the street and headed in their direction. It was the early dark of post dusk and its headlights caught them in its beam. The horn blared out angrily. As they moved out of its way, the driver lowered his window and spat in their direction. 'Fucking stupid kids. You all got a fucking death wish!'

The truck moved past, leaving a haze of dust and exhaust fumes in its wake.

Moth rolled his eyes and Gabriel smiled. For a few seconds, they shared the irony of that comment.

A breeze blew up from the direction of the harbour. It ruffled the hair on Gabriel's brow and he swept it away, his curled fingers resting on his lips as he scanned the area around them. Moth knew Gabriel's powers were stronger, but he still sent out his own probe.

They turned towards the harbour and fell into step. Moth felt unravelled, like a ball of string with too many loops. He wasn't used to just being with Gabriel. But then he wasn't used to Clove disappearing and Teal not waking up, either. He thrust his hands deeper into his jacket pockets.

Suddenly, Gabriel stopped mid-step and doubled over, his hands clutching his stomach. Moth stood there awkwardly as Gabriel threw up a mouthful of thin blood-streaked mucus. Moth was hungry, but Gabriel, in his infancy, must be starving. It wasn't only Teal who was in trouble.

He waited, scuffing his toe in the dust. Gabriel raised his head. His face was ashen. Moth tentatively put his hand out, but Gabriel had moved off.

Soon, they reached the same shipping yard Clove had walked the night before. The hulks of the metal containers were an easy place to use as camouflage, but Moth knew that it was also a place the hunters would look. But nothing moved in the concrete yard, apart from a few mice scurrying beneath the grain crates. The stone of panic liquefied and burned down his throat. Gabriel motioned for him to stop, then leaned against the side of one of the containers.

'I'm okay,' he whispered, but he didn't sound okay. Gabriel winced then pointed up ahead. Moth gathered his senses and something pinged his radar. *Prey.*

On silent feet, they edged towards the scent of blood. In a small enclosure, surrounded by a chain link fence, stood the truck that had passed them on the road. Right behind it was a portacabin with a large floodlight on its roof, covering the dented old vehicle with a blanket of harsh light. There were people in the cabin, and judging by the scent, more than a couple. A burst of saliva flooded Moth's mouth. His tongue flicked out. Gabriel growled low in his throat beside him. It was the sound of despair. They both knew they couldn't go in and kill indiscriminately.

The truck driver's voice sounded out from the cabin doorway.

'Fuck you, retard!' And then he laughed as though the insult was the most natural way of saying goodbye. 'Yeah, yeah, I know, keep it in my pants…that's not what his wife said.' And he laughed again.

Moth tensed, his muscles ready for flight.

Gabriel grabbed his arm. 'Wait, I think I've got this.' He pulled Moth towards him, catching his waist with one hand and sandwiching himself between the side of the container. Gabriel's pale face hovered only inches from his own as the sound of the truck driver's feet crunched on the gravel.

'Pretend we're making out.' Gabriel's voice hissed against his ear.

The ball of string that was Moth's nerves tangled in shocked surprise, but he was all out of any other option.

He pressed his hips against Gabriel as the gravel crunching came to a halt. Gabriel's lips touched the side of his neck and he froze, aware both of their breathing rates had hit the redline status.

'Fucking little faggots.' The man sneered. 'Hey, I'm talking to you!'

Moth couldn't see what was happening, but he knew Gabriel had a full view. The fingers around his waist tightened and Gabriel tensed. The man was right behind them.

Moth wheeled around to see a fist raised in anger. He grabbed it and twisted. The bone snapped with a satisfying crunch. There was one long moment as the man's mouth opened in pain and terror, and then the flash of a fang as Gabriel went in for the kill. Quick. Surgical.

Moth grabbed the weight as the man crumpled to the floor and dragged him away into the shelter of a group of abandoned containers. Sticky, warm blood soaked into his clothes, and he wanted nothing more than to drop the kill and tear into it. But he couldn't. It was too public. Gabriel's eyes were dark with hunger and Moth wondered how the hell he was keeping it together.

Finally, he couldn't take it any longer. He dragged the corpse under a rusted container and dumped it. They both collapsed, their breath laboured and urgent.

'Teal...' Gabriel's voice trembled as he crawled over Moth. Blood fever hung in his eyes. A trail of saliva glistened on one side of his mouth.

'Soon. Us first, otherwise...' He didn't get a chance to finish. The hunger took him into that red velvet place with Gabriel at his side.

CHAPTER TWENTY

It was no surprise to Clove to find that he was returning to the dwelling house of Emron D'Grey.

The master vampire wanted more morsels than Clove was prepared to offer, and this was D'Grey's way of letting him know this was his territory, that he ruled the roost. It wasn't unexpected. But seeing Olivia had been.

He wondered why she was prowling the deserted streets by herself. The fact she and Noah were present in the same place, and that things were starting to unravel, hadn't gone unnoticed. And he knew enough about them to know they would not take the fleeting glimpse of Gabriel lightly. They had presumed him dead and it was better that way.

This was not the time for Gabriel to be yearning for his old life, but undoubtedly the sighting had unnerved him, right when Clove needed him to focus. Moth and Gabriel walked a fine line between acceptance and all-out warfare. If he had hoped bringing Gabriel over would make up for Sasha, he had been mistaken. This trinity hovered on the edge of disaster; it was only Teal who kept them grounded. Now that Moth and Gabriel didn't have his guidance, he wondered how long it would be before someone pulled the trigger.

A firm hand pushed him forwards through the door and he turned slowly, fixing the hunter with a pitying stare. They were given special dispensation by the ruling body—which meant no vampire could harm them in the course of their 'duty'. But he would remember this one and teach him a lesson he wouldn't soon forget.

Emron D'Grey waited for him in the same room, although the searchlight was mercifully turned off. Clouds of blue smoke hazed the air. Another one of his vices. He lounged in a large leather armchair, his booted feet swinging over the side.

'Spice master.' He grinned, flashing two impressive fangs. 'Good of you to pop back. I feel I wasn't hospitable enough earlier. Come, sit.' He waved a hand at the semi-circle of soft seating surrounding his chair. Multi-coloured cushions in rich shades of orange and gold and purple lay scattered haphazardly, and if it wasn't for the fact that D'Grey had offered, it would have looked inviting.

Clove would have much rather stood, but he knew this was simply another game, one in which the rules could change at any given moment. He settled himself upon the middle of the couch, sinking into the deep, soft cushions. D'Grey was highly adept at making you feel welcome before delivering a punch to the gut.

'How is dear Moth? I trust you found him an appetising morsel to quench his thirst?' One booted foot swung like a pendulum.

'He is safe. Do not worry yourself about his well-being.' Clove replied with a smile, but his words were a warning.

'Oh, I'm not worried about him, spice master.' The booted foot stopped abruptly. 'What interests me is any *other* fledglings you might have hidden. Rumour has it you travel with three.'

'Rumour is over rated as you undoubtedly know.' Clove fought to keep the smile in his voice. Either D'Grey had known all along, or he had been sniffing around and calling in connections since Clove and Moth had left.

'Why don't I feel that you're telling me the truth?' A cold chill crept into D'Grey's words.

'It is of no concern how many fledglings I travel with, surely?'

D'Grey brought his feet to the floor in one fluid swing. The noise echoed from the low roof. 'Ah, but it is if I suspect you are harbouring one with the mutation.'

Clove kept his face expressionless. So, the news was out. He'd been a fool to think he could have kept it hidden, not in a place with so many eyes.

D'Grey leapt on his silence, clasping his hands together in what Clove assumed was a victory handshake to himself.

Part of him wanted to deny Teal, but he wouldn't. Nor would he agree.

'You might like to check the worthiness of your sources.' A muscle twitched in his jaw and he turned his face away from the light.

'Oh, my sources are excellent. And I have enough to hold you on suspicion of refusing to co-operate with the ruling body. You do realise that, don't you?'

Clove knew this had been a possibility, but he didn't think D'Grey would actually go through with it. A master holding a master was virtually unheard of.

'Or you can take us back to your bolt hole and show me you only have Moth tied to your apron strings. The choice is yours, my friend. Of course, as payment for my under-standing, I would expect a few hours alone with your little toy.' D'Grey grinned in a way a cat might, offering a mouse death by decapitation or disembowelment.

Clove pressed his lips together. He wouldn't give D'Grey the satisfaction of an answer. A flame of anger ignited in that dark space inside where his emotions were caged.

'And how long do you propose to hold me?' He swept a thread of gold cotton from his leg to the floor. 'One night? Two? Indefinitely?' The last word hung heavy with sar-casm. Even D'Grey didn't have the power to do that unless ordered to do so by a vampire of much greater standing. Clove knew he had no enemies in the hierarchy.

'Two at the most, my friend. This is all we will need to find the ones you have taken under your wing. They have to feed. They are young. They will make mistakes.'

Clove's mind was locked down. This, in itself, was a meas-ure of sin, but he could not risk picking up any signals from his boys that would give away their location. He could only hope fate would grant them a glimmer of mercy.

CHAPTER TWENTY-ONE

An odd feeling had wrapped itself around Tom Jacobson's shoulders, even though the day was bright and clear. Over seven decades on the planet had told him to listen to his intuition, and he wasn't about to go back on that this morning. So he let it sit whilst he fed the few chickens he kept for eggs and checked on his latest litter of piglets.

The sow, a huge Gloucester Old Spot who went by the name of Bacon, grunted as Tom came into the barn. Her piglets, ten in total, clustered close to her belly, all pale pink with varying degrees of spots. He would keep a couple of the stronger ones. Now he had so much time on his hands he couldn't be idle. At least that's what Betty would have said. A sudden sadness overcame him as he stood in a patch of sunlight with Jip at his feet. Life was cruel when it took away your life partner. The no nonsense side of him argued his life partner was a mere shadow of herself when she went. That had been the true cruelty.

He fed Bacon and brought in some fresh straw, lifting the bale with ease despite the ache in his fingers from arthritis. The odd feeling poked around in his gut and he sighed, turning his face in the direction of The Manor. Ella was away. He'd called in a few days ago and she had fed him homemade cake and enough tea to sink an army. She was taking a few days to visit a niece who had just had a baby. Carver, who had popped his head around the door to say hello, remarked she could stay as long as she needed. Ella's mouth had dropped and she'd tried to hide it.

Tom knew life in the house wasn't easy anymore. Most of the warmth had left on that night. As far as he could tell, he was the only one who knew the absolute truth. It had come out in dribs and drabs and each one he'd absorbed, never questioning or giving judgement. He trusted Noah and Carver implicitly, and Olivia, despite her thorns, was like a granddaughter to him, although he would never admit this to her. But she knew in her own way and that was fine.

'Better get myself over and have a nose around. Otherwise I'll be jumpy all day and that won't do, will it, Jip?' The collie looked up at him in adoration and waved his tail furiously from side to side.

Ten minutes later, Tom pulled up outside of The Manor. It looked serene, basking in the morning sun, but this was simply a mask it wore. His feet crunched on the gravel. He had a weird image of a mouth full of sharp teeth chomping down splinters of bone. His brow furrowed into deep lines as he knocked on the door.

No answer.

Carver would be working in the research lab, and Tom knew even if he heard the door, he wouldn't answer if the notion overcame him that he didn't want visitors. Tom pushed the door open. It was cooler in the hallway and smelled of lavender beeswax. The woodwork gleamed and the tiled floors looked clean enough to eat your dinner from. Ella poured her sadness into the obliteration of dust and grime, as though the act of doing so might bring back happier times.

'Carver?' Tom felt uneasy being in the house without an invite, but now he was here the strange feeling had magnified. He walked into the kitchen. There was nothing on the counters to suggest anyone had been in to even make a cup of tea. He toured the lower floor, checking each room, but found only an aching silence. He wondered how stillness could be so loud. Loneliness clung to the fabric of each room like a lost prayer.

The stairs made his knees creak. Were they always this steep? On the landing, the new carpet stuck out—far too bold, far too fresh. A memory of Ollie flashed before his eyes, chasing the chickens in the yard, his arms outstretched and clueless, hopelessly inadequate but eternally boyish. Life was definitely cruel.

He hesitated outside the research room, then knocked. There was no reply. No one behind the door when he checked. Similarly the other guest rooms, Noah's room, and even Carver's suite, held no clues. He scratched his chin thoughtfully. A crack appeared in his mind's eye and he shivered even though sweat had started to seep into the fabric of his worn work shirt.

The only room left on this floor beckoned to him, but no one ever went in there to his knowledge. Gabe's.

Tom's palm slipped on the handle as he pushed it open. The door moved slowly, as if it didn't really want to let him see what was inside. The air was stuffy and old, the room untouched since the night Gabe had left it. The bed unmade, clothes in the laundry basket, laptop on the floor. Tom's eyes swept over each thing, taking in the detail. His heart hammered in his chest at a rate that was probably not safe for a man of his years.

And there, on the floor, as Tom knew he would be, was Edward Carver, with an empty whisky bottle at his side.

CHAPTER TWENTY-TWO

It was Moth who pulled my head up right at the point where the new blood burned freely through my veins, warm and comforting, taking me to a place inside myself where I was aware of everything, but soothed. I wrenched myself free from his grip, a snarl falling from my lips before I could stop it.

'Teal.'

One word and I was brought back to reality with a hard jolt. I wasn't sure how long we'd been hidden away under the abandoned container, but I had a feeling Moth had taken what he needed then left me for much longer. I glanced at him, crouched down and alert, one knee in the dust, and felt something I never thought I would in his company. Grateful.

But now we had a big problem. How to get the blood-soaked man we'd killed back to Teal. It wasn't something we could parade through the streets. Moth chewed the edge of his lip, as if his thoughts ran alongside mine.

'The street we came up on runs behind this yard, I think.' I tried to remember the journey, but there were blanks.

Moth turned his head, his eyes darkening slightly as his location senses fired up.

'If we're lucky, it might mean there's a sewer opening nearer here. If it runs along the whole street, which it should.' My voice sounded hopeful to my ears, but hope wouldn't get us out of this mess alone. One of us needed to go check. 'I'll go.' It was my idea; I should be the one to take the risk.

'No, Gabriel. I'll go. Look at you. How far would you get?' I glanced down at my bloody t-shirt.

Moth was halfway out of the gap already. I grabbed his arm and he stopped. 'Be careful, okay?' As soon as the words were out of my mouth, I wanted to choke them back. What a freaking stupid thing to say. He was gone before the flush rose to my cheeks. God, I hoped I was right about the sewer system. Otherwise, we were screwed.

So, here I was, not technically alone if you counted the corpse beside me, but more alone than I'd ever been since Clove had taken my life and given me another. I thought back to the cathedral, and my internal monologue, debating on whether I should ask Teal to run with me.

This was my chance.

The voice sounded so loud I actually checked to make sure no one had crept up on me. But it was my own inner whisper. The truth of it turned my legs to jelly and I pulled them to my chest, wrapping my arms around my knees. I could leave right now. I was fed. I could probably find my way out of the town and if, *if*, the hunters caught me, I'd be okay. Clove had told me as much. Maybe I could find Noah and Olivia and persuade them to take me home? All I had to do was crawl out from under this metal box and run. The new blood thrummed in my veins, each cell a new world of possibilities. I felt alive, bright with energy and hope.

105

And then it hit me, a feeling so strong it seemed to suck all the breath out of my lungs. I heard Moth's voice in my head. *There is no going back, you know? What's in front of us. It's all we have.* I couldn't leave Teal to face what he might have to alone. I couldn't leave Clove, who had saved my life, and who might be in trouble himself. That was a thought I didn't want to dwell on. And I couldn't leave Moth, even if I wanted to. This was my family now.

I shuddered, the sensation running down my spine like the edge of a fingernail. My vision blurred and I blinked back tears, but I wasn't sure if I was crying for what I had lost or what I had found.

A torch beam swept under the container opposite. 'McGraw! Get your fat ass back here and move your truck. I got another delivery due at eleven.'

I froze in place, adrenaline spiking in my veins.

Another voice joined in. 'I don't like it. I'm sure that was blood back there. Think we should call the boss?' I picked up the fear from his scent.

'Nah. Don't be such a fucking pussy. And even if it was blood, it's probably dogs. I swear there's a pack of those mutts sniffling around most nights.'

I weighed up my options. I could bring them both down, but the kill would be messy and I didn't know how many others there might be. Clove's number one lesson fell into place: Don't bring attention to yourself. If that torch beam came my way…all hell would break loose. I inched back into the shadows, crab like, rolling out from under the other side of the container. Teal's supper lay with his blood clogging the dust into thick clumps.

It didn't take me long to find my way back onto the

street. It was busier now, the buzz of human nightlife, clusters of people standing outside bars, the stench of alcohol. I crossed my arms over my chest to try and hide the mess and skulked along. How the hell was I supposed to pop up a grating in this throng?

A police car cruised past with its window open, the crackle of static on the radio. I bent down and pretended to tie my boot lace. For the second time, I wished I had a phone to fit in. It was time to start thinking on my feet.

I picked up Moth's footfall as the police car stopped at the kerb a bit further up. It was behind me, the steps light but quickening. I fixed my concentration on the intricacies of knot tying. Then Moth's hand on my shoulder.

I stood slowly and greeted him with a 'hey', hoping I sounded like any other kid out on the street. The police car door opened. Moth extended his hand in a fist bump but his muscles were as tensed as steel rods. The smell of dank water rose from his clothes. A sudden shout filtered through the air from the container yard, sharp and urgent. The police car door slammed shut and the engine roared to life. I turned and saw it disappearing through the main gates of the compound, and the breath left my body in a long exhale.

Moth shrugged out of his jacket and handed it to me. A few people began to avoid us, crossing over the street. As nonchalantly as I could, I slipped it on. Moth set off before my second arm slid into the sleeve and I fell into step beside him. My heart was still trip hammering in my chest.

'I had to leave. I didn't have a choice.' I wanted to get in first before Moth pulled me down for abandoning our kill. But the berating didn't come.

His head was down, his mouse-coloured hair falling over his face.

'Moth?' My hand touched his wrist and he pulled away as though I'd burnt him. A sudden fear drained all of the moisture from my mouth.

'I went back into the sewer.' His eyes met mine, wide and slightly hazed. For an instant his bottom lip trembled. 'I went back to where we'd left him. But he's gone. Teal's gone.'

CHAPTER TWENTY-THREE

Emron D'Grey knew he was playing with fire. But the fact that he was bending the rules excited him to a point which could be called obsessive. He hadn't lied to Clove when he told him he had a special dispensation to hold him. The word 'treason' hadn't actually been said, but D'Grey knew the whispers ran along the underground web, each hushed expression of disbelief bouncing back to the spider at the centre. But this spider came in the shape of the grand ruling body of the vampire world, who for all intents and purposes had been slumbering quietly in their dotage, until a young pup came along and poked them in a tender place. And if one new voice could stir them up...D'Grey wanted his name to be the one other vampires talked about in the future.

It wasn't that he had anything truly against Clove, unless you counted the time when Clove left their bed one mid-winter's night without even a goodbye. D'Grey knew, deep down, he held onto grudges like some men held on to money. But the thought of some excitement coming into his life was more than he could turn down. The nights were all the same, despite all of his attempts to spice them up with fresh new blood and tender flesh. And a bored vampire ran the risk of the slow drip of insanity. He needed an outlet for his talents, and when this opportunity had turned up on his doorstep, quite literally…well, that had to be pure kismet.

He mused over whether Clove was lying. The spice master was a true vampire artist. If he didn't want you knowing something, you didn't get to know. But D'Grey's instincts told him Clove was, at the very least, bending the truth. His mind was on lock down. And this was probably the thing that served him up as guilty.

D'Grey had woken early with a flutter of what could only be called butterflies in his stomach. He pulled on his faded ringmaster's jacket and straightened his waistcoat, tying back his hair with a velvet ribbon. Clove sat in the next room, on the same chair as he had from the beginning. Only his eyes moved as D'Grey drew closer.

'Clove,' D'Grey tutted. 'Why didn't you use the guest bed? And after I changed the sheets, too.'

'I don't require anything from you, except freedom from this ridiculous farce.'

D'Grey pulled a wooden chair from the corner, spinning it around in a circle, then planting himself upon it, his legs astride and his chin resting on the back.

'Oh, it shouldn't be long.' He pulled a mobile phone from the slit pocket of his waistcoat and Clove arched an eyebrow. 'I know, I know. Abominable things. But needs must when the devil drives, and we are in the twenty-first century.' He grinned, but the smile didn't reach his eyes. 'When this rings, I will know exactly what we're going to do with you.'

'Even you wouldn't dare to harm me, Emron, and we both know that.' Clove's voice barely suppressed a growl.

'I won't be doing the harming, so don't worry about that. But if it's found you are harbouring a mutation, well...' He whistled three notes tunelessly.

'I think you know that after the last cleansing, they were all wiped out. Which makes it impossible for me to be harbouring one, does it not?'

D'Grey studied Clove's face for any flicker of emotion, but found none. This fact irritated him. His fingers tightened on the chair rails. 'Genetics is a fine thing, my friend. It can skip a generation or two. I'm sure there are a few specimens left. And now that the sun has set and the children must feed, we will find out who is telling the truth. I have hunters out at all points in the town. It would take a fledgling of extraordinary ability to elude them.'

He cracked his knuckles and smiled benignly. He knew Clove would never forgive him for whatever events might transpire, but he could live with that.

As if he knew, Clove bestowed on him a look that could break glass. But D'Grey was flying high on the thought of the next few hours, and what might come out of the woodwork now that the town lay in darkness.

The fact Clove could do nothing but wait was simply the icing on the cake.

CHAPTER TWENTY-FOUR

The phone call from Tom came through, right as Olivia and Noah were about to leave for their vigil on the cathedral steps. She thumbed the screen as Noah came out of the bathroom, holding up her hand and mouthing Tom's name. Noah's brow creased. They both knew if Tom was phoning there had to be a big problem.

'Fuck.' The word slipped out of her mouth after only the first few sentences, as a flush of shock chilled her skin. 'Is he stable now? What did the doctors say?' Her questions came thick and fast, but Tom didn't seem fazed. He answered them all fully before moving on to the next one. Olivia had an odd feeling she wasn't taking any of it in, as though her true self was running away as fast as it could so she didn't have to process what he was saying. 'Tell him we're thinking of him, Tom.' She passed the phone to Noah, who was pacing at the door.

Her heart began that quickening which had become so normal during those agonising weeks last year. Shards of it came back to her in glorious Technicolour recall—the sensation of spinning into a void as her car somersaulted into the ditch, the thick clog of coal dust in her throat as she fell into the cellar, the sound of her own scream when she learned her brother was dead. It had taken almost a year to climb back out of that soul-destroying pit, but right now it gaped open in front of her again. Gabe, Clove, and now Carver's collapse. This was no co-incidence.

'Olivia?' Noah's voice cut through the fog in her brain. She hadn't even realised he had stopped talking. 'Tom says there's no need to rush back tonight. Carver is sedated and won't know who's there and who isn't. But I feel like we ought to go home.' She knew he was fighting obligation and his friendship with Carver with the hope that Gabe might still be out there.

'He needs help, Noah. We can't pretend he's going to be the old Carver when he's good and ready.'

Noah sighed and chewed the edge of his thumbnail, a recent habit. His eyes clouded with worry. 'Tom says they are running tests on some bloods. He found him this morning but didn't want to ring until he had more news. The alcohol contributed to his collapse, but they think there might be more going on.'

She nodded miserably. 'So do we go back now or in a few hours?'

Outside, the light shifted one more shade into evening. Noah raised his head and stared out of the window. 'I say we give it a few hours, maybe until midnight.' He looked at her for clarification he had made the right choice.

There wasn't any right choice though, was there? But the least she could do was support him. She grabbed his hand and made for the door.

They walked in silence for a few minutes, both of them digesting the news from Tom. She wondered if they could have done more to help the man who had taken her in when no one else would. But how can you help when you're in over your own head into the thick mud of grief? Still, she felt a twinge of conscience over the fact Carver's unhealthy descent into research hadn't prompted more concern.

Noah glanced her way. 'Tom said he found a note on the floor with Carver. But it just looked like a book title. Do you think it meant anything?'

'Possibly.' But her gut instinct wanted to tear away that word and replace it with something much stronger. There were thousands of books in The Manor's libraries, more than even Carver could have read. So why would he take the time to write one on a piece of paper?

They paused at the edge of the pavement as a horse-drawn carriage went past. Its driver tipped his hat to them. The street lamp glow haloed around it. The lights in this part of the old town were gas lit, a nod to its history and a little fragment of nostalgia for the tourists.

Olivia's brain jumped from thought to idle thought as the spires of the cathedral came into view.

'I think you should ask Tom what it said. Follow up all possibilities.'

She laughed as her own words came out of Noah's mouth. He slipped his arm around her shoulders and kissed the top of her head.

'What gives, Mr. Isaacs?' She looked at him with a small quirk of a smile. They didn't do public affection.

A slight flush rose in his cheeks. 'I needed it. Humour me.'

The man with the pink umbrella was back, hustling his flock into the cathedral with all the charms of a rabid sheepdog.

'What will you do if you see him?' Olivia positioned herself next to Noah in the same spot they had occupied last night.

'Panic.' His eyes darted from person to person, his brain already in gear and focused. 'Because really it can only mean one thing.'

CHAPTER TWENTY-FIVE

Teal was dreaming. It was a thing of strange and fearful beauty because vampires didn't dream. It had been so long since images had danced in his head whilst he was sleeping, he almost thought that he must be awake. But the pictures were all in the centre of his mind vision, the area surrounding them blurred like an out-of-focus camera shot. There were fireflies, dozens of them, and he reached out, his fingers trembling. They swirled in patterns of dazzling light, and the brilliance of them made him want to cry. He wanted to tell Moth and Gabe about the wonder of it all, but he couldn't see them, couldn't feel them. But that was okay. For now, he would follow the fireflies. He travelled without touching the ground, skimming over the surface, aware of nothing but the seductive glow and the feeling of weightlessness. At the extreme edges of the haze came whispers, the voices all talking together in a Tower-of-Babel chorus. He veered towards them and the fireflies dimmed.

That's when he realised his feet were wet. Teal looked down into the dark water of the sewer. The dream crashed down around him, splintering into tiny pieces. He was suddenly very much awake and very much alone.

The seconds passed slowly in the dark. His heartbeat thudded in his ears, gradually increasing. His skin was covered in goose bumps. What did Sasha used to say? *Let's make them feel as if we're walking over their graves...*

But Sasha was gone. A sense of disorientation blanketed Teal, and he put one hand against the slick, cold bricks to steady himself. He had no idea how long he had been walking. As hard as he tried, he couldn't remember Moth and Gabe telling him they were going out either. But they wouldn't leave him. A small finger of doubt prodded his mind and he swept it away quickly. One thing he could rely on was the support of his brothers and Clove. Then he remembered Clove had not returned. He crossed his arms and rubbed his prickling skin. It was ice cold. He should be starving but he wasn't.

Teal had no idea where he was in the tunnel system. It looked different from last night. The bricks were newer with more concrete forming the curved roof. Somehow, he had to find a way to get back to the chamber. But was this fair? He stopped and let the thought permeate. Clove had said the hunters were looking for weak vampires.

In all honesty, he shouldn't have even survived his making. What if Moth and Gabe were better off without him? The realisation hit him like a blast of cold water. He tried to turn away from it, tried to breathe through it. But it was relentless. If the hunters found him, maybe they would be satisfied and leave Moth alone. But the thought of never seeing Moth or Gabe again lined his veins with despair. He wondered if he even had the courage to give himself up anyway.

It was strange, being alone. He couldn't remember the last time.

Well, he had two choices. Try and negotiate his way back down the maze of tunnels, or go above ground and get his bearings. He knew where they had climbed down, after all. Teal made his decision and pushed through the water until he came to a vertical shaft that housed a ladder. It might seem crazy, but how long would it be before the hunters did a detailed sweep of the sewers? Down here, he was a sitting target. There weren't many places to run.

He paused at the top and tried to hone his scanning powers. Nothing pinged on his radar, but that didn't mean it was clear. Slowly, he raised the grating a few inches. The narrow street was deserted. He climbed out and looked around, half expecting the hunters to leap out of the shadows. A row of shops, all closed, formed one side of the street. He darted into the doorways, which afforded some cover. At the end of the street, he paused, his heart skipping a beat as two men appeared. But they were too interested in each other to even notice him.

He caught his reflection in a window. Shoulder-length blond hair tangled around his face, and his eyes glowed like ocean embers. He didn't understand why he was different. None of the others stood out like he did. He remembered the fireflies and the way he had dreamed.

Moth had talked about something back in the chamber, about his visit to Emron D'Grey's. Teal thought back to last night.

Then D'Grey told Clove about the cleansing and about the hunters looking for mutations, but I don't know what they are.

Teal knew right there, in that moment, as the breeze brought the tang of the sea to his senses. He knew what the mutations were.

He was one of them.

CHAPTER TWENTY-SIX

Noah wasn't sure if Gabe's non-appearance was a good thing or not. Something deep inside was desperate to see him again, if only for a moment. His death had been so sudden. Even now, Noah couldn't think about it without feeling as if an iron fist was gripping his heart. All those hours of waiting for the demon to strike, and when it had, it had all been over in seconds. That it didn't claim Gabe wasn't a consolation at all. It had ended with the same result.

But what if the boy last night *was* Gabe? His mind grasped hold of the thought and turned it over slowly, as if it was scared about what it might find. What if, by some extreme miracle, Gabe *had* survived? Surely then he would have come home. Unless Clove had told him it wasn't safe.

The only other explanation reared its monstrous head and laughed in his face. Noah pulled his thin jacket closer to his body and Olivia looked up.

'I think it's time we headed back. We've been here for hours.'

Noah sighed. He knew she was right. A wave of disappointment flooded through him.

'Let's go back and hit the road. We can be home in a couple of hours, grab some sleep, then go see Carver in the morning.'

It was a sensible plan. So why did he feel like it was pulling him away from something more important? Carver needed him. This sighting of Gabe was only part of his hopeful imagination.

Olivia linked her arm through his and they made their way away from the cathedral. The crowds had thinned, apart from a group of people led by a tall woman in a top hat at the other side of the street. She stopped and her followers came to an abrupt halt behind her. Opening her arms in a theatrical wave, her long red fingernails caught the light from the street lamp.

'Right here in this house'—she pointed to a door below street level and all eyes wheeled in that direction—'lived the man who eluded police capture for over a decade. They only discovered him when a sewer backed up. With blood.' An *ooh* escaped from the crowd. She ushered them across the street, passing Noah and Olivia. She flashed a fake fang grin and slipped a business card into Noah's hand with a wink.

He studied it and laughed, without humour. "Lily LaBelle, Vampire Huntress."

'Jesus, that's fucked up.' Olivia grimaced, an odd shadow passing across her eyes.

Noah knew Lily LaBelle would wet herself if she ever came across a real vampire. But then, Noah had the benefit of hindsight.

They continued towards the hotel, passing deeper into the old district where the houses leaned together in their own conspiracy, and the price tags grew progressively higher. These were the old town houses owned by the port authorities, in the days when shipping had been the town's lifeblood. They were narrow in width and four storeys high, with basements below ground level, some of which were now trendy weekend haunts for migrants from the city.

The street was silent. The hairs on the back of Noah's neck rose. A sudden wind raced from the harbour, whipping Olivia's hair around her face.

Noah turned.

Under a gas lamp, at the far end of the street, stood a boy. A breath caught in Noah's throat. Even at this distance it was impossible not to notice his bright eyes. Olivia froze, her grip tightening on his arm. .

But Teal was gone as quickly as he had appeared.

'Still think we're wasting our time?'

Olivia didn't reply. Her lips were pale.

'So what do we do now?'

'You need to go back and check on Carver. I'll stay here and keep a lookout.' She tugged at his arm. His feet had suddenly become rooted to the ground.

'I don't want you here by yourself. It's not safe.' He frowned, glancing back to where Teal had stood moments before.

'I'm a grown woman and more than capable. Don't go all protective on me, Noah.' Her tone told him it was pointless to argue, but it didn't stop the odd fluttering of fear in the pit of his stomach. They walked in silence until the wrought-iron gate of the hotel came into view. Olivia ran her hand down one of the metal rails. Flakes of rust coated her fingers. Noah shivered. It looked like dried blood.

Inside their room, the mood was sombre. Noah tossed a few things into his holdall, trying to come up with a viable reason why she should come with him that wouldn't get him shot down in flames. He knew she was independent. He also knew she had been the one who had battled home with the palm crosses on that awful night. If she hadn't, Gabe might well be possessed.

A little voice flared up inside like a struck match. *Gabe is possessed now, but not with a demon.*

He shook his head in anger and Olivia bit. 'Just go, Noah. You don't need anything in that bag.' Her voice was cool and distant.

Noah opened his mouth to say it wasn't her he was upset with, but it was pointless. She hated goodbyes, hated the thought each one could be terminal. Ever since Ollie. He grabbed his car keys from the side table, pausing at the door with his holdall in his hand, feeling like he was getting thrown out. He took a step towards her and she dismissed him with her hand. His jaw tightened.

A sea fret misted in on the breeze, cooling his skin as he shut the door. He hated leaving her like this, but was unsure how to fix it. She would open up a new case file on her laptop, and document everything that had happened in a professional and concise way, as Carver had taught her. Any mention of Gabe would be distant. *A possibility the young boy sighted outside the cathedral, on the night of September eighth could be Gabriel Davenport, is noted.* He slammed the gate behind him in frustration.

It was a short walk to the old, abandoned railway station where his car was parked. He glanced at his watch. Just gone midnight. There was no need to be back at The Manor until morning. The hospital wouldn't let him visit until at least 9 a.m. Noah made a decision as the fine mist settled on his skin. First, dump the holdall. This would give him around five hours to go snooping around before he had to leave. He knew better than to check in with Olivia and tell her his revised plan. With any luck, she would be engrossed in the case notes before tumbling into bed. He thought about her scent as she folded herself against him in the night. Suddenly, his jeans felt much too tight.

God, if he was damned, she was his devil.

He stashed his bag in the boot of his car and headed out, into the night.

CHAPTER TWENTY-SEVEN

'So, what now?' I broke the silence that had fallen between us.

'I don't fucking know, Gabriel. I'm not Clove!' Moth bit back before I'd taken my next breath. His eyes were dark with anger and I swallowed my own retaliation, shrugging as though it didn't matter. If this was the way he wanted to play it, fine. He confused the hell out of me though. Every time I thought I'd scratched the surface, he would glue it back up again twice as tight.

'What do you think?' he asked, just when I'd come to the conclusion he couldn't give a damn about anything I said or did. He met my gaze then glanced away, kicking at a stone in the road.

'I don't think it's safe to go back to the chamber, at least not yet. The hunters will be all over below ground once they've exhausted up top.' It was a clumsy word choice. I drew in a gulp of air through my teeth. Moth appeared not to have noticed. 'Maybe Teal sensed they were coming so he had to leave?'

Moth fixed me with a stare, one eyebrow raised. 'This is Teal we're talking about. I don't think he has any kind of instinct, apart from the one to feed.' He paused and bit the edge of his lower lip. 'That's why we have to find him. He's a sitting target without anyone to look out for him.'

It dawned on me then: a lot of Moth's attitude right now was down to plain worry. I should cut him some slack. But he made that nearly impossible most of the time.

Something fluttered in the gutter. I bent down to pick it up. It was a ten-pound note. I rolled it between my fingers for a few seconds before letting it fall to the ground. It was so familiar, but so abstract at the same time. Part of my Before world.

By now we were skirting the edges of the old town, both of us as twitchy as alley cats. Moth looked back over his shoulder. 'Let's stop here and come up with a plan. We can't just walk around in a circle all night.' We had stopped on a cobbled lane next to a group of low buildings. The scent of hay and leather and horse shit hung in the air. This was the stabling area for the horses that pulled the town carriages.

There were a few people inside, but all were congregated in one area. Laughter came in bursts from a small room with harsh fluorescent lighting.

'Quick, in here.' I pulled Moth into the darkness of a rambling tack house by the gate. Standing against a wall was a pony carriage with bright yellow wheels. By its side, a couple of hay bales stacked together, a bridle in pieces on the top. The space was all old leather and summer dust. The scent of it took me back to my childhood. I shook my head to clear the image.

Moth settled on the floor, picking up a strand of hay and twirling it in his fingers. He looked miserable. It would be up to me to start a dialogue then. Why was he such hard work?

He glanced up at me. 'What?'

A flush of colour rose in my cheeks. God, I'd been broadcasting that thought loud and clear. He watched me steadily, his eyes searching for my weak spots.

'Tell me about you and Teal. How did you meet?' The words tumbled out on top of one another in their haste to break the silence.

'Why does it matter?' I'd expected to be shot down in flames, but his tone was even. He grabbed my hand and pulled me down beside him. The blood from our kill still ran in his veins. His fingers were warm.

'I figured it would be good to know, considering we're stuck with each other.' Any attempt at swagger failed. 'Look. I know I'm not Sasha—that I can't replace him.'

A small movement at the edge of the room. Our eyes wheeled together. A tiny mouse. Moth stared at it for a few moments before answering. 'I was already with Clove when Teal came on the scene. Clove went out one night and didn't come back until nearly dawn. I remember wondering if he'd dumped me. He was carrying Teal. His skin was scorched from the pre-dawn light. All Clove said was that Teal needed looking after. He never told me why he had picked him. I found out afterwards Clove had hunted down a rogue coven and destroyed them. Teal was the only one he spared. I guess even the spice master has a heart.'

He saw the question in my eyes. 'That's what D'Grey called him.' He rubbed the hay between his palms. I was drawn to the simple act as I listened. He was telling me more than I'd ever expected.

'At first I wasn't happy about babysitting, because I thought that's what it was. It was obvious Teal didn't have a vampire bone in his body. But you know Teal. He's a good kid, there's no agenda with him. He's all light, whereas I'm all shadow. Looking out for him is a privilege.' He stopped and brushed his hair out of his eyes.

I had been holding my breath as he talked, not wanting to break the spell and send it all crashing to the ground.

'No one is all shadow.'

He studied me again, his lips twisting into a half smile. 'I'm not good news, Gabriel. People get hurt when they're with me. Don't get too close.' He leaned across and traced the back of my hand with the hay strand.

I froze in place.

'There's something else you should know. Clove told me not to say anything, but I guess it doesn't matter now. This mutation thing.' He closed his eyes and rested his head back against the hay bale. 'Teal has it.'

The weight of his words crushed all the air from my lungs. I wanted to tell him to stop messing around, this wasn't funny, but one look at his face told me he was speaking the truth.

I'd wanted him to let me in, but part of me wondered what I'd trade now not to know.

       ✝

Moth stopped talking as he and Gabriel walked back to the old town centre. He wasn't sure what had come over him, unloading like that. What had happened to keeping it all close to his chest? He set his lips into a thin line. Gabriel stuck to his side, glancing across with those wide blue eyes full of questions. Moth knew he was being unfair, clamming up after delivering the news about Teal, but he didn't want to talk about it.

Moth was trying his best to keep Gabriel at arm's length, aided by his quick-fire temper and smart mouth, but each time, Gabriel bounced back. He had to give him credit for that. But it was pointless to push him away right now, with both Teal and Clove missing. Clove had prepared them for a lot this last year, but his disappearance hadn't been one. Now they were tied to a place when they should have been getting as far away as possible. But no way was he leaving without Teal.

It didn't take long for the façade of the cathedral to rear up again. Gabriel thrust his hands into his jacket pockets and the light mist coated the fall of dark hair over his brow. He craned his head to look at the spire, its tip swallowed by the sea fret.

Moth flicked his tongue, tasting the tang of salt as it settled in the moisture.

'That thing you do.' Gabriel stood motionless watching the sky, yet he had picked up on Moth's minute movement. 'How does it help?'

Pure bred. Those two words came back and jabbed Moth in a tender place. Gabriel might be young, but his blood and his instincts were strong. Something Moth would never be.

'Sometimes I can sense other vampires. They make my tongue tingle.' No one had ever asked him why he did it or how it helped.

Gabriel nodded. 'That's pretty cool.' He flicked his own tongue out and grimaced. 'All I can taste is salt and dirt.'

Moth smiled and shook his head. 'I don't think you need a vampire instinct for that, Gabriel.'

The smile felt odd on his face, a facial movement from his life before the man had dragged him away that Halloween. The sheer fucking cliché of it all still ground away under his tongue like crushed glass.

Gabriel laughed and turned his head slightly, his profile pale against the night. 'One thing I've always wanted to know. Your names, you and Teal, I'm guessing they weren't your human ones.'

Moth didn't ever think about stuff like that. A tree branch creaked in the wind and he followed the sound as it fanned out into the darkness. 'Clove named us both, for our looks, I guess. I don't remember what I was called before. Most fledglings don't. It's kinda a failsafe to help us forget. But not you, Gabriel. You came with a history. It's why you're different.'

A shadow passed over Gabriel's face and Moth wanted to take back his words. He hadn't meant to dig at him, not this time.

They passed in silence through the side alley, but this time no ghostly images greeted them. The streets were slick with rain, almost deserted.

The great doors to the cathedral were closed. Its stone steps were empty of even the pink-umbrella man and the dog with the neckerchief. There were no threats on the wind, only the damp emptiness of the fog, crawling in from the sea. It shrouded the tops of the trees in the small park between the cathedral and the road down to the port, billowing down to hang around the street lights, coating everything with the smear of early autumn.

Gabriel raised his head again and stared at the central spire. His concentration sharpened. Moth peered upwards, but all he could see were the stone grins of the gargoyles staring down and mocking them.

The central tower rose to its sharpest point—guarded by two stone angels, their wings outstretched to the heavens.

Moth registered Gabriel's shock as his brother's eyes widened, the slow ripple of his throat as he swallowed. His own eyes wheeled to the sky, searching through the gloom for what Gabriel had seen.

As a patch of mist cleared and the statues came easily into view, he was suddenly aware there were three figures up there. At the foot of one of the angels, a hunched form opened two bright eyes.

'Teal…' The name formed on his lips, setting off as a shout but ending up as a whisper. Teal was sitting far too close to the edge of the statue's platform, and it was one hell of a long way down. Moth knew some vampires could jump that distance and be unharmed. But Teal?

'He doesn't see us, Moth.' Gabriel's worried voice brought him into the present. 'Look how he's staring but it's not registering.'

Moth fixed his eyes on the unmoving form of Teal and waved his hand in a wide sweep. There was no reaction on Teal's face.

'Fuck. What's wrong with him?'

'I don't know, but I don't like it. Come on, there must be a way up to that balcony from inside!' Gabriel was off, sprinting down the alleyway. Moth hesitated then followed. Part of him wanted to make sure Teal didn't move. Or worse.

Gabriel stood outside the side door with his hands on his hips. The expression on his face made Moth's heart sink.

The sign on the door read *Alarmed. Do not trespass.*

'What the hell does that mean?' Moth's eyes were on Gabriel, but his instincts were waiting outside those stone steps.

'It means that even if we did break through, it would bring a whole heap of attention our way.' Gabriel struck his fist hard against the flint column surrounding the door. A fine dust flew into the air. Flecks of blood dotted Gabriel's knuckles. It wasn't like him to get so emotional.

The only way to Teal was staring them right in the face. It would mean climbing the walls of the cathedral. Which would be virtually impossible with people so close.

Gabriel's gaze settled on the end of the alley. Moth turned as a figure staggered towards them, one hand clutching at the wall for balance.

It was Teal.

Moth and Gabriel took off in unison, and it was Moth who caught Teal as he fell. Teal clawed at Moth's arm, his eyes burning with intensity. Strands of blond hair whipped across his face as the wind gusted and Moth swept them away gently.

'Where the hell have you been? Are you okay?' He tilted Teal's chin up to study his face.

A question he didn't voice hung heavy between him and Gabriel. How did Teal get down from the spire?

Teal shuddered and closed his eyes, letting Moth ease them to the ground. Gabriel crouched down beside them.

'Teal?' Gabriel put his hand on Teal's shoulder and he opened his eyes, the brightness slowly fading. He looked around in confusion then smiled, or at least tried to, and Moth bit his lip.

'I followed the fireflies,' Teal's voice was hardly more than a whisper, 'they told me I needed to find something.'

Moth exchanged a worried glance with Gabriel.

'What do you need to find?'

'The labyrinth. It's how we'll save Clove.'

CHAPTER TWENTY-EIGHT

Noah made sure to skirt the hotel on his way back to the old town. He doubted whether his plan was sensible. Sense would mean driving home, getting a few hours' sleep, and then doing what he could to support Carver. It didn't mean trawling the streets in the dark, looking for parts of his past that could only open up scars barely healed.

He let his footsteps lead him. To his surprise, they didn't end up outside the cathedral. They paused on the street where they had seen Teal only an hour or so earlier. Noah's hair lay plastered over his face and he shivered. The only thing that could come from this would be a case of pneumonia. But something inside spurred him on. It was a hair's-breadth chance in hell this might lead to Gabe, but he had to try. So much for letting the past stay where it was.

A pain twisted in his gut as Olivia's face swam into view. All of this had unpeeled the thin layer of healing skinning over the wound in her heart. He should be there with her, not outside searching for ghosts. He wiped his hand over his eyes.

A plastic bag danced down the street, carried by a gust of wind. Noah watched its progress with grim fascination.

It rose and fell, finally attaching itself to his shoe as it came to a halt. He bent to pick it up, but as his fingers closed over its rain-soaked surface, it skipped away. A speckled-gold fleur-de-lis spike, sitting atop a row of rusted railings, caught it, the bag whipping to and fro as it tried to break free. *I remember this*, he thought, as a memory unearthed itself from his mind. Only it was a flimsy shred of clothing on a fence post…

A chill froze his feet to the ground as his ears tuned in to the slightest noise. But the only thing disturbing the silence was the rain as it pattered against the pavement, and the manic rustling of the bag.

The railings surrounded a basement flat. Its windows were barred, but the gate stood open. A few steps led down to a weather-worn white door.

Noah crept towards the railings, taking hold of the bag and wrapping it around the spike. The noise was starting to unsettle him. It sounded too much like a voice. A car passed by, the rain streaming in his headlights. Noah paused. His heart began to hammer. This was ridiculous. He was letting his imagination run rings around his logic, and he was too damn old for that game. Emotion lodged in his throat. Frustration and hope and sorrow. This was someone's house, and he was loitering outside like some petty criminal.

Behind the single dirty window, a candle flared into light. Someone was watching him. He stepped back in surprise, his foot slipping on the edge of the pavement. Two seconds later, he was flat on his back as the air in his lungs left his body in a painful exhale. He rolled over onto his side, hauling himself up by the railings. Embarrassment joined his queue of emotions.

The door stayed shut and the candle was gone. Maybe he had imagined the whole thing?

Another car sped past. Its headlights caught the top panel of the door for an instant. Something glinted in the light, far too fancy for such a neglected entrance. A shuddering breath left his lips.

It was a gold door knocker. In the shape of a lion's head.

CHAPTER TWENTY-NINE

Clove contemplated the silence as Emron D'Grey sat by his side, picking at a loose thread on the worn brocade of a Queen Anne armchair. A small smirk hung on D'Grey's lips. He was enjoying this situation a great deal.

'You know you're not a prisoner, spice master. I'd just prefer it if you stayed and enjoyed my hospitality for one more night. For old time's sake.'

Something sparked in Clove's veins, a rare emotion, which hadn't seen light in decades. Anger. He well knew how dangerous this feeling could be if he gave it wings. The hunters would be no match for him if he decided to rip the smirk from D'Grey's face. He could be back outside in a small matter of minutes, but with the blood of a pure bred and the hunters on his hands, he would be a dead man walking. He smiled at the irony of that last thought.

'Share the joke, Clove. You know how I like to laugh.' D'Grey steepled his fingers together, his long nails shining in the lamplight.

'I was thinking of how small you will feel when the ruling body find out you have kept me without reason.' Clove laced his words with a ribbon of softness. D'Grey's probing bounced back from his mental shields with such force

Clove's ears rang. His reaction stemmed the rush of anger. Better to tease the lion, but stay in control yourself.

So far, D'Grey had said nothing about the search for his fledglings. Clove wasn't sure if this was a good thing or not. On one hand, he was becoming increasingly concerned for their welfare, but on the other, he could not think of them in D'Grey's not-so-tender care. He would not dare hurt Gabriel, but Moth and Teal? Especially Teal.

A knife of concern dug into the soft flesh of his gut. He would not dare harm Gabriel, but there were other things he would do to him, just to spite Clove. The anger threatened again and he bit down on the flesh on the inside of his lip.

'I know you were holed up in the sewer. My hunters found evidence of your whereabouts. Not like you to be so careless, Clove.'

Clove tightened the ring of steel around his mind shield. D'Grey was goading him, waiting for him to ask about his boys.

'Moth must be out by himself, no doubt looking for you. If what you tell me is true about not having any other charges? The old town is a dangerous place for a young single vampire. All kinds of unfortunate things have happened in the past. Such a shame to see immortal blood spilled before it has a chance to ripen.'

A scuffle broke out in the other room, the sound of voices and a slammed door. D'Grey sighed and glared in the direction of the ruckus. It had broken his spell. Clove almost felt sorry for whomever would bear the brunt of his displeasure later.

'Oh, it slipped my mind, spice master. An envoy from the ruling body will be arriving, possibly tonight, to hear your case. A rising star, so I hear, and one who is held in high regard already. I do hope they will be sympathetic to your cause. I would hate for you to go down as the first master vampire to be held accountable on treason.'

A tendril of flame crept through Clove's veins, but it left ice in its wake. D'Grey's words were not an empty threat. There was a possibility, if Teal's whereabouts were discovered, Clove's noncompliance would be seen as treachery. It broke the carved-in-stone rule that mutations must be reported.

Clove let the enormity of this seep through his skin. What he had thought was a mere ruffling of his feathers by D'Grey had turned into a much deadlier game. The serpent's venom ran black and deep.

Clove knew he could run. He could grab his boys and take flight somewhere. They could lose themselves in the windswept wilderness. But how fair would that be to his charges? And he knew full well he would always be looking over his shoulder. The bounty on his head would be impressive.

One of the hunters, a stocky man with a scarred cheek who went by the name of Saxon, entered the room. He whispered into D'Grey's ear. The slow smirk became a wide and feral grin.

'Let him join the party!' he motioned to Saxon with an impatient wave. 'The more the merrier, don't you think, dear Clove?'

A muscle spasmed in Clove's jaw. He found the nerve ending and silenced it. His heart rate increased as his mouth ran dry. Who had they caught? If it was Teal, they were both dead. D'Grey watched him, his eyes never leaving Clove's face. The ringmaster smacked his lips together and laughed as Saxon dragged in his captive.

The man struggled, but the hands that held him were made of iron. He fell to his knees before D'Grey. The tang of the sea rose from his wet clothes.

Clove's breath steadied.

'Ah. I see you recognise this poor, misguided fool who had the audacity to lurk outside my door.'

Clove didn't have to say a word. D'Grey was picking away at his captive's mind as if it was a chicken carcass.

Noah raised his head and met Clove's eyes, the smell of fear prickling from his skin.

'What have you done with Gabe?'

CHAPTER THIRTY

Olivia stared at her laptop screen as the letters all blurred together. She rubbed her eyes in frustration, leaving smudges of mascara on her fingers. Her notes were direct and professional. She hadn't left anything out. When she got home…she paused. Why would going home solve anything? The puzzle was here, and she knew it.

Her phone lay on the bed beside her. She thumbed the screen. No messages. After how she had treated Noah, what did she expect? None of this was his fault, but she had taken out her worry and irritation on him, knowing he'd shoulder whatever she threw his way. Why did she have to act like such a bitch? She slammed the laptop lid down and slid off the bed, padding to the bathroom to wipe away the racoon shadows.

Something churned away in the pit of her stomach. Things were rapidly spiralling into the kind of night she thought impossible to relive.

'Ollie, I miss you so much.' Her whisper fell into the silence as loss twisted itself against her lungs. She closed her eyes, trying to inhale slowly, to stem the rise of panic. Her fingers shook as she grasped the edge of the sink basin. Finally, she regained control, even though her heartbeat still hammered in her ears. It had been months since she'd had an attack like this. Fuck.

An overwhelming desire to hear Noah's voice surged through her, and she grabbed her phone before it passed. He should be home by now. The dial tone punctured the stillness in the room, and she held her breath. It went to voicemail and she listened to Noah's self-conscious attempt at a 'leave a message' blurb. Maybe he was still driving? He wouldn't answer if he was, but he would pull over when his notification light flashed.

She waited, willing her phone to vibrate. After ten minutes, she gave up watching it, avoiding the thought that he might have had an accident. Her brain was far too wired for sleep. She contemplated walking the streets, but what was she looking for? Besides, fate had given her enough nudges. Clove. Teal. The boy who looked like Gabe. She swallowed the lump of hope in her throat. The logical part of her brain had told Noah it couldn't be Gabe, but with all these other sightings…she rested the tip of her forefinger against the hollow above her lip and opened up the laptop.

Two hours later and with eyes that felt dusted with grit, she stretched her shoulders back and realised she had been going around in circles. Maybe she was going down the wrong track? She signed in remotely to The Manor network and opened up Carver's latest document. Scanning the words quickly, she didn't find anything to pique her interest. Most of it was rambling but that was okay. That was what he had taught her. Document everything. Every thought and every possible lead. Because someone might come along and join up the dots you were fighting to see.

Most of it was about the hidden secrets in paintings and how symbolism could silently tell the truth when no words were allowed. She read through five pages of notes about Gauguin and Munch before her brain shrivelled. Her phone lay cold and silent. It was quite possible Noah was severely pissed off, enough to want her to stew in her own juices until morning. But he didn't think like that. He was what society called a decent man, the kind your mother always hoped you'd bring home. Not that she'd ever had a mother.

She needed a stern talking-to before her head wandered into places it had no business going. There was another person who didn't treat her as if she was made of glass: Tom. But it was 5 a.m. Even he didn't get up this early.

Thank God he'd been around to find Carver, though. She wondered why he had gone over in the first place, and put it down to wisdom she could only ever hope to possess. A sudden thought poked itself from the depths of her tired brain. Tom had said he'd found Carver with a book title scribbled on a note.

Within minutes, she pulled what Carver had accessed recently from the database, cross referencing them against the curator's last document. All of the books in The Manor's massive libraries were meticulously stored by title and subject on the main server. The assignment was one all the new students got—or had got when there *were* new students. She remembered complaining bitterly about the laborious task with Ollie at her side, a grin of happiness on his face. *Don't think about Ollie. Just don't.*

She checked and double checked, finding each link, then applying it to others until she had come to what Carver always called the 'bare bones'. Some she tossed aside as red herrings. But one stood out, constantly reoccurring no matter how many rules she applied.

Rebirth and resurrection.

There was also a phrase, one Carver had used as he had picked away at his symbolism link: *There are no dead ends.*

So, she had something…but she didn't know what it meant. Wiping her sweating palms on her jeans, she glanced out of the window into the stillness of the pre-dawn.

Rebirth and resurrection.

Ollie was dead. They had buried him in the churchyard of St. Jude's on a bright-blue-sky autumn day with air as crisp as frost.

That left Gabe.

It didn't take someone with much common sense to piece it together.

CHAPTER THIRTY-ONE

Emron D'Grey gazed down upon the mortal man on his knees, and gifted Clove with a broad smile. The tip of one fang glinted in the light. This was possibly the most delightful night he had experienced in decades. Destiny had provided him not only with a warm drink before bedtime, but one who obviously knew Clove. The ripe tang of fear rose from the man's skin. D'Grey's mouth watered.

'Gabe? Who is this person, spice master? One of the elusive three that you don't travel with?' His eyes snapped back to the mortal. He studied him with a hawk-like scrutiny before hauling the man up by his shirt collar. To give the mortal his due, he did struggle as D'Grey held him at arm's length.

There was a steely resolve in Clove's expression, but a tiny quiver of his eyelids told D'Grey what he needed to know. The human would be useful. Very useful indeed.

He sighed as the image of his supper disappeared.

He dropped his hold and the man crumpled to the floor. One booted foot fell onto the man's neck. 'Tell me, or I will grind him into the dust.' For emphasis, he applied weight to his foot and the man cried out in pain.

'For the love of God, Clove, where's Gabe? Did you turn

him? Did you?' The man spat his beseeching words onto the dusty floor.

D'Grey sighed again as Clove sat back in his chair and folded his hands across his lap. A soft growl rose in the ringmaster's throat. 'If you don't co-operate, I will pick his mind clean and leave nothing, I swear!'

Something akin to the crackle of static electricity ran through the room.

'Gabriel is my fledgling, pure bred. Highly naïve. I thought it imprudent to bring him to anyone's attention as he is so wet behind the ears.'

A strangled sob rose up from the man sprawled on the floor.

D'Grey smiled and removed his foot. 'Now, wasn't that easier? There was no need for any unpleasantness. So finally, you have spawned, my old friend. This one must be incredibly special. I can't wait to meet him.'

The mortal staggered to his feet, one hand holding the back of his neck. He fell towards Clove, one arm raised, and Saxon swept in before the blow could fall.

Clove remained unfazed, his gaze fixed on the man's distraught face. 'Would you rather have had me leave him to die in the dirt?'

The man's jaw trembled.

'I thought not.' Clove lowered his voice. 'Believe me, it was not a decision taken in haste. I gave him a second chance.'

'You had no right. Only God has the right. And you are the devil.'

D'Grey watched this sparring with an expression of unbridled joy.

'Gentlemen, this reunion is all very touching. I can't tell you how surprised I am that you have a history. The chances of this happening right here in my little house…well, you've made an old vampire extremely happy. Haven't you, Noah Isaacs?' His tone chilled as he motioned for Saxon. 'Take him away and lock him up. I'll deal with him later.'

Saxon ushered Noah into the back room as D'Grey slowly circled Clove. He paused and placed his hands on the back of Clove's chair, lowering his head. He blew against Clove's ear, goading for a reaction. 'You're hiding something, spice master. But I'll unwrap it layer by layer. And if I find out what I believe is true, I will take your precious children and rip them apart.'

CHAPTER THIRTY-TWO

I don't know why we had picked the library out of all the other places looming up as we guided Teal off the streets. He was still confused, rambling on about Clove and finding a labyrinth. Moth and I stayed silent about it, urging him forward, both of us sure at every street corner we would run straight into a pack of hunters. The night seemed to have eyes in every doorway.

We broke a window at the back entrance of the building, expecting to hear the shrill wailing of the security alarm, but all was quiet. Maybe no one wanted to steal a few books anymore.

I sat with my back against a low area of seating. It was dark here, the only light the glow from the fire exit signs over the doors. The smell took my heart and twisted it inside out. It was the scent of page and ink, of words only silent because no eye hovered over them. It was the scent of home.

Moth clicked his fingers near my face. 'For God's sake, focus, Gabriel. I can't do this on my own.'

It was the first time he had ever admitted it.

However we'd imagined finding Teal, it hadn't been like this. We'd expected starving and scared and overjoyed to see us. I'd hoped Moth would know how to deal with him like this, but it looked like he was as clueless as I was. Right now, Teal sat at a wooden desk, a fine art book spread open in front of him. His blond hair fell over his face, pale gold in the minimal light.

'Do you think he made a kill?' I watched from the floor, my eyes flitting over the shadows.

'Are you kidding? He'd be covered in blood if he had. He's worse than you.' Moth paced before me, his hands refusing to be still as he clasped and unclasped them.

'Gee, thanks for the vote of confidence.' The words slipped out as they often did, and I steeled myself for a rebuff.

'What the fuck is this labyrinth stuff he's talking about?' His face was tight with worry.

I thought back to the great libraries at The Manor. And Carver. He would know. But I was dead to him. The old feeling of drowning in my own blood flooded back. I dropped my head and focused on a spot on the tiled floor. Then it hit me. We were already in a place with the answers to thousands of questions. My head jerked up as if it was on a string, and I sprang to my feet, dragging Moth off to the 'Alternative' section, where books were filed when no one had an inkling where else to put them.

'Books? That's your answer?' Moth looked at me as if I had lost all sense. 'You do know all this stuff in his head is crazy talk?'

I stopped, my hand resting on a shelf. Moth's jaw was set tight, but his eyes, those messed-up eyes, glistened. I never noticed the odd colours anymore.

'You think he's losing it?' I kept my voice low.

'Clove always said he was the runt of the litter, and he shouldn't have survived. What if all this upset has tipped him over the edge?'

148

The possibility lurked behind all the other jagged emotions flying about my head, and I didn't want to give it any breathing space. Moth's dejected expression mirrored how I felt. We were so out of our depth here.

I glanced at Teal's still form and my heart lurched. *Mutation.* The word sounded tainted and bitter, the polar opposite of what Teal was. I couldn't give up on him. Moth turned away and ran the back of his hand over his eyes.

I grabbed his arm, refusing to let go as he stiffened. 'But what if he's right, Moth? We have to consider it. Clove needs us. He would never abandon us unless something was seriously wrong. What have we got to lose?'

'You don't want me to answer that, Gabriel.' Moth's pain was etched in each line in his face. 'If you want brutal honesty, I think we're all living on borrowed time.' He held my gaze, the only sound the turning page from across the room and the wind rattling in through an air block.

'Tell me about Sasha.' I had to concentrate to form the words. But I knew, deep inside, I had to understand what had happened in order to make sense of what was happening now. Life is cyclical—Noah had told me that once. I said a silent prayer, hoping he was safe and far away. I couldn't bear the thought of him being dragged under again, into another one of my messes.

‡

Moth knew one day he would have to explain, but a huge part of him wanted to clam up or throw down another ice-cold barrier between him and Gabriel. His new brother had been all questions right from the start, and this had been waiting in the wings for a long time. It wasn't fair to keep the truth from him, not when Sasha's name kept cropping up like a phoenix from the ashes.

The old hurt reared up and punched him in the gut. Along with the guilt. He looked away and his eyes fell on Teal. Gentle, beautiful Teal, who right now was going quietly bad-blood crazy. It was all so fucking unfair. The thought of losing him too…Moth shook his head and tried to catch his breath. Gabriel's eyes watched him, non-judgmental and full of trepidation. Moth had tried to keep him at arm's length, had tried to make him feel unwelcome. That had been easy at first, because he did resent him. And Gabriel brought a shitload of worry.

Moth fought to control his feelings, but they were all galloping around his head like a herd of spooked wild horses. He got by playing it cool and acting like things slid off his back without leaving a mark, because that way he didn't have to face up to any fallout. But right now things had blown up in his face and the only friend he had was Gabriel. Unloading about Sasha would probably send Gabriel running off into the distance, but what choice did he have?

'Tell him, Moth. It's okay.' Teal's voice floated over from the other side of the room. Moth's eyes widened in surprise. He wondered how much Teal had heard.

He shivered and crossed his arms, hugging his elbows. Might as well get it over and done with.

'Sasha was everything I'm not. He was older than us, and probably smart enough to get by without a mentor. But he had tagged along with Clove to learn. When Teal joined, things got messed up for a bit. There were nights when all Teal could do was sit in a corner and throw up any blood he took. Sasha sat with him and coaxed him to try again. He stood by me when I didn't know what to do to help. And slowly, really slowly, we all bonded.

'Sometimes Sasha hunted for us if Clove let him. He liked that. Teal grew stronger and we all hung out, all of us so different but thrown together. We kept to Clove's rules and it was good. There was a line and none of us crossed it, although Sasha dipped a toe over it sometimes to see what he could get away with.'

Moth paused, the memories getting caught on the edge of his words. They were like dominoes and he wondered when they would all come tumbling down.

'One night, Sasha sent me out by myself to practise stalking. We were in a pretty isolated area, but there was a campsite in the woods nearby. He said I needed to learn to control my thirst, and the only way I could do that was to put myself in the zone, then learn to pull back.'

'Go on.' Gabriel's soft voice urged him on as he hesitated again.

'To cut a long story short, I fucked up. I misjudged the light and had to find shelter for the day. I had to dig a hole in the ground with my bare hands and cover myself with earth, and all the time my skin was blistering. I was so scared.'

Gabriel's eyes were full of empathy that Moth knew he didn't deserve.

'At dusk, I got back to our den and everything had changed. Clove listened to my explanation and then dismissed me. I felt like a little kid caught doing something stupid, and that was worse than his anger. Sasha was having none of it. He argued my case, refusing to step down as he normally did. There were nights of word-slinging and I tried to intervene because it was my fault, but they had reached a point where there was no going back.

'Sasha sat with us, but I could tell he was troubled. I was scared he would up and leave even though he promised he wouldn't. If I hadn't been such a fucking wimp, he'd still be around.' Now the anger ignited, spilling from his mouth, each word a flame. 'Sasha announced that he was taking me and Teal, and leaving. I thought Clove would be glad to see the back of us. But what he did next, I didn't see coming. I remember his face was deadly calm. He told Sasha leaving wasn't an option, and that's when Sasha flipped. It was stupid and courageous and I should have helped him, but all I could do was cower in a corner and stare.'

'What happened?' Gabriel asked.

'Clove grabbed hold of Sasha and pinned him to a tree. Sasha tried to fight back, but Clove was much too strong for him. I heard Sasha's neck break and he cried out. It was close to dawn then. I knew if we could get him somewhere safe, the break would heal whilst he slept. I hoped this was just a huge lesson. That Clove would haul him inside, give him another chance.

But he didn't. Clove sealed the entrance to our den and the world went black. Outside, I could hear Sasha screaming as the sun came up.'

Moth stood straight and fixed Gabriel with a stare. This was where Gabriel would re-evaluate all of his attempts at friendship and pull away. No one wanted a coward at their side, not when everything was turning to shit.

'That's why I told you in the stable not to get too close. I'm not a good person. I never was, and that sure as hell didn't change when I became a vampire.' Moth waited for the inevitable disgust to show on Gabriel's face.

From across the room, Teal suddenly cried out, his hands clamped over his ears. Flecks of blood-tinged spittle flew from his lips.

Moth and Gabriel sped as one to his side as Teal's eyes pulsed with light. That faraway look glazed his face and Moth's heart dropped into his stomach. This must be the insanity Clove had told them about.

Teal grabbed hold of Gabriel's arm, his fingers like claws. 'The fireflies are here, don't you see? We have to follow them.'

CHAPTER THIRTY-THREE

Behind several layers of brick and crumbling mortar, a sentient being stirred.

Cocooned in a web of her own red hair, she was aware on some cellular level of the existence of a kindred form. Instinct flickered inside the cavity that held her shrivelled brain. In the black sockets of her eyes, a light flared. It pulsed in the pitch black, gathering speed, then split into a myriad of tiny dancing stars.

One who carried her blood was near. But so was danger.

Her memories still existed, strung along the web of her consciousness like little blisters, waiting to be pierced. They had taken her life. They had taken her eyes. But they did not know of her power.

Witch! Burn her! The shrieks of distorted fear still rang in some chamber of her mind. Old, she was, and bent over with age, her beauty long since vanished. Easy to pick on the old woman who made herb tinctures for a farthing. Easy to pick on the old woman with the bright gold eyes. Sickness had taken their cattle. A harsh winter, their young and infirm. As the land warmed to spring they needed to appease whatever god happened to stop by.

She knew they were coming, even before they did. In the small, damp cottage she made soup from the roots of a fresh dandelion patch. Soup she would not eat. Soup she had not been able to eat for many a year. She was grateful for her magic; it helped to keep the blood thirst at bay.

But her life did not end that night. Their torches burned her cottage to the ground, leaving her homeless. Their voices ridiculed, their laughter a mockery of disjointed song to her ears. She had no choice but to leave, although to where her steps would lead she did not know.

She was the first of what would be called a mutation—the unplanned blending of the vampire gene with the witch spirit. Her bloodline would run for centuries. But now, she sensed him. One in who the mutation was strong, but the blood was weak.

Come to me, she whispered, and the fireflies in her eyes took flight.

CHAPTER THIRTY-FOUR

Moth's confession took a back seat as we led a dazed Teal from the library. As much as I wanted to be the voice of comfort, I couldn't stop the flashing neon sign in my mind that told me Teal was losing it.

'Maybe he's seeing things because he's starving.' But even as I said it, I crushed it underfoot.

Moth stayed silent, his usual brooding expression firmly fixed. I thought I had managed to chink away at his armour in the last few hours. His vulnerability in telling me about Sasha poked through the blanket of concern about Teal. I didn't think it was Moth's fault Sasha had met such a horrible end, but Moth obviously was carrying around a whole cartload of guilt about it. And Clove's ruthlessness chilled me to the bone. Would I become as heartless in the years to come? Some part of me still clung to what I once was.

But I killed people now. There was no easy way to sugar coat that. At first, it had haunted me. Not simply the cold, hard fact, but the way it didn't bother me as much as my conscience told me it ought to. It was only after unloading to Clove one night I found out why.

It was my bloodline. Instinct trampled any aspect of

morality that might be left in a pure bred. It was evolution, he told me, a way to keep the species alive.

Nothing could have prepared me for this life, not even half living in the shadow of the supernatural under Carver's care.

The cool night air chased away my thoughts. This wasn't the time for any internal massaging of my conscience. The drizzle had eased, but the air was still moist. It coated Moth's lashes and hair instantly. His tongue flickered out. I found the tiny window in my mind, the one where I could send out feelers into the night. It was becoming easier to locate now, the action more fluid. A small shred of comfort warmed my skin. We were working together.

Teal clung onto Moth's arm, but at least he was upright, in the punch-drunk kind of way I'd seen often in this town. Anyone seeing us would think we were staggering back after a night of bar crawling.

I led the way through the deserted streets, past the debris scattered outside the late-night takeaways, past the bars now in darkness. Something told me where we were going. It made only a fragment of sense, but I had nothing else to cling on to.

'You're not seriously saying we hide out in there?' I'd paused at a familiar door. The streetlight at the end of the alley cast a golden shadow onto the steps leading down to it.

Moth paused and slid an arm around a wavering Teal.

'The hunters have checked this out already. I don't think they'll come back to it tonight.' I waited for Moth to come up with something more sensible.

The door to the crypt gave easily as I shouldered it, the chain at the other side snapping as though it were made of paper. I wasn't planning on sleeping here, but we needed to get off the streets.

'Easy, Teal, easy.' Moth helped to guide him through the pitch black until we came to the end where the tombs lay. A single tiny light, connected to a sprinkler system, shone out bravely.

Suddenly, Teal stopped dead, his eyes rolled back as his whole body went rigid. Moth looked at me in horror, both of us powerless to stop whatever was happening.

Teal's head fell forwards, blond hair spilling over his face. His breathing became ragged, then slowly calmed to almost nothing. I didn't know which state scared me the most.

'Gabe...' He reached for me and I grabbed his hand.

'I'm here, Teal. I'm here.'

His eyes glowed with a fevered luminescence in the darkness.

'They want you to know they have Clove. They want you to know they have Noah too. Give yourself up, Gabe. Or they will die.'

CHAPTER THIRTY-FIVE

Noah awoke with a throbbing headache and dirt coating his lips. He spat at the ground and eased himself into a sitting position. Fragments of a bad dream swirled around his mind like autumn leaves. For an instant, he thought he was drunk and waking up with his head in an unknown gutter. That's when the truth descended with an iron fist and he spun around, his eyes searching for shadows from his nightmare.

Clove sat at the other side of the room, a candle flickering on a makeshift table next to him. Still as stone. Noah jumped when his head moved. The master vampire's eyes glittered in the half light and his face seemed sculpted from marble.

Noah straightened his back, his eyes now more accustomed to the dim light. Clove motioned to the candle. 'My apologies for the archaic lighting. Our host deemed it theatrical enough to hold amusement, and it is better than pure darkness. For you.' Those last two words were ice cold

'Is it true? Did you kill Gabe?' Noah wiped the grit from his lips and eased himself up.

He no longer cared he was addressing something he knew could take his life. All of the frustration and hopelessness of the past year came boiling out of his mouth. His body trembled with rage and indignation.

'Yes, it is true. But as for the taking of Gabriel's life, I must remind you the demon shattered his body to such an extent continued life was not an option. I merely tidied up the demon's attack. Then I gifted Gabriel with another life. Not the same as killing him, don't you think?'

A rush of blood raced to Noah's head and for the first time, he understood the phrase 'seeing red'.

Clove sighed and fixed him with an unblinking stare. 'Your anger is understandable, but futile. Is your faith battling with your need to see him again?'

Clove's words had punched a hole in Noah's indignation. The question of his faith hadn't raised its head, but underneath, it all came down to that, didn't it? His faith in a God who had deserted him and torn apart his adopted family. It wasn't that he didn't believe anymore, it was that his blind faith was now a lot more wary. In the war between good and evil, the latter always appeared one step ahead. And if he asked himself the tough question Clove had posed, he didn't have to think long about his answer. His shoulders slumped as he fixed his eyes on the floor.

A hand pressed down on his shoulder and he whirled around as his heart jumped into his throat.

Clove loomed above him. Noah's eyes flew back to the candle. It hadn't even flickered.

'I do not think it is to our best intentions if we remain enemies, Noah. Our host is an unhinged and vindictive creature. You are in great danger. But the most important thing to know is Gabriel and my other two wards are in danger too. You have to decide if you want to help him continue with the life he now has, or be an accomplice to his death. Whatever you decide, you will have to live with it. That is, if you make it out of here alive.'

That same black worm of fear from last year slithered around Noah's gut. He had no doubt Clove spoke the truth. The vampire would not lie. He did not have to. But could he ever live with himself if he joined forces with a creature that killed and drank from other human beings? Was he prepared to sell his own soul to save Gabe, even if this meant he was aiding more deaths? He clasped his hands to his head, digging his fingers into his scalp.

Olivia. Her name swam up from the mire, her hand clutching for his. How long would it take her to realise he hadn't gone back to The Manor? She would start nosing around for clues putting herself in harm's way. As strong as she was, could she get through another trauma? Another logical slice of his brain argued it was possible he could put himself in the same category.

Clove's whisper came from over his shoulder. 'Your saviour was reborn, Noah. Resurrection is not an evil state of being.' The vampire's breath was ice cold and Noah shuddered, crossing his arms over his chest in an attempt to preserve warmth, or possibly his sense of judgement.

'What do you believe in, Clove? Have you seen the devil?'

'I have seen much evil in my time. Some of it by man, and some of it by other creatures. But if you are asking me for knowledge about a creature with a forked tail and horns, then I must say no. True evil lays in the hearts and minds of things driven by their own greed and lust.'

Noah had expected to feel relief. But if hell and the devil did not exist, then could the same be said of God and heaven? His head ached. His bones ached. He was getting too old for sleeping on a hard floor…Routine thoughts sped through his brain, pinging from side to side like balls in a pinball machine.

'Tell me about Gabe. Is he okay?' He hadn't wanted to ask, because asking meant he had to accept that the boy he'd rescued from the clutches of a malevolent force sixteen years ago, was now walking in a different kind of darkness. But he couldn't help it. He wanted to know. And if this damned him, so be it.

'I cannot tell you much for the other vampire you met, who goes by the name of Emron D'Grey, will rip it from your mind in seconds. And he will not care what else he takes with it. Just know Gabriel is adapting well.'

Noah laughed and to his own ears, the sound had a touch of insanity to it.

‡

Clove calculated the factors to his advantage. And the factors against. Noah's appearance slotted uncomfortably with the latter.

If the priest started thinking about what had happened at The Manor, D'Grey could easily swoop in and take a few freeze frames. And it was probable Teal would be in one of them. Clove was under no assumption his bright-eyed fledgling had gone unnoticed, especially to a human eye. He did not want D'Grey to have any more fodder for incrimination. It was possible his old ally was lying, purely to unsettle him, hoping he would let down his guard. The ruling body was a close-knit and ancient hierarchy. Clove could not remember them taking in a new member. This new blood must be a force to be reckoned with. And they would be out to prove a point.

He did not think his life was in danger. But it was true he was committing treason by not giving Teal up. Still, Clove had never agreed to the unsavoury way the mutations were treated. It was barbaric. An inner vision played against his senses and his lips tightened. He couldn't put Teal through that.

And now there was the added complication of Noah. If Gabriel found out, Clove knew enough of his fledgling to know he would try to free him. This would be disastrous. Gabriel might be pure bred, but D'Grey could rip his mind open in seconds. He hoped his boys had somehow managed to leave the town, but this was the wish of a dreamer. They would be scared and confused. His sudden disappearance a worry. Hunger would drive them out from any hiding place they found, and too much hunger would make them careless. He wondered how long it would be before the hunters forced them into a corner.

Emron D'Grey knew full well Clove would fight for them if they were truly threatened. And there was no chance they all would make it out unscathed. If it came down to it and he had to choose, whom would he save?

CHAPTER THIRTY-SIX

Tom's phone rang a few minutes before his alarm went off. It was his landline, which meant he had to climb out of bed, go down the stairs, and into the kitchen. The ring tone jarred at his senses as he shuffled the last few steps. If this was a sales pitch, he would roast the caller. But even telesales didn't ring at 5 a.m. Jip raised his head in the doorway, his tail a blur of black and white fur. Tom lifted the handset of the 1950's Bakelite phone from the cradle. Now they were selling these in upmarket stores at crazy prices under the term 'retro'. The whole world was going to hell in a handbasket.

'Tom.' The voice at the other end of the line belonged to Olivia. Anyone else would have added that they hoped they hadn't woken him, but Olivia didn't operate like that.

A small smile touched the corners of his mouth. 'Yes, you did wake me, but you knew that.'

Olivia wasn't put off. 'Noah drove up last night and I can't get hold of him. Can you check his car is at The Manor?'

There was a tiny note of worry in her voice and Tom snapped himself wide awake. It was only in the last couple of months she had started to come back from Ollie's death.

That had been a dark time, but they had somehow managed to climb out of the gaping hole the departed had left. Grief shared doesn't lessen, but knowing others understand is sometimes all you have to hang onto. His Betty had died the first week of December, and The Manor had pulled him into her folds even though their own hurt throbbed like a raw nerve ending. When he'd found out the full extent of what had happened the night he'd dragged Olivia out of the ditch in the middle of that storm, he'd processed it the way he processed everything. He'd gathered up the details and ran them through his mind, using the wisdom of age to unravel the knotted edges whilst looking for any lumps of bullshit. He had known enough about Carver and Noah to understand, however far-fetched it all sounded, that it was the truth.

Olivia's determination that night had won him over, and her refusal to tell him he was too old to make it up the hill when his 4x4 died, still warmed his heart. But it was true. The climb, with the ground like quicksand, would have finished him off for good. He hadn't gone home after she clawed her way up the bank. He had pulled on his old waxed coat from the days when he was strong enough to herd half frozen sheep into barns, and trudged back up the field until he found a spot where he could watch the horizon. At one point, the night sky above The Manor had taken on an eerie green glow. But the northern lights didn't show this far south.

'Tom? Are you still there?'

He grunted and came back to the here and now. No point in getting caught up in what was already done. 'I'll go round after I've fed the pigs. Is Noah going to see Carver later?'

'Yes. We were both going to come back, but something came up here.' Her reply was vague, but Tom knew it had to be important for her not to make the journey home. His mouth twisted into a slight grimace.

'Can you get him to bring the note Carver was found with when he drives back, Tom? I want to look at it myself.'

Tom frowned. The line crackled with static. 'I hope you're being careful.' If Carver had deemed the note important, there was every chance that it was its own can of worms.

'I'm a modern woman, Tom. Don't worry about me. Just get Noah to call me, okay?'

The line went dead.

Jip trotted across to his feet and poked his nose into Tom's other hand. Tom placed the receiver back and looked down at his collie. 'I don't like this, Jip. It feels wrong.' Jip pressed his muzzle closer, a wet pink tongue offering comfort. Tom winced as his right hip locked. His joints didn't like an early start, but they would have to cope today. He made for the stairs, hoping the flurry of unease in his belly was only hunger.

‡

Forty minutes later, Tom set off for The Manor in Betty's old estate car. Once a vibrant blue, it could only be called faded denim now, but it still ran sweetly. He felt close to Betty when he drove it, could still see the determined jut of her chin as she peered over the steering wheel. The old 4x4 that had met its end on the night of the storm stood in the barn. One day he would get it fixed, but for now it had been put out to pasture.

Jip sat beside him, happy to be out and about, his head resting on the half wound down window. Bacon and her piglets had been fed, and Tom normally went in for breakfast then. He had decided food would have to wait. Betty's voice tutted in his ear as he drove along the deserted road to The Manor.

A slight mist and the promise of autumn hung over the fields, and as he turned onto the lane, the great house rose majestically out of that mist, the lead roof sparkling in the sun. Tom drove through the gates. He pursed his lips, squinting as the sun's glint pierced his windscreen. The gates to The Manor were never normally open. Edward Carver had the full resources to install an electronic system, which would make the local delivery drivers more than happy, but he wouldn't hear of disregarding the old iron gates. Yes, they were heavy and squeaked in protest at each swing, but he liked the feel of them and the history of what they had seen.

Noah's car was not on the driveway, nor was it tucked away around the side of the house near the garages. Tom's unease multiplied. If Noah had set off when Olivia said he had, he would definitely be home by now. The possibility the priest had stopped off at St. Jude's popped into his head. Leaving Jip in the car, he tried the Manor door, and on finding it locked, pulled out the key from his shirt pocket. As the paramedics had set about putting Carver in the ambulance, Tom had the presence of mind to take a key. Now, as he set foot inside the hallway, he didn't know whether taking the key was a blessing or a curse.

Noah wasn't here, this was obvious, but Olivia had asked for the note, so he would get it. But first he tried the vicarage from the phone in the hallway. No answer. He rang Noah's mobile. It went straight to voice-mail. Olivia was right to be concerned. Tom didn't like it one little bit.

The silence hung in the air as he went upstairs, trying to ignore the jarring pain in his hip. This house needed people, and right now everyone who belonged here were scattered like discarded toys. Whatever had poisoned the air a year ago had left a dark stain behind. Tom was a pragmatic man, but he was glad of the daylight. A strange sense of déjà vu loomed as he relived the day he had found Carver. He had known something was wrong, even before he'd set foot in the house. The same feeling lay in the pit of his stomach now.

The door to Gabe's room stood open. Tom paused before he entered, a sudden image of the boy as a baby in Betty's arms, his dark blue eyes wide and confused as Betty fussed over settling him in. This was the start of it. Of something they had all fought in their own way for fifteen years. And now, even with the loss of Gabe, it was still somehow not over.

The note lay on the floor where Carver had been found, the empty bottle kicked to one side. Tom picked it up and stared at the words. How Carver and Olivia made any sense out of what they researched was beyond him. He eased himself downstairs, using the handrail, and set the note on the side table by the door, picking up the few pieces of post as he did so. Turning an envelope over, he took a pen from the small drawer under the table and scrawled a quick message to Noah.

Tom didn't want to insert himself into a situation where Noah had more right and experience. If the priest was simply delayed, he would find it and be on his way before nightfall. If not, Tom knew he would be the one taking it to Olivia.

CHAPTER THIRTY-SEVEN

Teal's words had taken what little grasp I had on reality and sent it spiralling into the dust. I retreated inside my head, trying to find some sense, praying he was wrong, praying he was going crazy. I wasn't proud of that.

Moth brooded, his eyes occasionally flicking across to look at me. No one suggested moving on. There wasn't a chink of daylight down here, but I could feel the impending dawn in my limbs. Nothing Moth could say would make digesting this ultimatum any easier, even if he wanted to lessen my fears.

I roused myself and glanced across at Moth, sitting with his back against one of the huge supporting pillars. He played with a strand of Teal's hair as Teal lay sprawled over him with his eyes shut. There was a softness in Moth's eyes I'd never noticed before, or maybe it had always been there, but all I saw was his eagerness to belittle me.

An odd feeling spiked through my veins and I looked away, into the darkness. The door Teal and I had barged through had been temporarily boarded up with plywood, and its pale surface was easy to see. My eyesight was definitely getting sharper. But that feeling continued to irritate me, like a grain of dust in my eye. I knew what it was but I didn't want to acknowledge it.

'He might be just babbling, you know that, right? Don't think you have to go off and do the whole hero thing and get yourself killed.' Moth's voice interrupted my internal monologue.

'I'm not aiming to get myself killed.' My reply came out with harsh edges and Moth's lips tightened. It was so damn easy to say the wrong thing with Moth, and he bit back as easily as I asked questions. I shrugged, knowing I should apologise, but the moment had gone.

Part of me wanted to believe Teal was in crazy mode again, but another part, the part that ran on instinct, the part I was learning to trust more and more, said he was right on the money. Somehow, he knew. Someone, *something,* had channelled through him to get to me. Now that someone had Noah. Regret welled up in my throat and I wiped the back of my hand over my mouth. It was happening again. People I loved were in danger because of me.

Moth eased Teal from his lap gently and stood, brushing the dust from his jeans. 'You can sit here all day if you want, but I need to get Teal somewhere safe.' So, we were back to ice cold. As if the events of the night hadn't even happened. I had been stupid to think we had made a move towards friendship.

Moth tried the lid of the tomb, but it was solid against him. He looked around as I dragged myself to my feet, and for a second I thought he was going to haul me up. I scanned the crypt, my eyes cutting through the shadows, sure there had to be somewhere to hide. The possibility of having to dig a hole in the graveyard reared its foul head.

Under the steps, which led to the boarded-up door, the shadows shifted slightly. I honed in and Moth followed my line of vision. Set into the stone was a small hatch with a metal clasp. The opening looked too small for any kind of storage, but it might do. Moth tried the clasp and it disintegrated in his fingers. This wasn't somewhere humans went. He pulled open the door and a draught of musty air filtered up. I scrambled across and peered into the blackness.

'I can't see how far back it goes, but it runs under that door.'

Moth was already hauling a drowsy Teal onto his feet. Teal shouldn't be sleeping yet. I was always the first one to fall. How the hell were we supposed to protect him when all we had were ceaseless questions? My brain tried to form some coherent train of thought and ended up with a rail crash.

Moth wriggled into the gap and disappeared for a moment. 'We should be okay. There's no trace of any link to outside.' His voice echoed.

He pulled Teal through the gap. I sank to my knees, fighting to keep my eyes open.

'Gabriel, come on!' Moth grabbed hold of my jacket and yanked me through. I don't think I could have done it on my own. He banged the door back into place and wedged a lump of sandstone against it. More blocks stood to one side. This must have been where the stonemasons kept their offcuts.

I wanted to tell Moth I was sorry for snapping, I was just confused and worried and scared. For Noah. For Clove. For all of us. But I collapsed in a heap, unable to move.

I realized now what I hadn't seen before. Moth wasn't only looking out for Teal; he loved him.

And I was jealous of that bond.

CHAPTER THIRTY-EIGHT

Olivia knew she had rung Tom far too early, but the gnawing feeling in her stomach over ran any sense of etiquette. He had become a rock in her life, a man she could rely on to tell her when she was going off the rails, and a man who would simply listen when the anger inside her head had to explode. She was lucky to have these men. Tom. Carver. Noah. All much older, but each one a necessary balm when all the dark flames wanted to consume her whole. She tried not to think about Noah. It was pointless to leave him any more messages, but her phone itched in her hand as she slipped out into the early morning light.

The old town was beautiful in its stillness, the air fresh with a sea salt tang and a hint of chill. She crossed the street where the smell of coffee drifted from the hotel kitchen and debated whether to go back and grab a cup, but her feet led her away, not to the centre of town, but to the outskirts where the bed and breakfasts clustered together like old men in the park. She passed the small square of land where the market bustled on a Saturday morning. An empty coffee container rushed past in the gutter, caught by a gust of wind from one of the many alleys that led down to the sea. She paused and rubbed her arms, wishing she'd brought a jacket. And she listened, tuning out the usual bells and whistles of life and using the sense Carver had nurtured. The fine hairs rose in the nape of her neck and she turned slowly, the wan heat of the sun disappearing behind a cloud.

The gates to the old convent stared at her. Once thriving as a way to save the souls and chastity of the sea-faring captains' daughters, the building now stood unused and dilapidated on a prime corner site, with views of the ocean. A thick chain encircled the gates and a sign declared, *Acquired for clients by Broker and Dobson*. It had a certain smugness about it.

Olivia crossed the road and peered through the railings. The garden was choked with weeds and someone had thrown a dirty mattress over the wall. The darkened windows of the convent yawned at her. A shiver ran down her spine. Her sixth sense flared as her fingers tightened on the rusted bars. There were spirits here watching, drawing her closer, feeling her gift, calling their kin. She should step back. *Never go in alone if you can't tell whether or not they are malevolent*, Carver used to say. But this was daylight, and she could hardly call for any kind of back up. A deep yearning tightened her throat. She wanted Ollie. She wanted Noah.

The high walls surrounding the convent were topped with barbed wire, but maybe there was a place around the back where she could scramble over. She was glad to have something else to focus on, other than Noah's silence. And seeing Clove and Teal. And the elusive clues in Carver's note. Things were starting to spiral in a helter-skelter rush of chaos and she felt perpetually two steps behind. No one passed her as she cut through the alley to the convent's rear. The back wall faced a narrow street and the rear exits of a few shops. A green dumpster gave her exactly what she was looking for, and she scrambled up, not caring if anyone came out to deposit any rubbish. It was easy to reach the top of the wall from there. Somehow she managed to scrabble up, scuffing the toes of her shoes as she tried to find leverage. A barb spiked her wrist and she yelped, then gritted her teeth. Her fingers found the other edge of the wall and she pulled herself over, ignoring the scraping of skin along her shins. She clung like an alley cat whilst she got her balance, the glare of the sun glinting from the ocean. From her vantage point, she could see the Victorian roof of the railway station with its white-faced clock and the car park behind.

And there was Noah's red car, parked exactly where they had left it.

Her heart dropped into her stomach like an elevator in freefall. If Noah's car was still here, where the hell was he?

CHAPTER THIRTY-NINE

Moth opened his eyes to find two bright blue-green ones staring across at him in the dark. For a few seconds, he wasn't sure where he was, the sleep fog slow to clear. A weight pressed against his back and he half turned to find Gabriel wedged against the opposite wall.

'Do you think I'm going crazy?' Teal's voice was barely more than a whisper. Moth didn't answer. Teal sighed and gripped Moth's arm. It was an urgent gesture. 'I don't blame you. I thought I was at first. But I'm hearing voices, well, one voice, and it's telling me things I know have to make sense, even though they don't.' Teal paused and Moth tuned in to his anguish.

'We're going to get you out of here, me and Gabriel. We won't let the hunters take you.' He tried to make his words sound firm and decisive.

'They have Clove and Noah. What I said about Gabe is true. They want to see him.'

'And what did your voice say about what will happen if he does go?'

Teal stayed quiet for a moment, the light in his eyes dimming, then whispered against Moth's ear. 'What he sees might make him crumble. And if he does, we're all dead.'

Moth would have told anyone else to quit being so fucking melodramatic. But Teal was deadly serious. Right now, Moth didn't have anything else to cling on to. It seemed like they were screwed whatever they decided.

'How will Gabriel know where to go? I'm guessing it's not exactly signposted.'

Teal's fingers tightened. 'I can find out. But I followed the fireflies. It's how I got out of the sewer when the hunters went down there.'

'I'll go. I don't have a choice.' Gabriel's voice came from behind. It sounded weary even though he had just woken.

'You *do* have a choice. You could get the hell out of here.' Moth spit the words into the blackness, somehow angry at Gabriel for his bloodline even though none of this was his fault.

'Is that the kind of person you think I am?' Gabriel's voice trembled slightly.

Moth was glad of the dark, shame prickled his skin.

'We don't think of you like that, Gabe, I promise,' said Teal. 'This is hard. Really hard, for everyone.' As usual, Teal poured balm on a situation that could have got ugly very fast.

Moth knew he didn't deserve either of his brothers. He had a huge chip on his shoulder that even death hadn't managed to shift. He wormed himself down towards the hatch door and removed the sandstone wedge.

Gabriel appeared beside him. 'We're safe to go out. I checked.'

Moth's wrist brushed against Gabriel's as they moved to open the hatch. They both pulled away instantly. Carefully, they stole out into the body of the crypt, followed by Teal, who inserted himself between them as they made for the door.

A blast of cool night air swept the dust from their skin as they crept up the steps to the alley. Moth watched Gabriel from the corner of his eye, aware he was scanning in a way Moth wouldn't ever be able to. He could rage against him, but it wouldn't make any difference. He had to find the ability to accept Gabriel. To let him in, even though he was scared to death of adding another name to the list of people he had failed. Because he wasn't Sasha. And he wasn't trying to be. But if Gabriel went into this alone, he might never come out again. They needed strength, and this last year had proved Gabriel had a freaking truckload of that.

Something shifted deep inside him. Moth wasn't prepared to lose another brother. If they went down, they would all do it together.

‡

The past few nights, I'd felt like we were all on some kind of a demented hamster wheel. We had gone over the same ground so many times it just wasn't funny anymore. We were tied here because of Clove, and now Noah, when we should have been getting as far away from the town as possible. A heavy foreboding hung over my head like a thunder cloud. I'd had this feeling before. And look how that had turned out.

Moth seemed happy to go along with Teal's insistence about hearing voices and seeing fireflies, but I veered between needing to believe so I didn't have to think about the consequences, and wondering how on earth it could be true.

Moth's words from the crypt echoed around my head. *You could run.* Part of me wanted to. I'd take my chance with Clove afterwards. But a bigger part told me it was time to man up. I wouldn't be able to live with myself if anything happened to any of my family, past or present. And this included Moth. But his hot and cold attitude was confusing the hell out of me. I didn't know how to act anymore. Then I remembered last night in the stable, and the way he had softened enough to let me see behind that steel plated armour he wore. This was the Moth I wanted. This was the best friend that I'd never had. I wasn't proud of my jealousy, but for now it seemed to have simmered down. There were more important things I needed to concentrate on.

I didn't understand why I was suddenly so important. Clove had told me I was safe. But that was before he had been plucked out of our lives so suddenly. If a master vampire was captive, it didn't say much for my chances. But at least they hadn't insisted I bring Teal.

As we crept along the shadows by a wall somewhere on the outskirts of the old town, Teal keeled over, going into a state of trance again. Moth caught him before he hit the ground and we dragged him over to a gateway set slightly back from the road. I wasn't as scared as the first time I'd seen him like this, but Moth brought the back of his hand to his mouth and bit the skin over a knuckle. He was worried stupid.

I hesitated, then reached across Teal's chest to touch Moth's shoulder. 'He'll be okay. I think this is his way of tuning in to whatever is out there.' I kept my voice low and light, as if I knew what I was talking about. He tried to smile.

'Want me to go make a kill?' I offered in the time honoured way Ella would have offered tea. But I wasn't hungry. Fear had filled that gap in my stomach.

'No, stay...' His voice tailed off. I waited, picking up a pebble from the floor and tossing it between my hands, but he didn't continue.

I stared hard at the small, polished surface. 'When I leave, I want you to get Teal out of here. It's pointless waiting around, and it might be the only chance you get.' I hoped I sounded brave and sure. I risked a glance towards him. He was staring down the street, his mouse-brown hair whipping across his cheeks. I waited, willing him to answer, to say something. His silence spoke volumes. I knew if I didn't go now, then I might never make it. I closed my eyes and craned my head back against the railings of the gate. My heart was hammering so fast I could barely count the beats. Tears welled up behind my eyelids and I squeezed my eyes tighter, hoping he wouldn't notice. A tidal wave more lay lodged beneath a lump in my throat.

I sensed him move before I heard it, felt the air change as the molecules shifted. Moth was on his knees in front of me, probably about to give me a dose of snarky advice to send me on my way. I squeezed the pebble in my fist and waited. Then his fingers touched my cheek and wiped away a tear.

'Gabe.' My name fell off his tongue as delicate as a spider treading its web. I could cope with prickly. But I couldn't cope with empathy. Not now. My lower lip started to tremble. In an instant, he pulled me close, his arms around my shoulders. I laid my cheek against the thin fabric of his t-shirt and the dam broke, all of my uncertainty and fear

181

and distress pouring out with my tears. He never said a word, but right then he was my rock.

I hung onto every moment, my fingers clawing at his back, but he never flinched. I knew he would get Teal to safety or die trying.

CHAPTER FORTY

Clove sensed the approaching vampire even though it was trying to mask its steps. It was clumsy, attempting to be something it could never be. A shimmer of anger simmered under the cold, calculating shell he wore. When this was over, he would delight in exterminating the occupants of this poisoned dwelling. Emotion had become alien to him over the past decades, but since making Gabriel, it was rising from the ashes of his heart. How dare D'Grey imprison him and put his children at risk. His eyes narrowed in the dark, the solitary candle long since extinguished.

Noah was barely awake, curled up at the far side of the room where Clove had suggested. Clove would protect him, for Gabriel's sake. The man had courage. And his affection for the boy, even now, bled through in all of his words.

A key turned in the lock and Noah stirred.

'Master D'Grey will see you now.' Saxon's voice, one notch below cocky, came from the hallway.

Saliva ran in Clove's mouth and he ran his tongue over the edge of a fang. Being summoned like this was typical of Emron's belief in his own self-importance. But Clove knew he had to be careful. He opened the door to find Saxon leaning his weight against it. The stocky vampire stumbled, then righted himself. Clove graced him with an ice cold, full-fanged smile.

Emron stood at the far end of the room he called his lair. It was theatrically overdone in deep red velvets and pale voile drapes that obscured his lounging area. A dark wood four-poster bed, embellished with a gold tasselled hunting canopy, occupied much of the room.

'Spice master.' The greeting came with an open-handed gesture of supplication, but there was nothing humble about the vampire who used to be his friend and lover. Dressed in a finely embroidered gold frock-coat with a matching waistcoat and white open-necked shirt, he was a purposeful throwback to the times they had been close. Back then he had earned the name of the Velvet Viper for his dress sense and deceitful nature. Nothing had changed.

Distaste coated Clove's tongue.

'The envoy from the ruling body has arrived and is taking refreshment before delivering a verdict.' D'Grey rubbed his palms together. The sound grated against Clove's ears. 'Would you care for an appetiser before the meeting?' He snapped his fingers and the same girl from their first encounter stepped from behind a voile, her eyes downcast. Bruises stood out against her pale skin. Her chest rose and fell with shallow, terrified breaths.

Clove knew he should feed in order to keep his instincts in peak order, but he did not trust D'Grey and he would not take blood from such an abused creature as this. 'I find my appetite restricted. Keeping me against my will has that affect, ring master.' He dropped the old name as casually as a glance.

D'Grey's expression shifted, the smirk falling from his lips.

Those times had been their heyday. Young and trusted by the masters they served, they had both been in charge of finding newly turned vampires and bringing them into the safety of 'the fold'. Those unfortunates found out soon enough that safety was a relative word. Many were put into the pit, the cellar of a merchant captain's house on the quay side. Contests between masters were rife, and the hapless fledglings, some only a few nights old, would be made to literally fight to the death, the heart of the loser a trophy for the winning master. It was a cruel time. Clove and Emron had often been opponents, but never in the pit. They'd vied with each other like brothers, basking in the glory of living, knowing they were untouchable as long as their masters were happy. Emron's love of bloodshed was apparent even in those days. He would think nothing of culling an entire huddle of terrified fledglings for the sheer joy of the kill, like a fox in a hen house.

It was on one of these nights, as they hunted together, when they had come across an opium den on the outskirts of the old town. A group of vampires from another district had moved in, using the den as a way to lure victims in from the streets. The ships docking close by proved lucrative, both in their supply of sailors and their quantity of stashed poppies. But the group had made the fatal error of invading an area belonging to Emron's master. That night, they took no prisoners and blood fell like rain. For the first time, Clove had been caught up in Emron's acute and perverted hunger, and they had gorged on the dying vampires to the point of saturation. But the blood had been heavily tainted. Clove's senses had become muddled. Emron had taken full advantage of this momentary lapse and before the new day dawned, they were lovers. It wasn't Clove's finest moment.

The remembrances hung suspended between them as thick as a winter mist over the sea.

D'Grey's mask returned. But his sense of irritation slipped through. 'As you will. But don't say I was anything other than a gracious host.' He moved through the voile. It slid over his shoulders like skin from a snake. 'I know you keep a mutation, Clove. Your refusal to comply speaks of your dismissal of the rules. You won't be treated lightly. Your age means nothing. Moth and Gabriel will suffer, too, for your stubbornness.' He wagged a forefinger and Clove had an overwhelming desire to tear it off.

'But it will soon all mean nothing, because word has been put out on the Bloodvyne to your pure bred. Even as we speak, he is moving towards us, his steps monitored by my hunters. I want him here as a witness to your downfall. I want him to see the death of the priest. And then I will plunder his mind for news of the mutant. It will soon all be over, and your fall from grace will be complete.'

Clove wanted to believe D'Grey was using yet another ploy to wheedle himself under his skin. But instinct told him that every word was true.

CHAPTER FORTY-ONE

Teal floated back from the inner reality he couldn't ignore.

Moth's dusty eyes stared back at him, deep with worry, and he felt a pang of guilt for being the one who had caused it. But he couldn't stop the voices, and certainly not the one who shouted the loudest. He still wasn't sure whether or not he was going crazy, even though he had insisted to Moth he wasn't. What he did know was that he was the one the hunters were looking for. He had thought about running to save his brothers, but the voice had stopped him. It had told him about Clove and Noah. It had told him to send Gabe.

The absence of his latest brother was painfully apparent, the space where he had been lonely and desolate. He wondered what Moth had said before Gabe left.

'Hey, focus.' Moth waved a hand in front of his face and Teal blinked rapidly.

'Sorry. It's hard to come back. The voices are trying to tell me so much stuff it all gets jumbled up and then I get confused.' He took Moth's offer of a hand up and stared into the night.

'When did Gabe go?' The last words stuck in his throat.

Moth shrugged, his eyes downcast to the ground. 'Just before you woke up. He was so scared, Teal. He cried. And

I couldn't do anything about it.' Moth's anguish was swallowed by the darkness. He hadn't been like this since Sasha had died.

'We just have to trust him.'

'Trust him to do what, Teal? Die by himself because you sent him there and I didn't stop him?' Moth's words fell from his lips in an angry torrent and Teal felt them as much as a physical blow. Moth swung at the wall with his fist and the old brickwork crumbled under the force. Tears of frustration welled in his eyes when he turned. The wind picked up and blasted around the corner, carrying early fallen leaves in its wake.

A force propelled Teal's gaze towards the old convent behind them, brooding in the dark. It huddled there like a monster in the closet.

'We have to go in there.' Teal inclined his head, fully expecting Moth to lose patience. Moth opened his mouth, then swallowed back whatever he was going to say. His eyes carried a strange sort of acceptance.

They scrambled over the wall and stole across the blackness of the courtyard, both glad and edgy to be in the maw of the imposing but derelict building. A boarded-up window gave easily to Moth's nudge. Once inside, the darkness seemed unfathomable. A damp, dusty smell covered everything with a forlorn regret. Teal wouldn't have been surprised to see Miss Havisham floating past in her tattered wedding dress.

'What the hell are we looking for?' Moth whispered. It wasn't the kind of place to shout. It was sleeping and it would treat with displeasure any who disturbed its slumber.

'Wait.' Moth's arm snaked out and grabbed Teal by the elbow. The wet flicker of a tongue in the dark. 'Smell that? Human. A bit further on.'

'Maybe it's a tramp?' Teal couldn't think of anyone else who would willingly hole up inside here.

'Possible. But it's the first good thing that's happened tonight. Dinner might be ready and waiting. You must be starving.'

Teal wasn't starving. In fact, he wasn't the slightest bit hungry. He hadn't been since the night Clove had disappeared. It was just another item to add to the list of weird things. But Moth obviously was. He recognised the tell-tale stance of a vampire in stalking mode, the smooth, silent movements, the concentrated expression, eyes forward, all other senses tuned in to the pull of the blood. They rounded the corner. A large spiral staircase loomed, broken balustrades like missing teeth, a less than welcoming sight. Slowly, they both inched forwards, taking each stair one at a time, feeling for the rotten wood with their feet and edging past.

A wide corridor opened up, littered with pieces of fallen ceiling and the odd spirit bottle. Moth pointed, and this time Teal picked up the copper scent of warm blood. Maybe it wouldn't hurt to drink a bit. The chance might not come up again. A set of wooden doors with peeling paint stood at the far end of the corridor. They crept past other rooms, some open. From one, Teal thought he heard the soft murmur of a woman and he paused. But Moth urged him on.

Two ivory handles gleamed in the dark, highlighted by a sliver of moonlight slicing through a hole in the roof. The old floorboards were wet here, open to time and the elements.

Slowly, one of the doorknobs turned and Moth froze, one hand motioning for Teal to stay back.

The huge door creaked open, its hinges protesting. Teal's eyes glued themselves to something carved into the body of the door, an etching done after the wood was painted. His gaze followed the curves and lines and his eyelids flickered. Recognition stole the air from his lungs and he gasped.

CHAPTER FORTY-TWO

The tears dried on my face as I walked away. I didn't want him to see me wiping them off. So much for playing it cool and faking bravery. All it had taken was a gentle touch, and everything I'd been packing away in the recesses of my mind, all of the past year's pain and loneliness and horror, erupted like a salt-water volcano. All I felt now was empty. I couldn't decide whether this was a good thing or not.

My steps echoed on the ancient cobblestones of the narrow medieval alley, which led to the cathedral. It was the only place I could think of going. A sheen of sea mist hung in the air and the tops of the buildings floated in and out of it fitfully. In some places, the roofs of the houses almost touched, and the old wooden beams stood twisted at impossible angles. I knew this street dated back to the fourteenth century. Back then, it had been the main market lane, selling goods straight from the trade ships. A row of butcher's shops had stood at the far end, complete with a slaughterhouse at the back. That's why the cobbles I walked on were raised slightly; the gutters at either side would be running with blood on market day.

I shivered and thrust my hands into my jacket pockets. I knew all this because I had grown up in a house where history sang as loudly as the present. Carver had instilled it into me that, without history, we would not be where we were today. Sadness weighted my feet as I thought of him. How much pain had he gone through when he thought he had failed me?

The overhanging timber frames of the buildings loomed above me now as the street narrowed. A memory flooded back, walking with Noah and Carver the first time I had come here. I must have asked why they had built the houses all squiffy. 'To protect the meat from the sun,' Noah had said, grinning as he got in first with the history lesson. I remembered looking up at his face as I held his hand, in awe of this man who had taken me under his wing. And now that man was in danger again, because of me. However scared I might be, I owed him big time. After all, I should have been dead a year ago. Somehow it didn't make me feel any better.

It was darker here, the glow from the gas light at the end of the street hidden, but there was something in the shadows. I sensed it before it moved, my hearing picking up a sound even before a sound was made, when it was simply a motion of the air. I stopped dead, scanning behind me without turning. More movement there. They'd tracked me. But then I wasn't really hiding, and I was far enough from where I had left Moth and Teal for them to get away. I prayed Moth would do what I'd asked. There was no point in us all dying.

A figure melted out of the dark. I caught the glint of a fang and slammed down my mind shield. This time I locked it. The audible click inside my head made my ears ring.

The figure came forward, then paused and raised an arm. It pointed upwards, and my eyes followed. There, on the under hang of an old meat shop, was one of the original butcher's hooks, an evil curve of iron. He swung it and laughed. Two more ominous presences appeared at my shoulder: the same vampires from the night I'd run with Teal.

I plucked a ribbon of courage from everything else that was churning about in my stomach. 'What took you so long?'

One of them growled deep in his throat and grabbed my arm, his fingers digging into my skin. The figure in front stopped him with a glance and the hand fell away.

'Don't want to mark him. That's for Master D'Grey to do. This one's a fucking trophy. Clove's first born. Ain't that cute.' His voice carried a nasally twang, which grated on my nerves like a wet finger across glass. 'I reckon it's gonna be fun when this whelp gets pulled up in front of the envoy. That one won't stand for any pussy footing around.'

A shudder vibrated across my shield and the vampire's small eyes narrowed. If he'd hoped to take a few morsels back to D'Grey, he'd picked the wrong fledgling. Clove had spent weeks making me perfect this technique. Some nights I'd fallen into sleep with his harsh words echoing in my head. Nearly right wasn't ever good enough for him.

'Move.' A fist prodded me in the small of my back. Most of my senses were tuned into keeping that lock tightly shut. I couldn't risk thinking about Moth and Teal. But a single image flared, then fizzled out, as I extinguished it. Moth's face as he wiped away my tears. The pebble I'd been holding sat in my pocket. It was the closest I'd ever get to him again.

They closed in around me, leading me out of the cobbled street and across the front of the cathedral. A few people glanced our way, but it wasn't the kind of night for sightseeing. The sea fret had deepened to a miserable drizzle and my hair fell into my eyes. I peered through it, hating the feel of the other hunters behind me. I remembered Ollie telling me to stand back and give him personal space on the day when all I had wanted was to find out the truth. When I was naive enough to think I could somehow perform a miracle and stick my family back together again. So fucking stupid. I shook my head as we rounded another corner and headed downwind. Slipping my hand into my pocket, I closed my fingers around the pebble. Perhaps it could be my talisman.

Outside what was once a well-to-do merchant house, the vampire stopped and jumped down a set of steps leading to a basement door. A figure moved inside behind a dirty pane of glass. I raised my eyes to the sky and the stars gazed back indifferently. I wondered if this would be the last time I would ever see them. The hunters followed my gaze as I'd guessed they would. Very carefully, I placed the pebble on the stone gate post at the top of the steps. As much as I wanted to take it with me, I wouldn't sully my last moment with Moth by bringing it down into whatever hell awaited me inside.

Teal had said follow the fireflies, but all I had followed was death.

CHAPTER FORTY-THREE

After balancing on the wall and chewing over her thoughts, Olivia decided to retrace her steps and come back as dusk fell. It probably wasn't the sensible option, but then she didn't do sensible, not when her gut instinct told her to do something else. Her work came alive in the dark. It was pointless poking around in daylight. The feeling she was being called had eased as soon as she clambered onto the wall. Whatever it was had got her attention, and now it had quieted.

She spent the day poring over Carver's notes again, and drinking copious amounts of coffee. She had phoned Tom and told him Noah's car was still in Westport. Tom had made that whistling noise through his teeth, which meant he didn't like what he was hearing, and she had smiled in spite of the hard lump of worry that had lodged itself in her gut. He'd wanted to come down, but she'd made light of the situation and told him he was best to stay there and visit Carver.

The words she had found the night before blurred in front of her eyes. A dull ache throbbed above her right temple. She should eat. She should try to sleep. Noah would insist that she did. She rubbed her eyes with her fists like a toddler, a warm flush of frustration flooding her veins. If love was so great, how come it left you open to slivers of confusion right when you needed to be strong? Did she even love him, anyway, or was he just 'comfortable'? Her phone lay on the bed and she had a sudden urge to hurl it at the wall. But last time she had given in to a fit of temper like that, she had come to regret it. *Don't think about the past.* A small voice reminded her feeling sorry for herself wasn't helping anyone. She swallowed two headache tablets without any water, wincing as they sluggishly edged down her throat.

Rebirth and resurrection. If those two words didn't apply to Clove and Teal, she would join a modern-day convent. A small smile curled on her lips. She doubted whether a lifetime of praying would save her soul, having corrupted a priest.

She took the only clue she had, banking on Carver's knowledge and instinct, and teamed it with her sixth sense. The convent in the dark might be the only place she would find any other leads. But what if something else lurked there? That thought hovered for a brief second before she batted it away. Noah's disappearance had to be linked to all of this, and she wasn't about to let him down.

‡

Olivia opened the door slowly. The old door knob stuck to the sweat on her palm as her heart pounded. She could feel it echoing against her ears, knowing it meant she was alive. For now. In her other hand, she clutched a torch, borrowed from the hotel.

Something was on the other side of this door and it could very well snuff out her life in an instant...

Teal's bright ocean eyes regarded her with a quiet calmness. At his side, exuding surliness, stood Moth. She searched the darkness. She knew she was looking for Gabe. Words stuck in her throat as Moth studied her with open hostility. It should have been a relief that she knew them, but they weren't exactly friends. They were killing machines, and Clove wasn't around to referee this time. She forced her eyes away.

Moth's gaze shifted to the door at her side. 'It's a maze.' His voice split the silence. She raised her torch to look, letting the beam play on the curves chiselled into the door.

'No, it's not a maze.' She touched the peeling paint. Her fingers trembled. 'It's a labyrinth.'

‡

A rush of irritation spiked through Moth. He had sensed something human, had thought it a lucky break when everything else was falling apart. To find out it was Olivia, and therefore out of bounds, hadn't improved his mood. Gabe would never forgive him if he took her out. And what the hell was she doing sneaking around in the dark anyway? He should have guessed it as soon as he'd known Noah was in trouble. Olivia was not the kind of girl to accept a friend's disappearance lightly. And she had to be looking for Gabe. It seemed everyone was.

Still, her sudden appearance annoyed him. He felt like a cat with its fur rubbed up the wrong way.

'Same difference.' He replied to her observation about the carving on the door, unable to keep the feral glint in his eyes at bay. Saliva ran freely in his mouth. It would be so fucking easy to take her down.

She stepped back, a nervous twitch pounding in her jawline. Then drew herself up, her chin tilting in defiance. 'No, a maze has choices in its pathways. A labyrinth only has one. Look.' She ran her finger along the grimy edges of the carving, leaving a clear pale single pathway with no dead ends.

Moth shrugged. It didn't make sense. Nothing made sense. And he was rapidly falling down the rabbit hole.

'She's right, Moth.' Teal stepped into the warm circle of light from Olivia's torch. 'I think this is what the voices were telling me to look for.' He retraced her trail and Moth had to look away, the naive wonder in Teal's expression as clear as the light in his eyes. Moth was certain God didn't exist, and if he did, what kind of a game was he playing to mix such innocence with the need of a boy killer. An image of Gabe flashed up in his mind, the terror a mask on his face as Moth hauled him away from the demon who was swallowing his mother whole. All Gabe had been trying to do was save her, and look where that had got him. What was the point of being noble and courageous? He buried his face in his hands, his curled fingers digging into the sockets of his eyes, trying to stop the dark spiral of thoughts. This was so not the time to have a meltdown.

'Is Gabe with you?' Olivia's question floated from the darkness behind the torch beam.

Something clicked deep inside Moth's head and he leapt, a growl hurtling from his throat. The circle of light bounced upwards then fell like a shooting star as Olivia dropped the torch. He was aware of a moment of clarity as his hunger descended, a red veil of perfect instinct mixed with wild fury. It was probably the worst thing she could have asked.

Teal caught him in mid-flight, his arm blocking the death plunge. They both slammed into the door, its hinges protesting at the onslaught.

'Don't lose it, please!' Teal's face loomed above him, a fall of blond hair trailing across his face. 'I think she can help us. And if she can help us, she can help Clove. And Gabe.'

Moth stuffed his fist into his mouth and bit down on his knuckles, a swell of blood welling to coat his gums. Adrenaline, stopped in full flow, tingled in his limbs along with the drumming of his heartbeat in his ears. Teal's arm held him firm, one leg planted across his body. Moth never dreamt Teal had such strength. Or such quick reactions.

Olivia stood with her back against the wall. Moth could smell the scent of her blood oozing through her pores, mixing with her sweat. He closed his eyes and tried to concentrate on the taste of his own blood. Teal eased his hold slightly. 'Okay?'

Moth nodded, exhaling against his hand, trying to let the manic night and its events fold into space. Slowly, he stood.

Teal hovered, ready to jump in, then stumbled forward, distress etched on his face. He clutched his head with both hands, falling to his knees. A stream of jumbled words fell from his lips, a fevered nonsense of syllables. Moth dropped to the ground in front of him, grabbing Teal's arms. He was aware of the torch light moving, of its glow on Teal's tormented face. What he saw turned his blood to ice. Teal's eyes rolled back wildly, exposing nothing but the whites. But they weren't white. They were speckled with blood. A spittle of foam flew from Teal's lips and coated Moth's face. A strange gurgle echoed in his throat, as though something was trying to claw its way out. Then his head turned and fixed its blood-flecked gaze on Olivia.

'Find me, pretty girl. Walk the pathway with the blood. Speak the truth and watch them die.'

But the voice wasn't Teal's. It belonged to a woman.

CHAPTER FORTY-FOUR

The hunters ushered me into the front room of the basement. Their triumph and excitement throbbed around me
in thick waves. It made me feel slightly sick. The room was
pretty much derelict. A few pieces of battered furniture,
coated in grime. It didn't look much like the lair of a master
vampire with a personality disorder. I kept all Moth's words
about D'Grey firmly behind the steel door in my mind, but
I knew them off by heart.

A thin light oozed from under the next door, and a smell.
Human. My stomach twisted. Why hadn't I fed before walking into all of this? I imagined Clove shaking his head at
my mistake.

A hand shoved me forward and I drew on every ounce of
strength I could pull up. I prayed Teal had known what he
was saying when he'd sent me here. The door opened and
a haze of blue smoke drifted towards me. It was deep and
pungent, like burnt chestnuts. Through the smog, I could
make out dark shapes at the far end of the room. Two metal
uplighters cast wavering pools of light onto the ceiling and
a thin curtain wafted in a draught from somewhere. The
smoke curled into my nose, stinging my eyes and making
my legs feel sluggish.

'Good luck, pup.' The tall hunter's voice whispered sarcastically against my ear before he melted into the shadows.

I forced my legs to carry me forwards, concentrating on the glow from a kerosene lamp, lighting the gap between the floating curtains. Behind stood a large, wooden chair with a high back. No, not a chair. It was more like a throne.

A single step led up to this raised area. I planted my foot on the step and waited. The smoke eased a bit, or maybe I was getting used to it, but the feel of it lingered in my lungs and my head felt heavy, as though my brain had suddenly grown. From behind my locked shield, Moth's voice reminded me that D'Grey had used a harsh light to disorientate him. This master vampire did not play fair.

The nerve endings along my spine tingled as instinct over ran my musings. I was being watched. Raising my chin I scanned the room, using my intuition rather than my eyesight, even though that was as keen as any night creature. *Listen to what is not there. See only the truth and not what you imagine*…Clove's teachings, so much like Carver's.

'Master Davenport.' My name crept out from a concealed stairway, the gold thread from the figure's clothing sparkling in the lamp glow. 'How noble of you to call. The chase was becoming a little tiresome, don't you think?'

Emron D'Grey stepped into the light, all finery and showmanship and nauseating niceness. His hair was pulled back into a long ponytail, exposing the harsh lines of his cheekbones.

I could feel the fury bubbling underneath the uncertainty in my gut. 'Noble had nothing to do with it. You wanted to see me. You've seen me. Now where's Clove?' I didn't mention Noah. Better for D'Grey to think I wasn't bothered. It was less ammunition for him to throw at me.

'No formal greeting, Gabriel? I thought Clove would have taught you better than that.' He strode into my personal space and all I wanted to do was back away. The scent of the opium rose from his clothes, his skin, and danced on his breath. A long-fingered hand snaked out and grabbed my hair roughly, pulling my head back so I was forced to look up at him. His pale eyes held no light, only a flickering madness. 'I would advise you to watch your manners. It would be a shame to have to discipline you in front of your master. And the mortal.' He tossed the last part to me like a crumb to a bird, studying my face for any emotion. A stab of pain shot through my head as he probed my shield, its force meant to sweep any secrets from my brain with surgical precision. I held firm, grinding my teeth together and focusing on a spot behind his shoulder. He lowered his face and inhaled, running his lips along my cheek as he tightened the hold in my hair. The tip of his tongue traced the lobe of my ear and I had to force down a wave of nausea. 'I am going to take great pleasure in breaking you, beautiful boy.'

Someone moved from the shadows, its head cast downwards. I could smell the fear in its wake. 'Forgive the intrusion. The envoy is ready for you now.'

D'Grey paused, then released me with a hiss of frustration. 'Bring Clove in now.' He waved his hand in dismissal and I fell back, relief surging through my veins. I wasn't sure how long I could hold out against him, even with my powers.

A door opened behind me, but there were no footsteps. Clove appeared at my shoulder, his eyes flicking over my form. I had so many questions for him. I wondered if I'd ever get the chance to ask them.

'Gabriel is of no concern to you. He is of my blood and has committed no crime. I will meet with your envoy and comply with their demands, but let him go.' The steely determination of Clove's tone was a balm to my senses. His strength flowed through me, just like his blood.

'Your concern for your little family is touching, spice master.' D'Grey grinned, exposing his fangs, then cracked his knuckles. 'But the envoy specifically asked for Gabriel's attendance in your trial.' This last word ricocheted around my head like a stray bullet.

Clove moved closer to me. His hand pressed against my back, firm and supportive. He knew I was struggling. I stared up at his face, my eyes wide. His presence seemed to fill the room, surrounding me with an invisible protection he couldn't openly show.

D'Grey disappeared into the stairway, leaving a circle of hunters around the room. Clove turned to meet my gaze, and for an instant, his dark eyes softened. His lips moved, mouthing two words. *No fear*. Then his hand dropped away, brushing mine as it fell. That same electric shock I'd felt when I was human raced through my fingertips. I forced a smile. Surely the envoy from the ruling body was a reasonable soul. Envoys were historically diplomatic. The first heady quiver of hope flared inside me.

D'Grey reappeared, his face glowing with barely repressed excitement. 'Gentlemen, please lower your heads for the entrance of the newly elected Chief Envoy of the Vampire Ruling Body.'

It was though he was introducing a circus act. I suddenly understood the ringmaster's coat. I lowered my gaze, sharpening my senses, trying to smooth anything that gave me away as a naive fledgling. A rustle of soft fabric told me the envoy was now very much present. A cold chill ran its frosted fingers down my spine, and out of the corner of my eye I saw Clove's jaw tighten as his eyes lifted.

The chill seeped through into my bones as I raised my head. The envoy sat on the throne, one pale hand drumming slender fingers against the wooden arm. She was clothed in a high-necked gown of black and white. My legs turned to jelly.

'Hello, Gabriel. I'm glad we have the chance to meet again.'

My mother's face stared back at me, a cold mask of indifference. But her eyes glittered with triumph.

CHAPTER FORTY-FIVE

The voices filtered through the gaps around the old door. Noah stood like a dismissed child, trying to make out the words. It definitely wasn't a casual or friendly meeting. Of the words he could make out, all had barbs. The single candle had burnt itself out hours ago, but his eyes were accustomed to the dark now, and the faint light from the other room almost irritated his vision. Thirst thickened his tongue. He couldn't remember the last time he'd drank something. Pressing his forehead to the wood, he closed his eyes and prayed. Because this time there didn't seem a way out, and God might be the only ear that would listen.

Another voice drifted in. At first, Noah thought he was imagining it. His fingers splayed at either side of the gap around the door, as though he was trying to prise it apart. A prickle of tears blurred his vision and he blinked them away. That voice. He would know it anywhere. It was Gabe.

His hand closed over the doorknob and he rattled it in exasperation. All he wanted to do was see Gabe again, to make sure he was alright. But how could he be, with what had happened to him? Noah slumped to the floor, a dejected huddle in the darkness. Clove's words came back to him, *he is adapting well*. And that was pure Gabriel Davenport spirit. When life pulled the rug out from underneath him, he refused to fall with it. A swell of pride and love rose in Noah's chest. If Gabe could cope with this, the least Noah could do was support him. Cowering away and steeping himself in self-pity was a miserable waste of the time he had left. Raising his fist, he banged on the door as hard as he could.

After several bouts of thumping and shouting, Noah's hand cramped. He cradled it to his chest, hissing through his teeth in frustration. The door swung open. Saxon regarded him coldly, his thinning hair barely hiding the pale mound of his skull. Noah shielded his eyes from the sudden light, glad to block out the pasty appearance of his jailer.

'What the hell do you want?'

'I want to see Gabe. Tell D'Grey at least he owes me that.' Bravery didn't come naturally to Noah. He was one of life's introverts, but this time it was personal. The tone of his voice surprised even him.

'No one tells Master D'Grey to do anything. But I can't expect you to understand, mortal.'

For a moment, Noah wanted to laugh. If mortal was the best put down Saxon could come up with, Noah didn't think he would crumble. 'I know he's here. And you won't hurt me, because Master D'Grey will wipe the floor with your sorry ass.' The phrase *playing with fire* flashed up in front of Noah's eyes like a jackpot sign, but he ploughed on. 'So it might be better to let me have my way. For your sake.'

As Saxon contemplated this sudden change in his captive's demeanour, Noah took his chance. The vampire might not be the brightest example of his species, but his reactions would be far quicker than Noah's if he tried to run. Noah took the only other option. He screamed Gabe's name at the top of his lungs. The sound echoed down the long, neglected hallway. He waited for retaliation from Saxon, but none came. But the growl rumbling in his chest told him more than words.

A young girl appeared at the end of the hallway, as pale and thin as a bleached bone. She waved them forward, her eyes lifting only once. Noah had never seen such haunted misery before and his heart ached. Saxon grunted and grabbed Noah by the arm. It was all about saving face, Noah realised. If Saxon wanted D'Grey to think Noah hadn't come willingly, so be it. But from what he knew, nothing got past the vampire who had Clove in his grasp. Whatever had happened to make that possible must be of deadly importance. Clove wasn't exactly a pushover. All of these thoughts flitted around Noah's mind as he followed Saxon. Pungent blue smoke drifted from the room beyond, and an old fear surged in his veins. Saxon turned slowly and leered, a dribble of saliva dripping from one fang. His parting gift was a hefty shove through the door.

The smoke stung Noah's eyes, filling his nostrils with a burning richness that made his head spin. He floundered through the fog, aware that at the far end of the room were figures. None of them came to help. With his eyes streaming, Noah stumbled forward, coughing and spluttering. Everything was indistinct, like that hour after a heavy drinking session when your eyeballs wanted to fall out of your head. But the smoke was clearer here.

Clove stood with his back to him, his spine ramrod straight.

And beside him, a wilder version of the boy he'd once thought dead.

CHAPTER FORTY-SIX

In her hole beyond the wall, the stream of her consciousness began its long, laborious journey back into life. It had existed in a twilight world since her crude burial, and she still remembered the stench of fear as the men worked at breakneck speed to entomb her. They knew she was still alive, but they did not care. An old woman was of no importance. And yet she did not hate them, poor misguided creatures that they were. Men had shunned her when she was but a young woman, scratching an existence from the forest. Witches were to be feared unless their babes needed a tincture for a fever, or their daughters' bellies swelled, a parting gift from the many travelling men who roamed the land. Her small cottage stood at a crossroads in the wood, and that's where the devil loitered. She was happy with their assumptions. They would leave her be, and that was a good place.

But it wasn't the devil who had found her one wild night. Or maybe it was. When a man comes knocking on your door at the midnight hour, he can only be after one thing. Her instinct had told her that. But the tall man in the silk-lined cape and leather boots had looked like a gentleman. His hair had been soft and long, tied back with a black ribbon, and he had smelled of roses. *Forgive my interruption, miss, but my horse, in fear of the wind, unseated me.* He'd shown her the muddy patch on his cape as proof, and smiled with such fine teeth that inviting him for a cup of soup and a spot by the fire seemed the only proper thing to do. By the time she realised her offering had remained untouched, it had been too late.

But he had not killed her, even though the blood ran freely down her pale chest, soaking the harsh bodice of her dress. In fact, he had acted quite strangely, backing away and wiping her blood from his lips with the back of his hand, the fine lace of his cuff stained pink. She had known what he was. Had been expecting a visit, in a way. She was an easy target, but her blood had not been to his liking. This had perplexed her, and all through the night she had sat by the dwindling fire, waiting for him to revisit. By morning, she had been in the throes of a fever and had taken to her bed of straw with a thirst that would not be quenched by water. By nightfall, the thought of food had caused the bile to rise from her stomach. Three hours later, she'd made her first kill, a twitching buck rabbit caught in a wire snare.

She knew then the vampire had left his dark gift even though she had not drunk from him, as all the old texts said you must. For a week, she had kept to nocturnal hours, sure daylight would burn her skin. It did not. On her first visit to the village, for flour from the old mill, people had stared, some with mouths agape. Her fingers had traced her face, sure she must have developed a pox, but her skin was clear. It had only been as she passed the well and glanced down that she'd seen what the others had. Her hazel eyes now burned gold with the fiercest of intensities.

It did not take long for the news of her abnormality to spread. In a time of crude understanding and superstition, she had been an easy scapegoat. Children had hovered in the clearing outside her door, daring each other to run and touch the willow animals that adorned her doorway. She had found this creative talent soothing, even though the bark would make her hands bleed. Calming indeed to lap that blood like a kitten. But her thirst for blood was not overpowering, tempered somehow by the white magic that ran in her veins. She was, as always, an anomaly.

Her hopes for others of her kind had vanished with the years. Some nights, vampires roamed the darkened forest, and her acute hearing had attuned to the sudden cessation of the owls and scurrying creatures. Standing by her doorway with a lantern, she had beckoned them in, desperate to know more about what she had become, but they'd stayed away, wary of a being that shouldn't be. She was the white lamb in the black flock.

But that was then. A time of changing seasons.

Now belonged to the one whose bloodline called to her over the web of linked minds, spiralling into the dark with a thousand winding paths.

But there were no dead ends. She was the labyrinth.

CHAPTER FORTY-SEVEN

Clove stared into the triumphant eyes of the woman who had once been Gabriel's mother. They glittered with malice, the dark blue now jet black and focused intently on the boy standing beside him. After nearly a year the demon had returned, hell bent on revenge.

He moved closer to Gabriel and sensed the cold terror that ran through his body. The tight shield around the boy's mind wavered like a heat haze. He felt it shimmer on the edges of his vision. By the demon's side, Emron D'Grey hovered, the smirk on his face a gluttonous thing. Clove wanted to tear it from his head. Yet again he had underestimated the demon's intellect. What better way to find them than to worm its way into the favour of the ruling body. He had no doubt it had hidden away and licked its wounds at first, coming to terms with its new host and capabilities. If he had hoped for its demise, he had been sorely mistaken. It had used its time well, delving into vampire history and law, until it found a soft spot to probe and utilise. Hearing about the mutation must have been a source of unbridled joy.

Teal, instantly recognisable, had been the key. Putting out the hunters to find the mutations was devious and well executed. It was only a matter of time before they closed in on Teal. Clove growled, a rumble in his throat that rever-berated through his chest. The demon had played its hand and Clove had walked right into the trap. It knew he would bring his fledglings out of hiding to discover the latest news on the vampire network, doing all he could to protect them. The icing on the cake stood beside him—Gabriel's face, bone white with shock.

'No words of love for your mother, Gabriel?' The saccha-rine sweetness of the voice mixed with the opium smoke to form a swirling, nauseating fog.

'You are not Gabriel's mother. You only use her human form as a host. I will not let you play your games this time.'

'Clove.' Two black eyes fixed him with a frozen stare. 'I was not talking to you. Unless you have severed Gabriel's tongue, I am sure he is capable of answering for himself.'

Behind him, Noah's breathing came in shallow gasps. Clove was grateful for his silence. Another reminder of his mortal life would not help Gabriel now. The boy opened his mouth to speak, but no words came out. Clove slipped his arm around the slender shoulders. As much as they had all known the demon would return at some point, its absence so far had given them the illusion of time. It had softened them, made them pliable and easier to hurt.

The ruling body were all old, and not as wise as they liked to think. The fact they were dealing with a being that was not entirely vampire would not have crossed their minds. Aka Maga, or whatever name it was now known as, must have wept tears of joy at their ineptitude. Clove turned his attention to D'Grey, who was perched on the arm of the carved chair like a trained monkey. Triumph emanated from him in waves.

'Don't you think this is all a little too well planned, Emron? Does it not twinge your instincts to readily accept the new envoy also happens to be related to my first born? And has an obvious grudge.' D'Grey might be a venomous snake, but he was far from stupid.

'I find it amusing your fledgling's human mother is herself a recipient of the blood. It is called keeping it in the family, is it not?' D'Grey smiled, bowing his head in a gesture of their vampire youth. It was pointless to try to argue reason. He had decided long before the envoy had arrived that Clove was guilty.

'You are sorely misguided. But this should not come as a surprise.'

'Enough. Your whimperings are of no concern.' The envoy leaned forward, the rustle of the silk lapping at the floor. 'I know you hold a mutation, Clove. Do not dare to deny it. Bring him here, or I will gut your fledgling and hang him in the sun to dry.'

Clove had no doubt the demon still craved the body of the boy by his side. But if it admitted this need, it would alert D'Grey to the fact something was severely amiss with the rising star of the ruling body. The air crackled with volatile energies held suppressed. He was damned whatever he said or did. Tread carefully. He would need all of his centuries old wile and instinct, and his first task was getting Gabriel out of here, by any means he could manage.

‡

If Clove hadn't been by my side, I knew I would have crumpled, boneless, to the floor. The air in my lungs faltered. I wanted to run, but my feet were anchored to the floor, and all the while that vile blue smoke tempered everything with a sickly hue. Blind anger took my words. All I could do was stare at the creature who looked like my mother, but had been the cause of my fall from grace. Words sparred between her—*no, not her, it*—and Clove, but I couldn't grasp their meaning. To make it worse, I knew Noah was watching with his own horror pulsing in his heartbeat. I didn't want him to see me like this. My fingers curled into my palms, nails slicing into the skin. I hung onto the sudden sting of pain as the whole room blurred into a throbbing mass of hopelessness. How could Clove and I walk away from this? And Noah's chances were even worse. Teal had been right all along.

Someone was calling my name from a distance, but I didn't want to creep out from the storm clouds in my head. I was hiding underneath them. It hurt too much to think. A hand cupped my jaw and Clove's face swam into view, his dark eyes boring into mine, demanding my attention. His touch was ice cold.

'Gabriel, focus. Listen.' He dug his finger hard into the cleft of my chin and somehow I dragged myself up from the sludge in my head. 'You are to leave here and go and get Teal. Bring him back. Do you understand?'

I didn't. His words were crystal clear, but the meaning behind them? Why would he give Teal up now? Clove wouldn't cow down before anyone, not even the demon. I'd seen it with my own eyes. He would fight for us all. The ring of steel around my shield slid a little as I tried to ask him why. His eyes narrowed and his grip tightened. With effort, I regrouped.

'Splendid, spice master. At last you see sense. I'm sure Nekhbet will look favourably on your assistance.' D'Grey rubbed his hands together, the delight rife on his face. A surge of fury flared in my chest. I wanted to tear him apart with my bare hands.

Clove pulled me back yet again. 'Go now and be quick.' He grasped my arm with his hand, his long fingers almost spanning a limb that didn't seem a part of me anymore. 'May I walk my fledgling to the door?' He directed the question with all the humbleness of a monk, at the same time as he literally dragged me across the room. The grip on my arm was vice-like, but his face revealed absolutely no emotion. The hunters stood to the side as we passed, all except the tall vampire who had led me here.

'Better make sure you do as you're told, pup.' He grinned, but his eyes were dead. Clove pushed past him as though he wasn't there, opening the door with his other hand. I stumbled on the threshold, my face turned up to his, begging him with my eyes to tell me what to do.

From inside, D'Grey's form hovered, watching our every move. Clove pulled me close and kissed the top of my head. I pressed myself against him, trying to absorb some of his strength. His breath came in chilled bursts against my scalp, the scent of time on his coat, the freedom of the basement steps behind me. A whispered word, as quiet as a falling leaf, escaped against my hair.

Run.

He closed the door in my face with a resounding *bang*, and I stood there for a moment, that single word bouncing around in my head. Fleeing up the steps, I ran down the street, not stopping until I'd put enough distance between that house and where I was, to be able to think. Relief tangled up with the shock and I wanted to scream. But I couldn't risk drawing attention to myself. Relief that Clove didn't want me to find Teal, relief he wasn't giving them Teal's heart on a plate. Because one thing was for sure, once Teal was inside that house, he wouldn't come out again. The demon had used the mutation angle purely to find us, and I knew damned well it would carry out its 'duty' to the ruling body. Bitter blood rose in my mouth and I doubled over, letting it stream from my lips.

Clove had given me permission to run with Moth and Teal. This should have been all the urging I needed. He would stall D'Grey and…what had he called her? Nekhbet.

The name fired up in my memory. Egyptian history with Carver, a subject I'd excelled in. Days spent with my head over a book, letting my mentor's words cover me like a blanket. The warmth of a fire, Ella's cooking from the kitchen…I snapped my mind back into place, wiping the back of my hand over my mouth. Nekhbet, an ancient goddess and the original city of the dead. In hieroglyphics, her name contained a vulture. The irony and warning behind this pierced through my skull, shattering the lock of my shield. I felt it splinter almost physically, my eyes searching the ground, expecting to see the pieces. A breath of wind stirred the stillness, waking up the few leaves by the edge of the road. The rustling unnerved me and I stepped back, my brain still playing about with the name. I mouthed the syllables then froze, the breeze lifting my hair from my brow with salt-stained fingers.

'You bastard.' It was a whisper through clenched teeth. *Nekhbet.*

The last four letters formed my mother's name.

CHAPTER FORTY-EIGHT

As Teal floated back into reality, he found both Moth and Olivia looking at him intently, and with some degree of shock. He blinked hard to clear the wooliness from his head, his old self not quite comfortable being the centre of attention.

'What happened this time?' Sometimes he could remember fragments of his journey down the rabbit hole, but this time was a complete blank. He'd learned to stop trying to fight it when it swept in, but the fear of it taking over him completely was starting to nip away at his mind.

'Your voice. It was a woman, something about a pathway and truth.' Moth grasped his arm and pulled him into the circle of the torch light, examining his face with great concentration.

'You, or whoever it was in you, were talking to me.' Olivia's steady voice crept out of the shadows. She quickly filled Teal in on the exact words. 'How long have you been like this?'

Moth interrupted before Teal had a chance to reply. 'It's none of your business how long. I don't know what you're doing here, but I'd advise you to fuck off whilst you still can.' His bicoloured eyes darkened as his shadow danced on the wall behind him like a wraith.

'Wait.' Teal placed himself between them, one hand splayed out on Moth's chest. 'What if she's here for a reason, Moth? What if she's part of the plan?'

Olivia started to speak, but Teal stopped her with a finger to his lips. 'I don't know what is happening to me, but I'm not going crazy. Something out there *is* channelling through me, and I have to believe it's on our side and that it can help us get Clove back. Do you think I would have asked Gabe to go if there was any other way? It broke my heart to see his face when he realised he had no choice.'

'Gabe? Where the hell did you send him?' Olivia's shoulders slumped. The torch beam dropped to the floor. 'Do you know how fucked up this is? Being here with you two again. Hearing that Gabe is alive.' Teal picked up a waver of disbelief in her tone. They weren't the only ones struggling with things they didn't understand.

Moth growled. Teal felt the vibration through the palm of his hand. These two together were like gunpowder and a lit match.

'Moth, listen to me. Go and hunt. You're no good to me in this mood. See if you can pick up any ripples from out there.'

'I can't leave you here.' Moth motioned to Olivia. 'You must be starving.'

A grin spread out on Teal's face. 'I've not been called by the blood since all this started. Right now I don't need it. But you do. I'll fill Olivia in on what I know so far and see if she has any ideas. Remember her profession? She could be really useful.' He leaned closer, his face inches from Moth's. 'I promise I'll be fine. Go do what you have to. Please trust me.' He pressed his lips to Moth's cheek in the faintest of kisses.

Moth touched his shoulder and then disappeared into the darkness. Now they were all separated, and Teal felt their loss like a phantom limb. Olivia appeared at his side, her face pale and tired, smudges of dirt on her cheek. Tension ran in the line of her shoulders, her heartbeat raised but steady. Teal explained what had happened since the night Clove had brought his little band into the town, his only wish to find out the truth about the rumours singing on the night air.

She listened intently, occasionally pulling at her hair, absorbing the implications. Each time he mentioned Gabe, her breathing changed, and empathy for her rose in his chest. She had thought Gabe dead for nearly a year. How could she compute his existence now, especially as a vampire? Teal saved the news of Noah until the end. He wished he could soften it, but the truth was Noah had little chance of getting out alive in a nest filled with warring vampires.

The shock registered in her eyes and a shudder of exhaled breath. But this girl didn't do defeated. Despite her hidden worry, she wheeled into action, stepping back to the door and re-examining it. 'What did the voice say again about the labyrinth?'

Teal told her. She pursed her lips and tucked her hair behind her ear, concentration etched into her frown as she ran the torch beam over the carving. 'If there's a clue here, I'll find it…' She turned to him, chewing her lip. 'There's something else you should know.' Now it was Teal's turn to listen as she recounted what had happened to Carver, and the note he had been found with.

A small ray of hope flared in Teal's mind. 'Do you think it's important?'

'My gut tells me yes, but I'm not going back to see if there's anything else there.'

Teal picked up what she didn't say: She didn't want to leave because Noah was here.

'I don't think we have time for that anyway.' Although the voices hadn't told him specifically, their urgency increased each time they demanded his attention.

'Fuck. It's just like last year isn't it? That night when everything was stacked against us.' She hesitated, a slice of pain contorting her face, her brother's name on her lips.

Teal hadn't thought about the similarity, there was too much else going on. But she was right. The awful possibility the demon could have something to do with this reared its monstrous head. He turned and stared into the black maw of the derelict corridor. A rat scuttled away in another room, its claws scratching against the rotting wood. Insects crawled through the damp in the walls. They were all aware he was listening. In his mind, on the edges of his consciousness, a firefly danced, and this time it called his name.

CHAPTER FORTY-NINE

Moth kept to the shadows as he left the old convent, even though he wanted to run until it was a distant memory. He didn't like the feel of it, the weight of its history hand in hand with the dark. He felt as trapped as a caged bird, wanting to fly but with invisible bars holding him fast, tying him to this place. Teal's face knifed into his mind. The way his eyes had rolled back and changed to a blood-flecked mass, the voice that wasn't his. Insanity didn't do that to a vampire. But possession? Now that was another level of crazy to deal with.

The chill of the night air coated his skin and he was glad of it. Pausing at the end of the building, he scanned for threats. The sounds of human nightlife floated back, the harsh laugh of a man, the slamming of a car door, the echo of a ship's horn far out at sea. Claws of hunger raked in his stomach. Time to feed. He couldn't put it off any longer.

A shape shimmered at the other side of the street, the slightest of movements, dark moving within dark. Moth froze. If it was a hunter, he would run, putting as much distance between the convent, and Teal, as he could. He rose to the balls of his feet ready to flee, his tongue flickering against the night chill. The taste was salt and stale air from too many doorways vomiting out the flotsam of humanity, high on drink or drugs or sex. Or maybe all three. But there was no danger. He tried again, concentrating all his senses, his eyes still fixed on that one spot. The molecules of taste rolled around his mouth. Then his heart jumped.

Gabe.

Within seconds, he sprinted across the grounds, vaulting the high gate and tumbling into the shadows. He didn't think about possible traps or consequences, though the logical part of his mind was screaming with them. But the shadows contained nothing. Had he imagined it? His sixth sense had never let him down before. He knew Gabe's taste—not from blood, but from the close proximity of the places they had shared. He knew the scent on his skin when he was warmed from a kill. Moth shivered as his stomach clenched. Fuck, he was beyond hungry.

He turned, trying to stem the pang of disappointment, aware that somewhere in the bowels of the convent, Teal and Olivia were discussing things he didn't understand. He should be there, protecting his brother. But his brother didn't need protecting from a mortal, and from the way he had acted when Moth had wanted to tear Olivia's throat out, Teal's instincts had ramped up a hundred percent. Whatever this thing was he had, it was taking him away from Moth and Moth hated that. He'd always said Teal needed him, but maybe it was the other way around?

Someone touched his shoulder as the dark thoughts crawled away into his mind, and he spun angrily, his fangs bared. Adrenaline quicksilvered through his veins.

Gabe stood behind him, one finger to his lips and a grim determination etched on his face. He beckoned with one hand, leading Moth through a narrow alley and into a hidden courtyard. It was a forgotten place, its stones covered with a fine film of green moss. A desolate tree grew in the middle, its branches bowed and constrained by the buildings around it. Beneath this, a fountain with a nymph standing on one leg and holding a harp. The stone was coated in grime, the puddle of water surrounding it a stagnant pool.

A tangled heap of rubbish lay at the other side of the fountain, empty cans and milk containers, screwed-up newspapers and beer bottles. This didn't make the stench any better.

Moth let Gabe lead him, almost glad someone else was taking charge. From a balcony above the mound of debris came the sound of a man snoring.

It was easy to use the tree to gain entry. Its boughs were almost made to sprint across, and the double doors to the room were open, the curtains laced with the same green algae that had made this decay its home. Inside, a TV screen stood on pause, some alien game with spatters of blood frozen in the frame. The scent of who lived here wasn't pleasant. Stale sweat filled the air together with the stench of tequila. His skin glistened and his eyelids flickered in drunken sleep.

An empty bottle lay in his hand, his fingers still clutching the neck, as he lay sprawled on the sofa bed. But his heartbeat was strong and with each beat, the blood pumped through his veins, vibrant and rich. Moth tuned into the call of it, letting himself trip down that pathway where everything around him faded to grey and only this one thing mattered. Gabe was at his side, their shoulders almost touching, his jacket discarded on the floor. Moth's fingers tingled. A slow drool of saliva escaped from his lips, falling like a spider's thread to the floor.

There was no need to battle for the kill plunge. This wasn't like the guy they had taken out on the moorland track. This was pure pack hunting. For close on a minute, they watched their victim as he murmured and flailed in sleep, studying him without compassion, with the simple single-mindedness of predators. Gabe knelt by the sofa bed and Moth followed, almost as if they were in prayer. The pain of waiting was exquisite, almost orgasmic. A shudder ran through Moth's body, taking with it the tension and fear of the night. Gabe's hand smoothed the lank, dark hair back from the man's brow.

The jugular vein, the carotid artery—a banquet of blood pulsing under the skin. Gabe's eyes locked to his, a small quiver of thought transmitting. Moth grasped it in the palm of his mind. The words *no fear* lay imprinted on his skin. Something had happened to Gabe. Something awful. Something that had broken him into tiny pieces, just as Teal had said. But he was here now, remade, a terrible and jagged understanding etched on his face.

Gabe reached across and cupped the back of Moth's head, cold fingers tangling in his hair. Moth heard his brother's breath escape in a sigh of concentrated focus. Gabe's lips drew back as his fangs descended. A single moment of clarity charged the air, obliterated by the copper tang of a severed jugular. The warm blood spurted into Moth's mouth and he gulped it down, the taste filling that space in his mind, the one place where the vampire in him lived and breathed. He didn't remember the plunge, but Gabe's fingers were still tangled in his hair, pressing his head to their kill. The man jerked robotically, his eyes flying open in shocked surprise as his bladder let go. It was too late for him.

The blood filled Moth's stomach, its warmth charging through his veins in an intoxicating rush. Little mewls of pleasure rippled from Gabe's throat as he swallowed. His eyes were shut. A droplet of blood hung on his lashes. They fed until they were sated, and then, soaked in blood, they relinquished the rapidly cooling corpse to the floor.

Moth flopped down on the bed, his head spinning, knowing they had passed a point Clove had warned them about. They were weak-legged, punch drunk on the blood as it worked its black magic. Gabe collapsed beside him, a lopsided grin on his face. His dark blue eyes dreamy with the aftermath of bloodlust. Moth's stomach clenched again. Too much blood.

'Sweet fuck, that was a hell of a ride.' He wondered if his words were slurred, but Gabe seemed to understand. They stared at the peeling plaster on the ceiling, their hands touching, sticky with half dried blood. Moth raised himself up onto one elbow. He wanted to ask about the words in the mind touch. What did they mean, what had happened? But he didn't want to break the spell.

Gabe studied his face, inspecting every detail. This was usually the point where Moth pulled away, sure such close scrutiny would only showcase his flaws. Gabe shouldn't get too close. He couldn't risk another Sasha. But still, that gaze penetrated any qualms he might have had. He could feel warm breath on his face, coming quick and shallow. Gabe's cheeks, flushed from the blood, his skin almost human. Moth remembered the touch of Teal's lips as they'd parted, and the strength it had given him. He could give the same to Gabe. Just a little kiss.

A shudder ran down his spine, the nerve endings at the base blossoming. He touched the side of Gabe's cheek, the downy hair soft against his fingers. He was aware of Gabe's eyes closing, his lashes dark against his skin, and his lips, slightly parted, warm and plump from their feast. A little kiss, a little kiss. But his restraint didn't listen. Moth slid a hand over Gabe's hip and pulled him close. Gabe's mouth opened to him and his back arched. A strange magnetism crackled between them. The urgency in the press of those lips against his was about to tip him over the edge. He groaned and Gabe swallowed it. His mouth was alive with taste. He let his tongue dart, feather like, expecting a sudden pull back. Gabe inhaled softly.

Not now, not now. That little voice in his head vied for his attention. He tried to think about the afterwards, about how awkward it would be between them. He broke the kiss for an instant and Gabe's eyes flared. The glint of a fang glistened under his parted lips. He wanted this just as much as Moth did.

‡

I could still feel the pressure of his lips, taste the gentle flickering from his tongue. I wanted to slip against his mind and find out what he was thinking, but I was scared of what I might find. Now he was looking at me with an unreadable expression on his face. Neither of us moved. It was a miserable place for my first kiss. And probably my last. The blood-soaked sofa bed and the stench of the man's waste oozing onto the carpet. The TV screen stuck on some alien war in the corner. The dampness, which covered everything in a cold sheet.

I'd seen Moth moving through the shadows by the convent, stealth in each step, and I'd watched him for a while. I'd wanted to rush across and tell him what I'd found out. But another part of me had wanted to keep it bottled up. It was such a personal thing, the reappearance of my mother.

The still voice of logic echoed in my head and I wanted to crush it. I didn't think I'd been followed, but could I risk getting Moth caught up in all of this if I had? And where was Teal? I'd asked Moth to take Teal away, hadn't really expected to see either of them again.

He'd sensed me soon after, and I'd panicked, cloistering myself away at the back of the alley. That's when I had found the courtyard and our next meal. I should have made my kill and vanished, but instead I couldn't stop myself from going back for him. I knew he was starving. It was in his eyes. I could smell his weakness like a small bird clinging to a tree in a thunderstorm.

Our joint kill played along the wavelength of my thoughts. I knew from Clove some vampires hunted like this, but it was a rarity, most preferring a solitary dance with their prey. But somehow we had an understanding, something that cancelled out the need for words or planning. I ran with my instinct, high on the anticipation and the need. For those few minutes, I didn't think about Clove or Noah or anything that had happened. It was just Moth and me, throwing caution out of the window and saying fuck it to the consequences.

We'd taken too much blood. It clogged in my throat, but still I craved more, and the sound of Moth feeding only made it worse. When we finally stopped, my ears were ringing and the new blood zinged in my veins like a copper-tinged current. Maybe that's why he'd kissed me. A blood-drunk reaction to his own feeding frenzy. It was only a kiss, no big deal. And yet I felt it was. I wanted so much more. He wasn't mine to have, though. He was in love with Teal, and there was no way I'd spoil that.

'What happened, Gabe?' His voice cut through my thoughts, a little uncertain, a little bit slurry with blood.

I sat up, running my fingers through my hair, knowing if I stayed next to him I'd make a fool of myself. My sodden t-shirt clung to my chest, and I ripped it off, hating the feel of it against my skin.

'The hunters found me. I let them. They took me to D'Grey's house. Clove was there. And Noah, just as Teal said. And…' I paused, not wanting to put into words what I'd seen, because that meant it was real.

His hand touched my spine, his fingers swirling around each vertebrae. It was almost painful.

'The demon came back, Moth. It's my mother. That's the envoy from the ruling body.'

'Jesus.'

But Jesus wouldn't save us. Not even with Noah's input. I sprang off the bed before the pressure of his fingers flipped me out completely. Tearing open a greasy, finger-marked wardrobe door, I rifled through a forest of plastic hangers and crumpled t shirts until I found one that might fit. Faded black with some band emblem on the back. It would do. I tossed another one to Moth, trying not to stare as he yanked his shirt off, then pulled it over his head. His jeans hung low on his hip bones. I'd reached the stage now where I couldn't be still.

I fidgeted with the hem of my t shirt, twisting a loose thread between my fingers.

'Where's Teal? Did you get him away?'

Moth fixed me with that mismatched stare. A furrow appeared between his eyes. 'Yeah, that didn't work out too well. He's in the convent. With Olivia.'

CHAPTER FIFTY

It was strange being alone with Teal.

Olivia didn't feel any sense of malice coming from him. In fact, if it wasn't for those eyes, he could be just a kid out for a night of scares in a haunted house. She wondered where that idea had come from.

His fingers caressed the door as though it was something alive, and she was sure the light in his eyes ebbed and flowed in its intensity, which was impossible. But Olivia knew impossible was never written in stone.

'So, this voice you heard didn't tell you anything else about how to find the labyrinth?' She waved her phone around in the air, trying to get a signal.

'No. It's a one-way thing. When it calls me, I can't seem to communicate with it. I'm just a listening device.'

'You're channelling something paranormal, maybe a spirit or a ghost. But I've never heard of a vampire being used like this.' She paused as Teal turned to her and grinned in such a boyish way an image of Ollie flooded her brain.

'What?' She tucked the mental picture away, honing her concentration on what was happening now.

'It sounds weird. You talking about vampires as if it's completely normal.'

She shrugged, not quite sure how to answer, then swore at her phone. 'I need to go outside and see if I can pick up a signal. This place is a black hole as far as technology is concerned.'

Teal followed as she made her way down the rotten staircase and out into the night air. His feet made no sound behind her. But still there was no ripple of danger from her instincts.

'How come you don't need blood?' Another surreal question. Two faint bars on her phone.

Now it was Teal's turn to shrug. 'I don't know. But ever since I heard the voices…no, that's not strictly true, ever since I saw the fireflies, I haven't been hungry.' He was perfectly still beside her, his face turned to the breeze. He's scenting, she thought, looking for danger like any animal who is hunted.

A cold hand opened in her gut. What the hell hunted vampires? 'Guess that's lucky for me.' She tried again with her phone, swiping Tom's number from her contacts and listening impatiently as it rang out. It went to a recorded message and she cursed again, irritation flaring up like a tiny stone in a shoe.

Teal's voice came out of the shadows. She hadn't even heard him move. 'Don't stand in the open, just in case.'

Part of her wanted to be stubborn. She didn't want the aggravation of trying Tom's number all night. But if Teal was wary, she had better run with it. *You don't want to end up like Noah.* A black cloud settled on her shoulders as pangs of longing rained from it. Missing him shouldn't be like this. They had a modern arrangement. No ties. No emotional luggage.

Teal led her back inside, this time along the ground floor. They bypassed the mouldering remains of the staircase and veered off to the right, stepping over fallen timbers from above and a few half-rotted blankets. A flotsam of drug paraphernalia littered the floor in an alcove, syringes and spoons and dirty pieces of foil. The smell of decay was richer here. She held her hand over her nose and mouth. Darkness clawed at them, but Teal seemed to know exactly where he was going. Blindly, she followed the young vampire. What if he was lying? What if he was taking her back to his lair? A sudden laugh burst out onto her palm. Teal had had plenty of opportunities to kill her, and she didn't think over-the-top vampire cliché was quite his thing.

The slow creak of a door opening, and then Teal's voice, sounding like it was in the hull of a ship. 'We might as well delve around in here till Moth gets back.'

She wondered what 'in here' was, until a sudden flare of light made her eyes twitch. The beam of the torch, *her* torch, which she hadn't even seen Teal take, danced around the room. It was immense, stretching up and up on two levels until it reached the glass dome of a roof. At first, she thought the floor above must have caved in, but there was nothing to suggest that on the ground. As Teal moved the light around, a dizziness flooded her head, until she realised the room didn't have any corners. It was a perfect circle. A circle that contained a disintegrating vast library, reaching high into the void above.

'How did you know?' Her voice came out in a raspy breath.

'I could smell the books. And look, we were meant to find this.' Teal turned and concentrated the light on the door. An identical shape decorated its surface. Another labyrinth.

She stared at the pattern, then at the rows and rows of festering books. A flutter of wings echoed up above and she froze, half expecting to see the magpie from last year, even though she knew it was dead.

Teal glanced up. 'It's okay. It's only a seagull. We must have disturbed it. The roof is full of them.' He ran the beam along the floor. A carpet of droppings, thick and glossy with damp.

The staggering task of looking for a needle in a haystack rose before her. But this was even worse, because she didn't even know what the needle was.

CHAPTER FIFTY-ONE

Emron D'Grey paced the small back room that led to his parlour. Irritation needled his veins like a bad drug. He had been dismissed. Like a schoolboy. In his own house.

His feelings of triumph and excitement now lay in a puddle at his feet. A bitter taste hung in his mouth. Nekhbet's arrival had come with no announcement and no fanfare, one of the first things that picked away at his need for control. There were things he had wanted to do in preparation, a ritual he'd wanted to complete before Clove's hangman came to call. To find out it was a hang*woman* was indeed a surprise. Not that he had anything against the fairer sex in principle, but the ruling body was entirely old school. A woman had never served in their ranks, or had such an important job as their envoy.

She'd arrived like a wraith, the only sound the rustle of the silks she wore like a second skin. Her hair was bone-white and lay around her shoulders in a fan, but those dark coal eyes were what he remembered the most, looking right through him as though she could see his soul. A shiver ran down his spine as he listened, trying to pick up the odd word floating from the other room where Clove stood before her. The priest was back in his hole.

He almost felt sorry for his old lover, scrutinised by those eyes of black ice. Almost. D'Grey carried grudges, and this particular one went way back to the times of their youth. No one left him without a word. No one left him open to all of those messy human feelings he had thought long buried. Not even Clove.

It was too dangerous to attempt to mind read. D'Grey knew Nekhbet would feel it immediately, and he had no wish to be made an example of in front of Clove. It was strange she had arrived without her own entourage too. It was if she had no need for anything but her own abilities and instincts, sweeping away any debris that might get in her way. D'Grey contemplated that he did not want to be part of that debris. He paced a little more, his hands clasped behind his back, the white ruffle around his neck hanging loosely where he had torn it off in annoyance.

The fact Gabriel was now free irritated him too. The decision to send him off on some kind of mission to gather his brothers and bring them back to the slaughter did not make sense. Clove had been too quick to agree to it, and the warning bells in his head had rung long before the boy left the house. True, they were holding the priest, who had been part of his life before, but would Gabriel risk returning to save one miserable mortal life? How long did he have to wait before sending out his hunters to drag Clove's bastards in?

Something else played along the centuries of knowledge he had accumulated. Nekhbet knew Gabriel. Clove's words came back to him. Yes, it did appear a little off. But he would never admit that to Clove. He couldn't shake the feeling that, even as a prisoner, Clove seemed to have the upper hand yet again. Anger simmered below the surface of his thoughts. Carefully, he tempered it, damping down the rolling ripple. This was not the time to lose perspective. He cracked his knuckles together, the gleam of a red ring catching the light. He liked this piece of jewellery, liked the way it resembled a fresh droplet of spilled blood. It was old, the gold thin in places, but still it had a certain draw. He looked through the circle of colour to the pattern inlaid on the gem's base, calming his thoughts as his eye followed the lines.

Saxon waited in the wings like a well-trained guard dog. As a vampire, he was lacking—a bumbling hulk of a man the dark gift hadn't endowed with any grace. But he was loyal. D'Grey swept a pewter goblet from the table, holding it out with a flourish. On cue, his guard dog appeared.

'Bleed our righteous guest, but be careful with him.'

This was another annoyance. Being out of kilter always made him hungry, but he couldn't leave in case Nekhbet summoned him. A little Godly blood would have to do. For now.

CHAPTER FIFTY-TWO

Neither of us mentioned the kiss, but it hung between us like a hangman's noose.

We crossed the derelict stretch of ground outside the convent in stealth mode, our senses attuned to the slightest hint of something wrong. I didn't want to go. Us all being together was like waiting to be delivered to Nekhbet on a platter. But now I knew Olivia was there, I had to try to get her away. Not that I knew how I was going to do it, not when she found out Noah was in a whole heap of trouble.

I gazed up at the battered windows and foreboding roofline. 'So, tell me again, why are we here?'

Moth followed my gaze. 'On Teal's say so. Then we found Olivia inside, almost waiting for us. They both got far too hyper about some carving on a door. A maze…no, a labyrinth, according to her. Same difference.' He scuffed a pebble out of the way with his boot.

'Teal told us we had to find a labyrinth, remember? And if there's one in here we must be on the right track.' I wish I felt as certain as my words.

It was easy to gain entry, most of the ground floor windows were open to the elements, although a few still had bleached boards hanging from them, clinging to a few rusty nails hammered into the frames. The air inside smelled dank and green and dirty. Pieces of abandoned furniture lay covered with filthy dust cloths, the shapes looming out of the shadows as we made our way into the middle of the building. The unmistakable scent of human blood crawled through the darkness. I turned my face to it, instinctively, then a wave of relief. She was in no danger. Moth and I were sated.

We picked our way along the winding corridor. My heart began to race. What would she think of me now? Not quite the adopted baby brother any more.

Moth nodded toward the pattern on the door as we stepped into the room. I could feel her eyes on me, feel the penetration as she tried to size me up, but I kept mine circling the room, taking in the mountains of mouldering books, the huge expanse of space reaching up to the stars. I caught the smile on Teal's face as he saw us, the glow in his eyes flaring as his lips quirked into genuine delight.

Olivia's hand lay on a stack of books piled on top of the remains of a library ladder with most of its rungs missing.

Teal knelt on the page-strewn floor, his fingers around the spine of something disintegrating in his hands. He stood and let the book fall to the floor, his face searching mine.

'Are you okay, Gabe?' Those laser-beam eyes fired through me and I fixed my gaze on him. Anything to avoid the confrontation with Olivia. 'I didn't want to send you there, but I had no choice. What happened?' The words lined up in my throat, thick and sludge covered.

Moth came to my rescue. 'I'll fill Teal in. You go talk to Olivia.' His nod towards her clearly said 'tell her about Noah.'

Her fingers trembled. She brushed her hair behind one ear and stared at me, eyes wide.

'Hey.' I greeted her as if I was still human because I didn't know any other way. I wondered how I looked to her. I was still a baby in my new life. I didn't have the mask-like skin of an older vampire, and I had fed. That always helped. Still, I must look different. Odd. Dead.

Her lips parted slightly and she swallowed, her heartbeat singing in my ears. 'Gabe?'

Teal and Moth whispered behind me. I could feel the pressure of their gaze. A downy white feather floated down from the rafters, dancing from side to side on its journey.

Then she launched herself across the small space between us, and threw her arms around me. The warmth from her body caught me unawares. It amplified her perfume, dark and woodsy, mixing with the salt tang her hair had picked up from outside.

Very carefully, as if she might break, I slid my arms around her shoulders and hugged her. She bunched the thin cotton of my t-shirt in her fingers. There was a dampness on my shoulder. Gradually she pulled away, studying my face with eyelashes glistening with tears.

'Are you...' She paused.

'Okay?' I finished her sentence. The lead weight of dread at meeting her again had dissolved as soon as she had thrown her arms around me. 'Yes.' I gave her what I hoped was an easy-going smile, lips closed. No hint of fang. But okay was relative. If I didn't return to D'Grey's lair soon, Nekhbet would send out her insectile feelers.

I had no intention of betraying Teal. So it was up to me to find another way, if it even existed. Moth appeared at my shoulder as Olivia swiped at her cheek then bent to pick up a book from the carpet of pages on the floor. His presence beside me was strong, reassuring. He brushed against my arm. I bit the edge of my lower lip as his eyes flashed to mine.

I wasn't doing this by myself anymore.

‡

The library wasn't Moth's favourite place. He had never had an affinity with books; his concentration span didn't let him dwell on one thing for long. Once, at school, they had made him see some kind of psychologist. They had known his home life was a mess and he was 'disruptive' in class. All she had done was to tell them he was late to mature, and the authorities had ticked the box that said they had tried to help him.

Moth hadn't liked school. He'd had better things to do. He had been the sole carer for his mother, who had severe rheumatoid arthritis, a condition that had appeared in her early thirties. She had been in constant pain, and this had led to bouts of depression that Moth hadn't known how to help. She'd refused any more medication, preferring to hide away in the dark, watching inane game shows and re-runs of old movies most of the day and night. Moth had learned to cook and clean when most of his peers were playing X-Box or riding skateboards at the park. She hadn't liked him going out, and would crave his company as soon as he walked in the door. Having friends over had been a nightmare. She'd plied them with questions to the point where most had made an excuse and left. They hadn't had any other family around to help, and Moth was terrified if he went to the social services, they would take him into foster care. So he'd kept quiet. He spent his evenings glued to social media, creating fake profiles on various sites, of the life he'd like to lead. People had wanted to be his friend, but by the time he'd realised they were only doing it because they thought he was cool or rich, he had been in too deep to stop it. He knew his mother needed him. This would have to do for connecting, even if it was all a lie.

The first night he'd slipped out to have some fun had been Halloween. He had been too old for dressing up and knocking on doors, but a group of his classmates were going to a new coffee shop in the next town. Moth didn't even like coffee, but it beat hanging out behind the bus depot swigging cheap cider from a can, which was their usual pastime, so he'd agreed to meet them at 9 p.m. For once, his mother hadn't objected.

He'd waited at the end of the street, his fingers curled around his phone in his jacket pocket, but no one had turned up. Angry and humiliated, he'd refused to try and find out why. This was the worst mistake of his life.

With his cheeks burning, he'd set off, first at a walk, then breaking into a run. He'd run fast and hard, to the point where a stitch creased him double, his breath escaping fast into the chill of a late October night. An old man had watched him from across the road. The streetlight had bathed him in a harsh glow, turning his wrinkled skin to an unhealthy grey. Moth had given him a middle finger, hating being watched, squirming in his discomfort.

After a few seconds, the hair had risen on the back of his neck. Somehow the man had wound up behind him.

And the rest was history. Vampire. Halloween. Teenage boy. What a fucking cliché…

'Moth?' Teal's voice cut through his thoughts. Why was he even thinking about that night anyway? What's done is done. He glanced down to see his fingers covered with tiny flecks of paper, like charred ash. Gabe was over by one of the fireplaces, his eyes flicking over the rows of books. Olivia stared at the shelves, occasionally pointing to an area she thought might be useful. Moth wondered if Gabe was keeping away from him on purpose, but that was stupidity talking. They all had a job to do here, not that Moth was helping much. His thoughts, dark and brooding, hung over him like a storm cloud. He had failed his mother by not returning that night. He had failed Sasha by not keeping to the rules. History has a habit of repeating itself.

'This is fucking useless.' He kicked at a pile of torn pages at his feet, scattering them like dirty leaves. 'Even if we looked at every book here, it would take months.' He waited for the inevitable chorus of determined voices.

'He's right.' Olivia sighed and rubbed her arms. It was cold here. Grave cold. The stone walls seemed to radiate it. 'It's not as though we're back at The Manor. There, we'd have a chance to find something.'

As soon as the words left her lips, Gabe flinched as if he had been hit. Moth was half a second from sprinting across, but somehow he managed to glue his feet to the floor. This wasn't hard, considering the remains from the stomachs of hundreds of seabirds oozed over the toes of his boots, fastening him in place with a sticky, foul-smelling paste.

Teal was with Gabe and Olivia now, both of them offering the kind of support Moth could never have done.

He scrubbed his boot on the floor, trying to dislodge the fish paste shit, scooping up a heap of pages to finish the job. His foot left a trail in the rank grey slime, exposing the floor underneath.

At first he thought the marks were deep scratches, but as he dislodged more and more of the sea bird ooze, a pattern emerged. Moth crouched down, clearing more with his hands now, not caring about what his fingers were running through. He could hear the voices of the others, but he ignored them, his focus honed in on this one task. The concentration span he had lacked in school emerged in one spectacular effort.

Someone called his name. Then two hands grabbed him and hauled him to his feet, slime dripping from his fingers. They encircled him, stopping him from dropping down again.

His heartbeat rang in his ears. 'Is this it?' He gazed down at the markings on the floor, directly below the domed ceiling. The labyrinth lay before them.

Teal's eyes pulsed in the darkness. Delight hummed from him like an electric current. 'This is why we're here!'

A sudden warmth flooded through Moth. Gradually, Gabe's grip on him loosened, but Moth didn't move away. He felt unhinged and a little light-headed.

'Remind me never to doubt you again.' The grin on Gabe's face was reward enough for Moth.

‡

I took myself away from Moth because I didn't know how to react to him.

We'd been drawn to each other since our kill like a magnetic force—attracted, then repelled. I wondered if his thoughts mirrored mine as he leafed through books at the other side of the room. The slump of his shoulders gave me my answer.

Maybe he was going over what had happened and was chiding himself for kissing me. Maybe he felt like he'd been disloyal to Teal. I couldn't work it out, so I focused my energy into helping Olivia. I tried to soak up her methodical restraint, but something trip hammered away at me, and all I saw was a mental egg timer with the sand rapidly running out for all of us.

Her expert eye ran over the blotchy, ink-written name cards on the front of the mildewed shelves, occasionally pointing at a spine for me to pull out. It was all so *normal*. But when she glanced at me, her racing heartbeat told me this was as far away from normal as it could possibly get.

And I still hadn't told her about Noah. I knew she'd want to go there, to try and see if there was a chance we could rescue him. And I wasn't about to put that idea into her willful head. For all of her professional calm and logical approach, anything personal tended to be met by a knee-jerk reaction, and I wasn't going to give Nekhbet any more ammunition with which to take us down.

Olivia's reply had taken all the breath out of my lungs with one innocent mention of my old home. So much for thinking I was holding it together, that I was keeping both my lives neatly separated with a bold line that couldn't be crossed.

Teal and Olivia were with me in seconds, but my eyes were on Moth and his sudden flurry of activity. I saw his concentration go from brooding anger to focused determination. His tongue flickered out as his eyes swept across the floor. The stench of the disturbed seagull shit filled our nostrils, and I sensed the crazed confusion from Moth along with it. I was by his side and hauling him away before I had a chance to wonder if it was a good idea or not.

With her hand over her mouth trying to stop the nauseating smell, Olivia studied what Moth had unearthed. The labyrinth gleamed in the torchlight, its undulating pathways free at last from their toxic blanket.

'It looks like a human brain,' Teal whispered.

'The pattern closely resembles the biological structure of the brain,' Olivia answered as though she was in a lecture, 'at least in this form of labyrinth.'

Moth gripped my forearm. Our newly discovered clue didn't resonate with anything I knew, even though Carver had spent many hours discussing the various kinds and their meanings. I should have listened more. Moth stared at the floor, and I studied his profile. His eyelashes were far longer this close up, pale brown with lighter tips. I'd never noticed before. Teal glanced up at us and his lips settled into such a sweet smile. He was like sunshine. No wonder Moth loved him.

I remembered Clove saying we would drift apart as we grew more comfortable in our second skin, that we would view each other as enemies in the long years ahead. I couldn't even begin to understand. Not now. Moth and I could have easily run, together or apart, as soon as Clove was taken, leaving Teal to his fate. That would have saved us. We could have gone anywhere, running until our betrayal was lost in the miles. But you can't outrun your own moral code, and so we were here together, bound up like flies in Emron D'Grey's poisoned web, with Nekhbet the black widow spider poised at our throats.

Moth's arm dropped away and I pulled back, crouching down beside Olivia and Teal. Olivia photographed the pattern with her phone, the flash illuminating the darkness in a single blinding light. Moth watched me from over Teal's shoulder, his expression imprinting itself on my retina. He was back to that unreadable book, the one in another language. I forced my eyes towards the labyrinth.

High above, in the glass domed ceiling, a ray of moonlight sliced through the weather-stained glass. It penetrated the darkness, bathing us all in a cold white glow.

Olivia gasped, the sound of her breath catching in her throat.

In the centre of the labyrinth, invisible until now, three points were marked.

'Look.' The lines formed in my mind. 'See? It's a triangle.'

It was easy to see, now I had joined the dots. Each point of the triangle met a pathway. And at each junction, a small circle contained a single letter. The letter R.

'Rebirth and resurrection.' Olivia's eyes widened, her lips moist and slightly parted. Undeniable excitement. 'That's from Carver's note, before…' She paused and looked at me, biting back the rest. But I knew.

'Before he collapsed.' I wanted to go to him, to tell him things would be okay, but I couldn't. And they weren't.

CHAPTER FIFTY-THREE

Noah sat in the dark, grateful for its soft press. He was still badly shaken from seeing Gabe again.

And Beth. *But it wasn't Beth, it wasn't.* He didn't know what was worse. The confirmation that Gabe was a vampire had come from Clove, but actually seeing him standing there, flesh and blood, had muted his voice as easily as if someone had flicked a switch. Then there was the fact the demon had returned, as he knew it would, and this time it had wormed itself into the favour of things even Clove seemed powerless against. The master vampire was playing a game with words, that was obvious, and his skill was consummate. But could you ever reason with something as deadly and as devious as Aka Maga?

The door opened and Saxon appeared, his bulk blocking most of the light from the hallway. Noah dragged himself out of the torrent of his own mental river reluctantly. The vampire, carrying something in one hand, advanced slowly like a battleship approaching a harbour, then pulled an ugly-looking knife from his pocket with a flourish. Noah raised his head, his eyes glued to the curve of the knife blade. He wanted to pray, to ask God to absolve all of his sins and his weaknesses, but all he could do was stare.

Saxon grabbed hold of Noah's arm and rolled up his sleeve roughly, tearing the cotton of his shirt. The sound grated in the darkness and Noah tried to pull away, but his arm might as well have been in a vice.

'Stay still.' The vampire slid the knife against Noah's forearm. It was cold and crusted with dried blood at the tip. 'If you struggle, I'll make sure you regret it.'

In one practised sweep, the blade nicked Noah's skin and he watched in horror as the blood welled up in a thin line. Saxon brought what he was carrying into view—a metal goblet. Probably pewter, Noah's mind added, and he laughed, a short, coarse sound, as his civilised brain made notes.

Saxon grunted, glaring at him. He rested the goblet against the cut and Noah watched as the fine stream dripped slowly into the bottom. He couldn't take his eyes from it. Relief flooded his limbs. This wasn't an artery. It would heal. He had more time. Closing his eyes, he recited the Lord's Prayer in his mind, feeling the calm from it as his blood fell into the goblet. A cold touch slid along the wound and Noah's eyes jerked open. Saxon ran his finger along the line, then licked it, a hideous grin splitting his face. Noah tensed every muscle in his body, his teeth grinding in his jaw. This was like being touched by a corpse.

The vampire retreated with his offering, leaving Noah alone again. He sat in the dark, trying to formulate some kind of plan. The blind fear had trickled away, leaving him with a cold resolve. He might end up dying here, but if he could be of help to Gabe, it would be worth it. Olivia's face appeared in his mind. He banged the palm of his hand against his head. As much as he liked to think she was tucked up safe and warm at The Manor, logic told him she was prowling the streets looking for him. That feeling shredded any fear he had left.

He listened at the door. The voices still lingered, a cat and mouse game that could only end in disaster. But not before the cat had tormented the mouse to the point of extinction. Noah tried the doorknob. The metal moved in his hand, the catch clicking as it loosened. The click seemed as loud as a gunshot and Noah paused, holding his breath. But nothing came down the corridor to investigate. He peered around the edge of the door into the still hallway, searching for possible means of escape, but all he could see were two other battered doors. He inched out and turned left, for no other reason than instinct, and crept along the corridor, his feet testing each worn floorboard for creaks that might give him away. The door loomed in front of him. Old blood trails smeared the bottom amidst fragments of hair. Human hair. Revulsion rose in his throat as he tried the handle. It opened.

This room was much like the last, but smaller. It faced the road and the light from a street lamp filtered through a tiny window at ceiling height. But even this route was barred. He searched with his eyes, not wanting to risk his footsteps being heard. But this seemed like another dead end. Dead. The thought was heavy in his mind. The only thing in the room was a filthy, threadbare rug. He moved it with his foot. The floorboards beneath were newer, a little paler. Crouching, he peeled it up. Dust rose from its surface. He fought the urge to cough, summoning saliva to coat his irritated throat.

Underneath the rug was a trap door with a single clasp. With trembling fingers, Noah eased the clasp apart, sure it wouldn't budge or that suddenly the door would fling open and Saxon would drag him out to face the demon again.

The edge of the metal dug into his fingers, slicing open a knuckle. He fumbled for a handkerchief in his pocket, remembering all the times Olivia would tease him about his old-fashioned habits. Noah had no idea where this would lead. It could well be a simple cellar. What if it was somewhere the vampires kept their victims? He thought of the hair on the door.

Slowly, he raised the trap door, staring into the black void below. Nothing had emerged to grab his ankles, yet. He sat on the edge of the hole with his legs dangling and prayed, then lowered himself into the blackness, pulling the trap door shut above him.

CHAPTER FIFTY-FOUR

Most of the voices had faded into the recesses of his mind, but there was still one, incessant in its whispering, impossible to avoid in its feather-soft caresses. Teal had tried to talk back using all of his vampire mental powers, but it was like speaking into the wind. She did not hear him. Or she didn't want to hear him.

They stood around the uncovered labyrinth, all of it now visible. It was well over six feet wide.

'This place was a convent?' Olivia broke the silence, her frown deepening. 'I don't know why this would be here...' And then she stopped, her hand halfway to her face. 'Fuck. I think I have it, or something.' As one, three pairs of eyes wheeled to her. 'It looks familiar, or rather, the concept looks familiar. What kind of symbology would you normally find on a floor?'

'Pentagrams,' Gabe answered, his mouth slightly open. Teal knew something had clicked into place.

'I don't get it.' Moth scratched the back of his head and Teal smiled. Something had happened between Moth and Gabe, something beautiful and wild. Whatever wall Moth had built, Gabe had managed to breach it. A fluttering unfurled itself inside Teal's stomach like a butterfly opening its wings.

'Aren't pentagrams to do with witchcraft? This was a holy place, so it's way off base.' Moth's eyes challenged Olivia.

'That can be misinterpreted. A pentagram is actually a witchcraft symbol of protection.' Olivia's eyes swung to Gabe. Teal studied her, feeling for a moment like he was watching from afar. *She's trying to tune into his energy*, he thought, *but she doesn't know she's doing it*.

'Pagan symbols can be found anywhere, even in churches, so it's not unusual.' The excitement of discovery hung on Gabe's words and Teal didn't miss the way Moth was drawn to its light.

'Let's think about this logically,' Olivia continued, walking the far edge of the labyrinth with her hands raised, as though she was trying to pull answers from thin air. 'If this is some form of protective symbol, and let's forget for a minute this place is religious...'

'And that this isn't a pentagram,' Moth reminded her, his words quick fire and irritated. Gabe drew alongside him and touched his arm gently.

'But what if they couldn't use a pentagram because people associate them with witchcraft, so they used this instead?' Olivia twisted her mouth sideways in concentration. 'A pentagram was the preferred symbol for amulets for early Christians, and the ancient scriptures are full of it. But people do connect it with black magic. It's not such a crazy mix. So if we substitute this for a pentagram, what are we left with?'

Gabe crouched down, dark hair falling over his face. 'It was protecting them from someone or something, but they had to keep it secret. But the labyrinth means something.'

He glanced up at Teal. 'You've been saying all along we have to find it. There's a link somewhere.'

'The document Carver was working on—it was all about symbolism. He was on to something. But he hadn't connected all the dots.' It was like she was talking to herself, voicing thoughts that had only now strung themselves together like fairy lights, each little glow like a spark in the connection.

Teal knew she had her place in the plan. They would never have unravelled this puzzle piece without her. Knowing the demon was part of the chaos hadn't come as much of a surprise to Teal. A part of him had known it, right from the moment the fireflies had appeared. What he had, this mutation, had played right into its hands. What better way to get to Gabe than to use Teal as the bait.

'Hey, are you okay?' Moth stood in front of him, his face taut with worry.

'Yeah, just trying to put everything together whilst I'm still on a level with you. I never know when she'll call me back again.'

'We're not going to leave you. You know that, don't you? No matter how fucked up this gets.' Moth's breath was warm. He had fed recently. With Gabe. The knowledge came to him as surely as if it had been voiced out loud. Teal wanted to tell him to take Gabe and run. Go as far and as fast as they could. But the voice murmured away, underneath his conscious thoughts, like the drone of a bee. She needed all of them.

Behind them, Gabe and Olivia were deep in conversation, exchanging remembered facts from countless hours of studying. Teal wondered if Olivia had forgotten Gabe was a vampire. He looked so mortal standing there in the glow of the torch, his skin flushed from the kill, his eyes bright and animated. Moth watched him too.

'You and Gabe,' Teal whispered.

Moth looked down at the floor, his muscles tensing. 'Don't.'

It was one single word, but it had the meaning of a hundred.

CHAPTER FIFTY-FIVE

Despite the chill of the abandoned room, Olivia was flying high on managing to piece together a fragment of the puzzle. This was where she excelled, chewing on a few sparse bones of maybes until they turned into a feast. She didn't mind if she ran with an idea and it ended in a brick wall; the possibilities were always there, and sparring with Gabe had ignited the flame to a degree where she no longer felt cold. For a few minutes, she had almost forgotten what he was. It was like the old days when she would throw things at Ollie and he would ruminate on them until he was sure of the answer. There had been so much teasing on her part, he had never come out with a sentence until he had polished it to perfection. But this wasn't Ollie in front of her. He was dead. This was Gabe, and he was dead too, but in an entirely complicated way. She wondered what Noah would think if he could see them now. The slice of longing cut through her chest when she thought of him again. For the past hour, she had been doing a damn good job of forgetting about him.

Gabe was looking at her in an odd way, his head tilted slightly, his tongue visible between his lips. She wasn't scared, he didn't look threatening, but he should know about Noah in case he could throw any light on his disappearance.

'Noah was with me.' There was no point flannelling. She wasn't the kind of girl who wasted words. 'But you know that, don't you?' Her mind flicked back to the night on the cathedral steps.

Gabe had the good grace to look a little sheepish. His downcast eyes gave him away. That hadn't changed. He was still Gabe. Her throat tightened.

'Yeah, I know. Clove didn't want me making any contact.' He paused, scanning the labyrinth again. 'I know where he is.'

He had barely got the words out before she was up in his face, her eyes blazing. 'And it took you till now to tell me? Jesus, Gabe, what kind of game are you playing? Is he okay?'

She studied Gabe's face. Right there, in his expression, was the haunted mask of desolation that had been looking back at her in the mirror so often in the past year. 'Gabe… you're scaring me.'

A form appeared in her peripheral vision and her legs burned with a sudden spike of adrenaline. Moth. Now he *was* looking at her oddly, those crazy eyes shifting with shadows. Meeting him in a dark alley would only end one way. He pulled Gabe away. 'Gabe hasn't had much chance to tell you. And anyway, he's still digesting it himself. Who are you to get all high and mighty with him? He's not the boy from The Manor anymore.'

Somehow she managed to stand her ground, but her legs had turned to jelly.

'I'll make this simple' said Moth. 'That fucked-up demon is back. It still looks like Gabe's mother. It's out for blood and won't stop until we're all dead.' She stepped back on boneless legs. 'It has Noah, too, so you might as well...' He looked back at Gabe, swallowing what he was going to say.

'We have to help him, Gabe!' She tried to push past, but Moth grabbed her arm and she winced.

'Leave her be, please.'

Moth dropped her arm as if it had suddenly burned him.

'She didn't ask to be part of this anymore than we did.' Gabe turned his attention to her, the same sadness pulsing behind his eyes. 'I'm sorry I didn't tell you. But there's nothing we can do, not until we solve what the labyrinth means.'

For a few seconds, she wanted to scream at him. But that wouldn't have done any good, although it might have released the pent-up frustration boiling in her veins. She pressed her lips together and counted to ten. 'Okay, here's what I want to do. I need to go back to the hotel, grab my laptop, and see if I can get hold of Tom. If I sweet talk him, he might be able to have a look around and see if Carver made any more notes.'

'I don't know how much time we have,' Teal said. 'It doesn't feel like long.' His head tilted forwards and he staggered as though someone had caught him off balance. Moth and Gabe flew to his side.

'I don't know how much time Nekhbet will give me to bring Teal back either, but hurting Noah or Clove wouldn't be her style, not without me there to watch.' Gabe's voice was almost devoid of emotion. A shiver ran down her spine, dead fingers slicing her to the bone.

Pulling her shirt cuff back, she checked her watch.

Teal's legs crumpled beneath him and Moth swept him up into his arms. 'We need to get him somewhere safe, Gabe.'

Teal's eyes flickered open and then rolled back, his body spasming for a few seconds.

Olivia watched in horror.

'It's okay. He's done this before, but it weakens him each time. Where the hell do we take him?' This time Gabe's voice held a trace of panic.

'There must be dozens of hiding places?' Moth's answer was more of a question.

He wants someone to guide him, she thought. *For all of his snarky bravado, he's scared.* Something poked out of her memory banks, a fragment of digested information, filed away from one of countless history books.

'A priest hole.' She had their attention immediately. 'This was a convent. There must be a priest hole somewhere, probably in a fireplace or under the floor, anywhere that could be a tunnel.'

The building was cavernous and no doubt structurally unsafe. Still, it was worth a try. Although she didn't want to think of Gabe, lying here in the dark all day. Another idea pushed through.

'Come back with me to the hotel. The bathroom doesn't have a window. I'll stay and make sure no one disturbs you.'

Some sensible part of her tried to take the words back, but it was too late.

CHAPTER FIFTY-SIX

Would they run? Were they now on the boundaries of the town, breathless but safe, fleeing into the darkness with at least a slim chance of survival?

Clove allowed himself a shimmer of reflection as Nekhbet dismissed him, her face as expressionless as a death mask. He had held his own, firing back answers with just the right amount of humbleness. But there were barbs in his words and she had felt them, sliding under her skin to wedge there like a thorn. If he could make her show her true self, it was possible D'Grey might realise all was not quite as it seemed. Clove had no false hopes his old lover would join with him, but all Clove needed was a fraction of time to make his escape. Without D'Grey's assistance, it would prove problematic. Apart from the hunters in the house, there would be groups staged at various points close by, on high alert, waiting for his attempt at desertion.

There was also the added problem of Noah. Clove had no ties to the priest, apart from a respect for his relationship with Gabriel, but he did not want his blood on his hands. Nekhbet would not harm either of them, not when she was awaiting Gabriel's return with Teal in tow. He knew enough about her warped need for an audience to her deeds, to understand he might be playing for time. But so was she.

But the thought that returned again and again, settling like a blanket of snow, was what would happen if Gabriel came back, his fledgling naivety hopeful for a resolution that would get them all out alive? Then it would become a bloodbath. Clove surveyed the room, still laced with the cloying stench of opium, the fine furnishings of D'Grey's corner, the old, dried blood trails on the worn floorboards, and he wanted to burn it to the ground. It would be the only way to cleanse this poisoned place.

A sudden commotion came from the hallway. Raised voices and slammed doors. There was fear in those voices. Clove trained his senses in that direction. A few seconds later, Saxon ran past, his lumbering form surprisingly fast. But yes, panic in his eyes. He didn't even glance Clove's way, pausing outside the door that led to D'Grey's inner sanctuary.

'How can he be gone?' Another voice rattled down the corridor.

A slow smile curled onto Clove's lips. So, the priest had found his courage and seized his chance. But, more importantly, where had he gone? Behind him, the furore escalated. Another door slammed and the tall vampire appeared, wringing his hands together as D'Grey stormed from his room.

'He used the covered trap door in the other room. I've sent a team down after him. He won't get far.'

Clove almost admired his false bravado. D'Grey grabbed the vampire by his throat, pinning him to the wall like a butterfly on a board.

'If he escapes, I'll make sure *you* take his place.' His words shook with fury and, Clove suspected, a sprinkling of humiliation. D'Grey's hunters were his responsibility. Nekhbet would not take this calmly. Her absence from this heated exchange concerned him. D'Grey's grip loosened and the vampire fell to the floor in a crumpled heap, his swollen tongue protruding from his mouth.

'Her Eminence is resting and taking refreshment.' D'Grey pulled at the hem of his waistcoat as though the mere act of doing so could straighten his thoughts. 'I will inform her of this setback shortly. Don't get any ideas yourself, Clove. Once we find the priest and drag him back here, I will personally make him accountable for his actions.'

CHAPTER FIFTY-SEVEN

Noah clawed his way through the suffocating darkness. It disoriented him until he had no idea what direction he was heading in. For all he knew, he could be going back to the vampire house. This sobering thought jabbed away in his brain as he slowly made his way. Sometimes the tunnel narrowed. His hips bumped either side of the wall and he was sure at times it was going to lead to another dead end. Sometimes it fell away to nothing more than a rat run, horizontally winding and twisting. This was the most frightening. What happened if he got wedged inside and couldn't scrabble back out? It would be a long, slow death. He tried to cage these thoughts as his hands slipped into a nauseous slime and the sound of running water came from above. It wouldn't be long before they discovered his absence, and they would chase him. They were things of the dark, this would be home ground for them. He thought of Gabe. He thought of Olivia. He thought of Carver. Anything to stop his imagination from spiralling. Sometimes the rumble of traffic came from overhead, reminding him there was still a normal world out there. Dirt fell into his eyes and mouth, and his knees were skinned from crawling.

The noise came suddenly, and he thought he had

imagined it, because when he stopped and listened, there was nothing there. But it came again. And this time, there was no dispute. It was the sound of scratching. Noah froze. His heartbeat galloped in his ears. *It must be rats. There'll be hundreds down here…*

But the noise wasn't consistent with tiny, scampering feet. It was a long, drawn-out scraping. A sharp screech that found a raw nerve in Noah's head and lapped at it repeatedly. It stopped as suddenly as it had started, but Noah could still hear it. He drew his hand over his mouth and spat out a wad of grit-encrusted saliva. Salt. The unmistakable taste danced across his tongue. It could be sweat. But it just might be sea water—and if it could get in, maybe he could get out.

From far behind, sound rolled along the tunnel like an ocean wave. They were after him. He set off again, one hand trailing along the wall, one held out in front of him like a blind man, and he prayed.

A hand grabbed him by the shoulder and wrenched him backwards with such force his legs left the ground. The next second, his back hit the tunnel wall with a thud that made his teeth rattle. A surge of blood welled in his mouth as his incisor dug a hole in his lip. The air exited his lungs painfully. It was pitch black. All he could think of was that this was a terrible place to die.

His other senses took flight. The dank smell of standing water, the sound of traffic overhead, the metallic taste of his own blood…Noah shook his head and pain shot through his skull. In the battle of bone against brick, the wall will always win. It was pointless to resist, their presence hung around him like a suffocating black cloak. At least he had tried. He swallowed the blood in his mouth as his heartbeat hammered in his chest. But death hadn't come for him yet. Rough hands hauled him away in the dark, dragging him back to D'Grey's house, and pushing him through the trap door unceremoniously.

It's the lion's jaws, he thought, and laughed, the sound a hard, dead thing in his throat, because he remembered Gabriel's nursery.

‡

Noah came to as a torrent of iced water hit his face. Instinct forced him to his knees, head lowered, as he coughed and spluttered, his stomach heaving.

As his focus cleared, he found himself staring at the black biker boots that belonged to Emron D'Grey. Slowly, he raised his head, wincing as a sharp pain rocketed across his temple. D'Grey bent down and grabbed his hair, yanking Noah's head back.

'I'm trying to decide whether you are stupid or courageous, Noah Isaacs. Tell me, how far did you think you could possibly get?' D'Grey's pale grey eyes fixed him with a pitying look. Noah didn't have any option but to stare back and refuse to answer the question, because he didn't know himself. But damn it, he had tried.

'Leave him, Emron.' Clove's steady voice came from behind. 'You have him now. Your attention should be on Nekhbet, and on the things that make little sense. You always were intelligent. I see no reason why that intelligence should have deserted you now.'

The fingers in Noah's hair tightened to the point where he thought it would be pulled from the roots, and then D'Grey pushed him away. He got to his feet, shakily, and felt the side of his face. A lump the size of an egg rose from his right temple. It was hot and didn't take kindly to being prodded.

'Stop trying to confuse me with words, spice master. There was a time you could have swayed me with anything that fell from your lips, but that time is long gone. If you are playing for time, you have lost that game. My hunters are in conference with Her Eminence. Your children will be dragged here soon, and then we shall see if words have any power.'

There was such arrogance in D'Grey's words, and something else, an extreme animosity. Noah swallowed the bitter taste in his mouth. He didn't want to be here if Gabe was once again fighting for his life.

Noah studied Clove's face, the expressionless eyes, the slightly tilted face as though he was talking to a child, his firm stance and lowered shoulders. If there was any tension in him, he wasn't showing it. But looks were deceptive.

'We're going to keep this God-fearing man until our young guests arrive. It isn't fair that he should miss the show.' D'Grey finished this with a chuckle and a single hand clap, circling the floor where Clove stood, his eyes flicking up and down, almost hungrily.

The door to the parlour opened and the tall vampire exited first, followed by half a dozen others, a group of intimidating darkness.

An image flooded Noah's mind: Mid-winter. Gabe's loss had shredded layers of his heart daily, would it ever stop? He had been walking in the woods, up by the crypt, drawn there by a sense of longing for the desolation. His fingers had been stiff with cold, but his emotions were caught in a never-ending current of boiling confusion. A sound had come from behind. He'd whirled, his breath escaping in a sudden white fog. The birds had been studying him. In every tree, on nearly every branch, crows perched, bright black-glass eyes drinking in his fear. And he had fled, the winter bare branches whipping his face, unable to outrun the weight of loss and fury at a God that had deserted him...

They were like those crows, these killers clothed in black. A murder of crows. He wanted to laugh at the sheer insanity of his thinking. From the corner of his eye came the quietest of movements. In what seemed like slow motion, he turned. Clove calmly moved one hand, a subtle sweeping of the air with outstretched fingers. It said, be still.

The rustle of silks announced Nekhbet's entrance and all eyes turned to that sound.

'Your hunters have their instructions.' Her cold eyes swept over D'Grey. 'I tire of the games the fledglings play, and the sand of time has run out for them. Before the dawn, I wish to return to the ruling body with this mutation.' Her eyes settled on Clove. A smile greeted the master vampire. It was a smile of triumph. 'I will make my decision on the one who harboured it before I take my leave.'

Clove curled his fingers into his palms slowly. 'If you think you will prevail, you are sorely mistaken. Demon.'

Nekhbet's eyes narrowed to hard, black slits.

'If there is blood to be spilt,' said Clove, 'yours will fall too.'

They were brave words. Noah wasn't entirely sure if needling her was a wise move, but it did prove her skin could be irritated. Carefully, he filed that knowledge. D'Grey strode across, his pale face a fraction away from Noah's. There was blood on his breath and Noah recoiled.

D'Grey's fangs curled over his bottom lip. 'Don't get any stupid ideas, priest. Perhaps take the time to reflect on your own miserable life? When those bloody little killers get here, and let's hope for their sake it's before dawn, you're going to be the entree.'

CHAPTER FIFTY-EIGHT

The young vampire girl's body lay in a crumpled heap on the floor. She wasn't dead, but drained to the point where movement had become impossible. Her veins had all but collapsed in on themselves.

Nekhbet wiped the trail of blood from her mouth with a white napkin. A small smile broke the mask of her face. Her host was a man who appreciated the finer things in life. But he was a cockroach. A bottom-feeding fish who lived off what he could trade of others. Still, he was useful. Her elaborate dress chafed her skin, but this was a small price to pay for its impact. And what an impact that had been. The deep, heart-wrenching shock rising from Gabriel was worth a thousand nights of silks and satins. And they had not expected her return, which was the most delightful thing.

Her disappearance and subsequent silence was down to two things. One, the longer she stayed away, the safer they would feel. Two, she needed time to adjust to her new body and its limitations and its skills. This host, made of the shell of the human, Beth, whose blood ran with the saliva of Moth and Teal, was now fused together by the power of her old demon spirit.

Aka Maga, all seeing, all powerful, had evolved into a

dangerous tri-bred.

The first few months had been challenging. The human body, overcome with its sudden onslaught of powers, had to adapt. Occasionally a trickle of the old Beth had flared up, but it was caught and quashed. Systematically and in unison, the demon and the vampire genes had worked to banish all memory and all emotion until only the husk remained. A new name had been chosen, not only for the connection with the Egyptian depiction of a vulture, and therefore a timely reminder of its other feathered host, but also as a link back to Beth.

And Nekhbet had plotted, night after night, huddled over old texts, separating myth from fact, discarding the chaff and absorbing possibilities. Gradually, as she became more comfortable in her skin, she had sought out the company of other vampires, happy to prowl on the outskirts of their nests, listening to conversations and placing those that interested her into her mind cell marked *revenge*. She had used Beth's appearance as a weapon, asking questions of older vampires, always careful never to alert suspicion. She had learned what killed a vampire. She had learned of the ruling body of old masters closeted away, overseeing what was done and what was not done. She had learned no one questioned their authority. And she had smiled, in the dark, awaiting her chance to be the cat amongst the pigeons.

But she had known she needed a plan. A plan cast in stone that would not only lead her to Clove and his whelps, but also one which would put her in a seat of power. Destroying the vampires who had vexed her demon self would only be the beginning. The cold heart of revenge still wanted Gabriel, though the host she occupied now had served her well. The boy had caused an unmeasurable amount of frustration by siding with Clove. He would pay. They all would be broken.

Her breakthrough had come suddenly. A snippet of conversation overheard as she was debating the usefulness of this particular group.

'They thought he was a mutation, but it turned out his eyes were that colour all along. Some kind of freaky albino thing.'

She had drawn close, humble and open, asking what was this mutation they talked of—she was young but wanted to learn. They had taken her bait without a glimmer of uncertainty, both of them more than happy to fill in any missing gaps in her education. And she had repaid them well, luring them away with a promise of a personal thank you, then ripping out their throats as the first rays of sunlight tripped over the horizon. The ability to tolerate a small amount of natural light had been a most useful addition to her blended parentage.

The information she had gleaned was the key to the ruling body. She had learned mutations were feared and abhorred, with unsound blood that weakened the species. If they bred, their offspring further spiralled into abnormalities. In essence, they should be destroyed, at birth, like the runts of a litter. She had learned they were rare, that hunts were organised to cleanse them, and that vampires with any knowledge of one should report it immediately or face the consequences.

She had schemed and reasoned and had slowly fed the ruling body small morsels of information. They had been in power for so long, they'd actually welcomed her unique brand of infiltration. Not that they knew. Power comes with complacency. They were the proof. It hadn't taken long for them to agree to another hunt, and it hadn't taken long for them to make her an envoy. She'd given them no choice, but coated it with a mixture of lies and ego stroking. They swallowed it much better this way.

Their only request had appealed to her sense of justice. The mutation, if there was one, would be brought back to them. But she knew what would happen then. For all their loathing and disgust, they would draw lots for one thing: The honour of taking Teal's eyes.

The time for triumph was nearly here. This time, she would not fail. She did not know where Gabriel's loyalties would lie. If he returned, they would be to Clove and to the priest. It would be interesting if he chose his fellow fledglings. Interesting, but foolhardy. It was quite delicious to have him dangling by a string, to imagine how conflicted he felt, distress gnawing at his resolve. She knew he wouldn't leave, not with his maker and his old friend held captive.

But now it was nearly dawn, and all vampires, even the ones co-habiting with a demon, must sleep.

CHAPTER FIFTY-NINE

Olivia stared at the bathroom door. Behind it, in their death sleep, lay three young vampires. One of them was the boy she had thought she would never see again, who was very much alive. Or as alive as something dead could be. Goosebumps prickled her skin, but it wasn't her guests who caused it. The ceiling fan rotated with an oscillating whine. Since when did the English weather need a fan in September? It was an unhinged thought, but all her thoughts seemed like that now. Exhaustion weighted her limbs. She couldn't remember the last time she'd slept.

Those boys in the next room had trusted her with their lives. Somehow, Gabe had managed to convince Moth they didn't have a choice, but Moth wasn't happy. His eyes had settled on her and she'd had the distinct impression he was like a cornered animal. That glint in his eye that said *one wrong move and I'll retaliate*. He was like a stick of unstable dynamite.

The convent contained many hiding places, but there was a possibility they might be discovered. It was a slim chance, but the board outside had stated it had new owners, and the way their luck was going, today could be the day they decided to renovate.

Moth carried Teal back to the hotel like a small child unable to keep its eyes open after a long day. She didn't know what was happening to him, but he was definitely channelling something. This was unique and exciting. Or it would be, if it hadn't been happening in the middle of a situation that was so deadly serious. Her heart wanted to think about Noah but her brain didn't.

The early morning sun slanted in through the wooden blinds. She closed them and checked the sign hanging on the door to the pathway, which led down to the main hotel. Noah knew she hated being part of anything corporate, so he had booked them into a 'boutique' suite, which was the name for a small row of single-storey rooms behind the hotel. There it was again. Noah.

The sign swung from the handle on a rustic piece of string. A rectangular slate board was attached and the hotel provided its residents with a stick of chalk so they could write their own messages. Her message read: *Do Not Disturb. Sick.* If anyone tried to get in, she would haul their asses down to hotel reception and go into Queen Bitch mode.

Closing the door and locking it from the inside, she stuffed a couple of pillows against the bottom to block out any light, then checked the other two at the bottom of the bathroom door.

The last thing Gabe had said as they entered was, 'Don't, on any account, come in'. He could hardly keep his eyes open and she was reminded of the first New Year she had spent at The Manor. They had all been in the parlour, which Ella had decorated to the hilt in traditional festive trimmings. It had been a fairy-tale week of laughter and food and family. Even though they had only arrived the month before, Carver had treated her and Ollie as if they had always been there. That was a memory carved into her mind forever.

Gabe had been a boy of eleven, all long limbs and serious eyes and incessant questions. His quick mind, even at this age, had astounded her. He hadn't been able to keep his eyes open, and by 2 a.m., he was sprawled on the couch, fast asleep. Someone had covered him with a blanket and tousled his hair. Noah. She shook her head, bringing her focus back to the present.

It was dangerous to disturb them, and she didn't want to find out what happened if she did. Part of her internalised that Gabe didn't want her seeing him in his vulnerability. In his corpse-like state.

Fatigue covered her body with its dull weight and she lay down, the soft cotton of the pillowcase cupping the side of her face. There was so much she wanted to do before nightfall, but if she closed her eyes for a minute that would help…

The sudden ping from her phone woke her, slicing through her head. The dream fog hovered as she tried to get her bearings with sleep-heavy eyes. On autopilot, she swung her feet to the floor, knowing in some cerebral place she might have to move quickly. But the bathroom door remained tightly closed, the pillows intact.

With numb fingers, she checked the screen. Voice mail. Her throat felt full of dust and the water bottle at the side of the bed was empty. Whoever had left a message better be prepared for her sharp tongue. Dialling her mail box, she stretched her back, rotating her shoulders, stiff from carting armfuls of books at the convent last night.

Tom's voice hit her ear. 'Saw you'd been trying to get a hold of me.' There was a pause whilst he cleared his throat and she smiled, imagining him battling with the new technology. 'I don't like using these infernal things. If you want me to come down, call me back.' He paused again. 'Be careful.'

The words he didn't speak spoke louder than the ones he did. He knew something was wrong. She shot him a quick text, saying the signal was bad down here (which was true) and she didn't need him (which was a lie), but the last thing she wanted was Tom getting caught up in all of this.

Confusion waged a storm in her head. There was something she just wasn't getting. The need to get out of the claustrophobia of the room simmered behind her senses. But what if someone from the hotel came knocking to ask if she needed anything, and then used their master key to get in, full of concern for her wellbeing?

The image of the labyrinth danced in front of her like a whisper from a dream. There was something familiar about it, but she couldn't quite grasp what.

Grabbing her bag, she rustled through it and found her hair brush, dragging it viciously through her tangled hair. A face wipe removed the blotchy imprint of yesterday's mascara and a fresh breath mint would have to do in lieu of a toothbrush. She headed out of the door. The patio was deserted, but the two rooms at either side of her stood empty, their doors wide open to the morning sun. A cleaner's cart sat by one, with its selection of luxury toiletries. When they had checked in, the immaculately presented receptionist had informed her, quite seriously, that if she didn't like the orange blossom and green tea shower gel, to ring nine, and they would change it for something more suitable. Noah had actually sniggered at this, and then blushed, which was so endearing she had wanted to hug him.

Olivia slipped a twenty-pound note to the young girl who emerged from the room on the left, her arms full of used towels. 'Forgetting' about the room housing her young guests carried a price tag.

Olivia rested her forehead against the closed door. Now would be a good time for a prayer, but she had a feeling it would go unanswered, like so many other things had. A year ago, she had struggled to The Manor with palm crosses on the words of a ghost, to kill a demon. It hadn't quite worked out like that.

Today she was looking for something else. A clue to solve the mystery of a hidden labyrinth, to save a young group of vampires and the man she loved.

There, she had said it. And as soon as it saw the light, she knew it was true.

CHAPTER SIXTY

I opened my eyes to pitch black and the feeling that I was trapped. Before my senses could work out where I was, my body had already gone into fight mode. Muscles tensed, lips drawn back on fangs.

'Hey, it's okay.' A hand touched my arm and another figure stirred in the dark. The warm air of the tiny bathroom shifted against my skin. Moth. He was curled up behind me. I didn't remember him doing it, but then I was always asleep first. The bathroom floor space was small, but he didn't have to be that close. Something stirred in the pit of my stomach, something strange and not altogether unpleasant.

'She came through. Olivia.' He seemed to add her name as an afterthought, as if he didn't want to acknowledge her. I didn't know why he didn't like her; as far as I could see, all she had done was help. But Moth wasn't the kind of boy who liked immediately. You had to earn his trust. I was the poster child for that.

'Teal?' I rolled on my side and looked up at the side of the bath.

'Leave him. He must still be sleeping, and he needs it.'

We'd dumped Teal in the bath as soon as we'd got in, not quite a luxury bed but better than an insect-riddled hole under the rotten floorboards of the convent.

'These episodes he's having, Gabe, they're getting more frequent and longer. I'm scared one time he won't come back to us.' The same thought had crossed my mind too, but I hadn't wanted to vocalise it. Saying it made it real.

Moth rested the weight of his hand on my hip and my heart rate rocketed. I saw us together last night as clear as if I was watching a movie, saw the way his eyes darkened as he let the hunger in, saw the way he had trailed that piece of hay across my hand at the stable. Don't get too close, he'd said, and here he was, doing just that. I should move. I should break the spell. Laying here in the dark wouldn't help Clove or Noah. But it felt safe. And I was clinging to that. It would be a miracle if any of us survived until another dawn.

His hand moved to my waist and I gasped. But I didn't stop him, even though Teal was laying asleep not a few feet away. Why was he making a play for me when he loved Teal? Confusion danced across the butterflies taking flight in my stomach. If this was wrong, why did it feel so good? I had zero experience, but my body somehow knew how to respond. I reached across, brushing the hair from his face. A few strands slid between my fingers and I tightened my grip. This time, he was the one who gasped. It was such a sweet sound.

His fingers trailed along my cheek and I turned to them, smelling dust and blood and *him*. He rested his palm and, tentatively, I kissed it, part of me waiting for him to laugh and say this wasn't right, what was I playing at? His hand moved to the small of my back and he pulled me close. Hip to hip, his need was obvious. I tensed.

'It's okay, it's okay.' His voice softened. 'I just want to be close.' Then he laughed, but not to mock me. 'And some more, but we can't.'

Our situation was hopeless, in the truest sense of the word, but we were clinging onto these stolen moments, our shadows caught on the barbed-wire edges of what reality had planned for us.

His face was so close to mine, each exhaled breath sang against my skin. My fingers were still anchored in his hair, as if I was hanging onto what little sanity I had left.

I opened my mouth to him.

His tongue flicked against my lower lip, lapping up the saliva that trailed across it. My grip tightened and he groaned, the sound falling into my mouth. He rolled me over, pressing my back into the side of the bath. My head hit the porcelain with a bang, but it barely registered. Now I knew what need was and I didn't want it to end. He darted his tongue inside my mouth, delving it across my fangs and I cried out. Pleasure surged through my veins, and for a few heaven-sent seconds, I forgot where we were and what we would have to do. I responded to his urging with little noises of pleasure in my throat that only seemed to spur him on. We were breathless, consumed, caught up in our own rollercoaster ride to hell. In my fumbling, the edge of one of my fangs grazed his lip and I sensed the small droplet of blood as it welled. Sensed and smelled. He hesitated, and for one heart-pounding moment, I thought I'd blown it.

'Kiss me.'

I didn't need asking again. I licked it from his lip with the tip of my tongue. The taste of him exploded in my mouth, all salt and copper sparks. It only fuelled the fire screaming around my body. I was breathing hard now. Quick, shallow breaths escaped my mouth and he was right there, inhaling each breath as if he couldn't get close enough to me by body contact alone. Reason tried to raise a hand—*this isn't the time. There won't ever be a time.*

I wanted to rip off our clothes and feel his skin against mine. I wanted to explore every inch of his body, my fingers memorising each curve and hollow, to close my eyes and let my tongue become my sight. So I could forget about being brave, about facing the demon who now wore my mother's skin.

'Me too, Gabe.' He stopped and kissed my forehead. My thoughts must have been broadcasting loud and clear, which was so irresponsible a wave of guilt consumed me.

We stayed, clung together, for another minute, our ragged breathing slowly settling. A pang of sadness choked my throat. We had started something sweet we wouldn't ever be able to finish. Unless we could snag a miracle.

Moth moved away first, giving me a shaky smile then pulling himself up and peering over the side of the bath. His eyes widened and he froze, and I felt that chill glide right through me. I scrabbled to my knees, not really wanting to see, but having to.

The bath was empty. Teal had gone.

CHAPTER SIXTY-ONE

Teal didn't remember waking up. He didn't remember getting to where he was now. But he had been here before, hadn't he? The skin on his face and hands felt tight, as though during his death sleep, his bones and tissues had all enlarged. His vision swam. It was hard to make out anything in the dark. At least he hoped it was dark.

Inside his head, the countless voices had all faded to a distant hum, still there like a background drone of traffic, but one voice led him, telling him to do things he had no control over. His body responded to her words while his brain was a silent passenger. It was as if he was floating over his own lifeless body, watching it but untethered from any emotional bond. He tried to think about Gabe and Moth, but every time he dredged their images up from the recesses of his mind, she covered them over until he couldn't remember what they looked like anymore.

They were shapes in the mist, circling the beacon that was…a witch. She's a witch. It broke through, piercing the membrane of his thoughts, without kindness.

A sudden breeze chilled his face and he turned towards it, like a new-born to a mother's breast. Something wet and cold rolled down his cheek and over his lips. He flicked his tongue, like someone he knew once.... Tears. But for whom? He didn't know anymore.

You need to know where I am. I am the unknown centre, the mystery of death and rebirth. It is only in the risk of the search and the danger of losing your way that I will find the ability to return. Teal, it is the quest and the finding...

Her words washed over him like storm waves, incessant and repeating, soaking into his mind, but he still didn't understand.

My poor child—her voice softened now, became like sunlight—*I ask of you a great deal. But what you have inside you, this gift of brightness, is stronger than mine. I need my revenge to die. I can be your symbol of destruction, against those who would see you mutilated and buried. It is a great unpleasantness to be aware of everything on The Bloodvyne and be powerless to intervene. Waiting for you, Teal, I was always waiting for you.*

He clung onto the unyielding stone angel in front of him. His fingers clawed. It was colder than death.

A wavering image of Moth and Gabe swam up from the waves and a small sigh left his lips. He rested his cheek against the stone.

A searing pain knifed through his head and he cried out, falling to his knees. Then a weightlessness took him and he was impossibly floating, looking down on the old town, ethereal and without fear. Strands of hair whipped across his face and he laughed, the sound lost to the night. A rush of blood filled his head and the vessels pinged at the onslaught. Was this finally death?

No, my child. This is not your death. This is enlightenment. Open your eyes and see.

Teal obeyed; he had no choice. The haze across his vision gradually cleared and he gasped, the cold night air cascading into his lungs.

The labyrinth lay before him, sprinkled with light.

CHAPTER SIXTY-TWO

Moth stared hard into the empty bath, fear replacing the passion thrumming through his veins. Teal was gone. How could he be fucking gone?

A few seconds ago, his world had been filled with warmth and the blinkered hum of sensual tension. Now the walls had all fallen in around him, again.

'How could he leave? I mean…'

It was obvious how he had left, but Teal never woke up before Moth, and Moth felt like he had been awake for hours, content in the curve of Gabe's body against his, weighing up the well of feelings inside. When had it all changed between them?

Gabe made for the door and swung it open, kicking away the pillows on the floor. A thin glimmer of dusk poked out from under the window blind, but the room was empty. He moved the slats and winced, stepping back quickly.

'We can't go out yet.' Gabe's face was grim. If they couldn't go out, how could Teal?

Footsteps sounded on the path outside and Moth paused, ready to run, ready to fight.

'It's okay, it's Olivia.' Gabe opened the door, shielding himself from the half-light, and Olivia almost fell in, Styrofoam coffee cup in hand.

'Jesus, Gabe!' She righted herself as Gabe slammed the door shut. 'What are you doing awake now?' There were dark circles under her eyes and she was still wearing yesterday's clothes.

'I thought you were staying here to make sure no one came in.' Moth couldn't help mentioning this small fact.

'It might have escaped your notice, but you were occupying my bathroom.' She fixed him with a glare. 'And I needed coffee. Some of us have been awake for hours.'

'You two fighting isn't helping, you know.'

Moth knew Gabe was right, but there was something about her that made him react.

Gabe sat on the edge of the bed, his fingers curling into the white duvet. He had a faraway look in his eyes and his lips were moist. Moth remembered the feel of his tongue, and a tremor ran down his spine. Olivia sipped her coffee. Moth watched as the steam wavered in the air like a mirage.

'I did, however, slip out earlier because I had to,' she said. 'There was something bugging me and I had to walk it off—'

'Teal's gone,' Gabe interrupted, his voice hollow.

She stopped, the cup halfway to her mouth. 'But it's not quite dark, and where would he go without you?'

There she was again, Miss Stating-The-Fucking-Obvious. Moth slammed his fist into the wall. Fragments of plaster fell down behind it, a rattling that sounded too much like the skittering of insect feet. They all looked up.

'He's gone to D'Grey's.' Gabe voiced what Moth feared the most. It made sense. Nekhbet wanted Teal, or she had to play along with wanting him to keep her plan intact. It was just like Teal to give himself up to save the rest of them. Yet something about that prickled in his mind. The voices in Teal's head were all about finding the labyrinth. What-ever was calling him had a determined purpose. Surely it wouldn't let him sacrifice himself now?

Gabe's hand squeezed his shoulder and Moth closed his eyes. Why was everything so fucking difficult?

'How long will you need?' Olivia glanced outside.

'About ten minutes. But we still need to keep to the shad-ows. If you have a plan, I'm right with you.' There was an undercurrent of steel in Gabe's voice.

'If what you told me about the hunters is right, they'll be out searching in all the places they haven't checked. They won't expect you right in the middle of their sights.'

'So we're going where exactly?' Begrudgingly, Moth was glad someone had at least the glimmer of a plan.

'We're going to the cathedral,' said Olivia. 'There's some-thing there that ties this altogether, I swear. You need to trust me.'

Gabe's eyes met his. 'It's a big ask, Moth. It puts us right on their radar and Nekhbet isn't stupid. But I don't think we have a choice.'

They were damned if they did and damned if they didn't. But weren't they damned anyway?

Ten minutes later saw them creeping along the streets. Thick clouds blanketed the sky, but still the whispers from the faint light stung the back of Moth's eyes. Gabe didn't seem to have a problem. That was the pure bred in him again. They were so different in so many ways. How could it work between them? He caught the heavy cloak of anx-iety before it settled. This was no time for self-pity. He told himself to enjoy walking alongside Gabe. It could end any minute. And he tried not to think about Teal.

They skirted past D'Grey's lair, following the curve of old houses that clung to the edge of the cliffs. Centuries ago, people had built their homes not in straight, uniform lines, but respecting the lay of the land. It was quirky, and one reason why Westport Quay still thrived to this day when so many other little towns were forlorn and forgotten.

Olivia walked with Gabe, her gaze fixed straight ahead, mouth set into a thin line. Moth caught her thoughts even though he wasn't prying. Noah. She's thinking about Noah.

Moth hadn't given much thought to the priest, but now he wondered just how well a human was holding up in all of this. Being a guest of D'Grey's was like staying in a room in an executioner's house.

People streamed past and a few gave them wary glances, like you might peer at a wolf cub until you realised there was no cage between you.

This was worse than last year, and he hadn't thought that was possible. At least then Clove had held them all together. Back then, there hadn't seemed to be a single thing on this earth that could have fazed him. A burst of anger popped in his head like a blister and he stamped on an empty plastic water bottle out of sheer frustration. Olivia spun around, her heartbeat increasing, and glared at him. He shrugged. It wasn't his fault she was jumpy. Gabe didn't even appear to have noticed. He was deep inside his own thoughts, his head bowed, tension tightening his features.

They rounded the corner where the road led down to the quay and walked past the line of shops where Olivia had first seen Clove. Tiny fairy lights swayed from the store fronts, a remnant from the summer. Some of the bulbs lay dormant and no one had bothered to replace them this late in the season. The breeze from the sea had turned colder, like the kiss of a dead lover. A chill ran down Moth's spine.

The front of the cathedral came into view through the veil of trees, and Moth half expected to see D'Grey there with his viper's smile. The great door stood open, an old carriage lantern lighting the stonework above.

Olivia paused in front of the old town street plan, her mouth twisting in concentration. But something had sparked Gabe's attention. He stopped and scanned, his lips slightly parted. Moth could almost feel his instincts clicking into place, the pure bred blood in his veins oiling the cogs, his sight and smell and hearing becoming one single probe into the darkness. Moth drew close, darting his tongue, using the only instinct that had never let him down. The air tingled with an effervescent energy, a grounded force that seemed to come from the earth itself.

Gabe slowly lifted his face until he was looking at the indigo sky. *He's done this before*, thought Moth, and then it hit him, and he cranked his head back hard.

There, in almost the same place as he had been before, was Teal, with his back pressed into the fold of an angel's wing. In the new dark, his eyes glowed like blue-green embers.

Don't shout to him. Gabe's voice touched his mind, a split second before Teal's name came from his lips.

As one, they bolted to the steps. Moth knew it could all be a trap but it didn't matter. He'd wondered how Teal had got down from there before, but somehow there had never been the time to ask him. They both barged through the cathedral door, the candle flames from the prayer table dancing as they passed, feet skidding on the marble tiles.

Gabe hesitated then set off again through a thin door to the right. It led to a narrow staircase, winding its way upwards. Taking the steps three at a time he raced up, Moth hard on his heels. They sped along a small walkway open to the night, then ducked under a low arch, the sign above it reading 'Strictly no admittance to the public'. It was easy to see why. This last reach of steps had a dizzying view of the ground below, and was pock-marked by the droppings of sea birds and pigeons. The platform the statues stood upon loomed above them, its lip hiding the figures. And Teal. It took all Moth's resolve not to call out.

Gabe threw himself up the first few steps then grabbed hold of the wall and scrambled up, using the weather-worn gargoyles as footholds. Moth followed on autopilot, trusting Gabe's instincts, his heart lodged in his throat. After a few long, drawn-out seconds, Gabe's fingers curled around the platform lip and he hauled himself up, scrabbling onto his knees then reaching down to grab Moth's hand.

In the damp, cold air, they both stared at the dead stone eyes of the angel, his arm outstretched to the heavens, asking for a blessing, asking for redemption.

There was no sign of Teal.

CHAPTER SIXTY-THREE

We stared at each other in disbelief. I didn't know what I'd expected when we got up here, but finding Teal gone wasn't on the list. The only way down was the way we had come. Or…Moth glanced down at the square of grey stones outside the cathedral. Clearly his mind was set on the same wavelength as mine. The breeze lifted his hair back from his face and I found myself staring at his profile.

'Is that even possible?' Even though I knew some vampires had unbelievable abilities, voicing it still sounded so far off base.

Moth stepped back from the edge. 'Clove told me it does happen. But usually to those that are old and powerful. Teal doesn't tick any of those boxes. And he's not pure bred.' A shadow passed over his eyes, like clouds obscuring the sun, and then it was gone. He was still hiding things from me. I wondered why that hurt so much.

Far down below, Olivia still stood in front of the town plan, her hand outstretched towards it. If Teal had jumped, surely she would have seen something? Or felt something. She was intuitive and in tune with things most people didn't even believe existed. But Moth didn't like her, and I didn't understand why.

'Hey, what's wrong?' Moth reached for my hand, then stopped, his eyes softening.

'Too much to think about. Don't worry, I'll be okay.' I wanted to hold his hand. I wanted to feel his arms around me. But I couldn't take comfort, not when everything around us was falling to pieces. I think he felt it too, but when he pulled away, the night seemed colder. Whatever was happening and whatever the outcome, it had nurtured something between us.

I stared into the night, at the old town laid out beneath us, at the ocean to our right and the tiny lights far out at sea from passing ships. The salt tang seemed stronger tonight, the wind skipping across the swell of the ocean. I ran my tongue over my lips to taste it, the points of my fangs catching. They still felt unnatural sometimes, but then wasn't I completely unnatural? Reflection coated my thoughts and I tried to chase it away. There was a surreal feel to the air, as though questions and answers were caught up in the very fabric of it.

Most of the old town lay before me, the only lights at strategic places deemed needed for public safety. But the old gas lamps still glowed, their softer light flickering against the night. I studied them, mesmerised, letting my eyes move from light to light, like I had done when looking at the stars with Noah or Carver. *Please hold on*, my thoughts told them, but that thought passed swiftly, caught up in the rhythmic pattern my eyes were tracing.

'Oh. Fuck. Moth, look!' I grabbed his arm and pointed. 'Look at how the streets run around the old town. See, in curves, as they fit in with the hills.'

He followed my instruction, his eyes travelling the same path as mine. 'I guess so, but why's that such a big deal?'

293

'Think about what we saw on the convent floor. I swear this is the same shape. I think the old town is the labyrinth!'

His head jerked around, his eyes wide and bright. For the first time, I saw the light of hope shining there. It was a thing of beauty in all of this twisted chaos. Together, our eyes were drawn to the darker central core, away from the soft focus of the gas lamps.

'That's the convent.' He pointed to the far end of the centre. From there, the harsher lights grew more common, the old giving way to the new.

Something clicked against my mind. The shape inside the labyrinth at the convent was a triangle.

My thoughts went into freefall. I was aware of Moth staring at me, of his hand holding my arm, of the crystalline quality of the air crackling with invisible words. There was a definite line from the convent to where we were standing. I tracked right, towards the sea, searching for something I recognised that would make the last point of the triangle, but there was nothing. Frustration flooded through my veins. I was so sure…

Footsteps sounded on the stone steps leading up to where we stood. Moth flicked his tongue and I stared, still hypnotised by how he did it. He mouthed Olivia's name to me.

'Gabe?' Her voice rang out in the stillness, echoing from the surrounding stonework.

I looked over the platform.

'Gabe, I know what the labyrinth is. It was on the town plan!' She had joined up the dots at the same time as me. Her eyes shone as the wind whipped her long dark hair around her face. Reaching down, I offered her my hand, not sure if she would trust me to pull her up to where we stood. She didn't even hesitate. She weighed almost nothing.

'Where's Teal?' Her hand smoothed back her hair as she asked the same question, a frown deepening as she logged his disappearance.

'The labyrinth, look.' I pointed again. Each time I went back to it, it seemed clearer, but I was still missing that final point.

'Fuck, yes.' Her reply was all breathless excitement and the drumming of her heartbeat vibrated in my ears. It was a song and it sung to me, like it had sung to every vampire who had ever existed. I silently thanked the guy from last night who had fed us to the point of saturation.

'The convent and here are two points of the triangle, see the line?'

She nodded. 'I saw that too, although it's clearer from up here. I don't think the plan is true to scale. So, that would make the other point about there.' She waved a hand into the darkness. 'What's there, besides the sea?'

Moth joined us, taking a place at the other side of Olivia.

'The sea. And the harbour. Gabe, didn't Clove tell us he came here when he was a child, on a ship during the spice trade?'

My next breath caught in my throat as the third point of the triangle fell into place. If that was right….and it had to be, didn't it? I was grasping at straws, but the fit was too perfect, too seamless. The triangle stood out for all of us, as clearly as if it had been marked in neon.

'Is there anything in the centre of that triangle?' Her words were whispered, as though she didn't really want to know. My eyes searched, and then the breath left my body in a rush.

'Yes.' I forced the next words through gritted teeth. 'It's D'Grey's house.'

CHAPTER SIXTY-FOUR

They stared at the recently uncovered labyrinth on the convent floor, but this time with new eyes. It was crystal clear now, the curves of the outer shell, the lines between the points they had plotted. Hindsight deserves more credit than it gets, Olivia thought. She was fidgety with unease and annoyed at herself for not figuring the clues out sooner. The town plan was so obvious, now she thought about it properly. She had stood in front of it only a few nights ago—the night Noah had first seen Gabe on the cathedral steps. She bit her lip and tucked her hair behind one ear. Gabe knelt, tracing the lines with his finger, his brow furrowed in concentration.

On the floor were four metal lanterns containing thick church candles Olivia had taken from the hotel patio. She had ducked into her room, grabbed a sweater and a small backpack, coming out to find Moth with his hand on Gabe's shoulder. The attraction between them sizzled in the crisp night air and she wondered how that had happened. They were so unlike. But look at her own relationship. What the heart wants, it wants, and fuck anything that tries to get in its way.

She pulled herself out of her thoughts and forced herself to concentrate. 'So we know D'Grey's house is in the centre of the labyrinth, and that's what Teal had to find, yes?' Gabe nodded. 'But how can going there help anything?'

Moth fixed her with that mismatched look. 'And what about what Teal said when he went all weird when Gabe wasn't here? The "find me, pretty girl" thing.'

She didn't miss the slightly raised eyebrows that went with this, but her annoyance was quickly replaced with a rush of thought as she recalled Teal's words, spoken in a woman's voice, and the feeling of dizziness sweeping over her as he had spoken them. The hair at the nape of her neck bristled and Gabe glanced up as she repeated the rest of Teal's words. 'Walk the pathway with the blood. Speak the truth and watch them die.'

Moth and Gabe exchanged a glance. Could they read each other's minds?

'What if the pathway is the labyrinth itself, like Theseus and the Minotaur?' Gabe's question hung in the cold, damp air, in the small space of light they had carved from the darkness.

Olivia pulled up the myth from her memory and flicked through the pages. 'King Minos hid the monster in the labyrinth because he didn't want to kill it...' She paused as Moth moved away into the shadows.

Gabe nodded. 'The monster. It could be Nekhbet. We already know the clues we're getting are riddles, the labyrinth being the pentagram for one.' He looked up to where Moth stood in the gloom.

Olivia glanced down at the labyrinth. 'We can't take anything at face value, Gabe, you're right.'

She continued, walking the outside curves of the pattern as she spoke, aware of Moth's eyes burning into her back. 'Minos imprisoned his enemies in the labyrinth so the Minotaur would destroy them.' She shivered. If Gabe was right and the monster was Nekhbet, Noah might already be dead. She blinked away the burning in her eyes. 'Let's focus on how Theseus won.'

Gabe took up her train of thought. 'He went into the labyrinth with the golden thread from Ariadne, killed the Minotaur, and found his way out again. So we find what links us to the golden thread, and use it to go get Clove and Noah.'

It all sounded so simple, but her head pounded with all the dangling trails they could follow and end up lost. She laughed, its sound bouncing from the high walls.

'What's so funny?' Moth, of course.

'Everything links back to this fucking labyrinth, and however we look at it, there's always a monster in the middle.'

Gabe watched her plant a foot in the centre of the triangle and something clicked into place behind his eyes. 'You just walked the pathway, Liv. I think you have to do it for real. Moth and Teal and I, we're the blood.' The logic in his words and the sound of the nickname only Ollie had used for her settled in her throat. Her emotions swirled up underneath it, a sea of feeling wanting to crash to shore.

'She's there, waiting for us.' Teal's voice came from the doorway. No one had heard him enter. Cobwebs clung to the strands of gold in his hair, as though he had been in a forgotten place.

Moth ran across, scattering loose pages like fallen leaves. '*Who's* there? And where did you go? From the cathedral roof?' He bombarded Teal with a barrage of questions before sliding an arm around his shoulders.

'I don't really know what I did, but she let me see this time, told me what I have to do.'

They came into the light. Olivia was mesmerised by the glow in Teal's eyes. It was as if the ocean was on fire. It was too easy to get caught up in the snares of their plight and to forget what they actually were, and then something like this would come back to remind her.

'Who's waiting for us, Teal?' Gabe repeated Moth's question, his face half in shadow as he moved.

'The White Witch. She's the one who's been talking to me. We have to find her and set her free.'

‡

We'd managed to make some sense out of all the mess at long last, and now here was Teal adding another layer to what we were fighting through. I knew I was right about Olivia and the labyrinth, but it didn't make me all that happy. She was here for a reason, like everything else that had just slotted into place, but putting her in the firing line didn't sit well. I didn't want anyone else to die because of me. Remorse rolled over in the pit of my stomach.

I turned to Teal, hugging my arms across my body. Unease crawled over my skin. 'So, The White Witch is at D'Grey's?' It didn't make sense.

Teal knelt down by one of the lanterns and put his hands out, as though the candle flame was a roaring fire. My heart ached at his innocence. Why did he have to be the one this was happening to? A fall of hair obscured his face and Moth looked at me with pain in his eyes. We were trying our best to make it right, but every time we moved forwards, another boulder came crashing down upon us. The mouldering odour of rotting paper welled up from the floor, and somewhere upstairs, an old door creaked.

'She's in the dark somewhere. I saw through her eyes, only for a fraction of a second...' He paused and pressed a finger against the glass front of the lantern. 'They buried her there because they couldn't kill her.' His voice sounded small in the dark.

'How can freeing her help us, or Clove?' Moth put his hand on Teal's shoulder and I bit my lip.

'I don't know yet. But Olivia has to do it.'

Olivia's pulse quickened and I tuned into its pace. Her face was pale in the shadows, but the steely look of determination she gave me told me more than words. Once again, she was the one who would be racing against time, and a surge of love swelled up in my chest.

Teal stood and stared down at the labyrinth on the floor. All the time I had known him, he had never been anything but the voice of reason and light, even when Moth and I were verbally tearing each other to shreds. But now the weight of the world seemed to be on his shoulders.

'What are you going to do?' But I knew the answer before the words had left my mouth.

He smiled, and those ocean eyes darkened for an instant.

Moth's intake of breath filled the silence. 'No! No, Teal! There must be another way!' He grabbed Teal by the shoulders and his fingers trembled even as he protested.

'There is no other way. Nekhbet wants me. If I give her that, it gives you all a chance to find The White Witch. If I take away their attention, you've more time to get in undisturbed.'

His words made perfect sense, but letting him face Nekhbet and D'Grey by himself? It was suicide.

'What happens if she takes you to the ruling body right away?' I wanted to make him aware of all the risks. A part of me wanted him to say he had changed his mind.

'She won't. She'll be so triumphant she has me that she'll want to show it off. And that means playing to D'Grey and whoever else is there. We'll have the first part of tonight at least. After that...' Teal shrugged.

'This place was a Catholic convent,' Olivia said. 'But the more I think about it, I think that was only part of it. The labyrinth on the ground for a pentagram, and the carvings on the doors. What convent has those? This place had a darker side.' She thought, and her brow furrowed. 'Before I go to D'Grey's I need to go back to the hotel and do a search on this place. Maybe even log in to The Manor database if I can.'

'You're not going alone, I'll go with—'

'No. Not you, Gabe.' Teal's voice came softly, but power shadowed his words.

'Moth, will you see Olivia is safe? Please.'

Why would Teal want Moth to go? Especially as they both rubbed each other up the wrong way, but I wasn't going to argue. I trusted Moth enough to know he would protect her even though he didn't like her very much.

He frowned and shrugged, his eyes meeting mine for a moment before he headed for the door.

Olivia opened her arms to me and I hugged her close, breathing in her scent and burying my face in her hair. She smelled of cold nights and woodsy perfume. She smelled alive. 'Be careful, okay?'

'I won't be long.' Fortitude edged her words. 'If I'm right, we might have more to go on with The White Witch. I think she's linked to this place.'

She followed Moth and paused before the darkness swallowed her whole. 'Don't do anything stupid, Gabriel Davenport. You're still my baby brother.'

And then she was gone.

Tears burned in my eyes. One escaped and rolled down my cheek. She had accepted what I was and still loved me. If anything happened to her...I curled my fingers into my palms tightly.

Teal appeared silently at my side, his arm touching mine.

'You're going now, aren't you? That's why you sent Moth.' I took him in my arms and held him, whispering his name over and over, winding my fingers in that golden hair, wanting to keep an imprint of him with me always.

Finally, he pulled away, stepping back until he was only holding my fingertips. 'Find her for me, Gabe. Find The White Witch. She's the missing puzzle piece.'

I didn't watch him leave. It hurt too much.

But I heard his voice come back from the doorway. 'I love you both.'

And then I was alone.

CHAPTER SIXTY-FIVE

Moth hung around the doorway of Olivia's room. The door was slightly open and he could hear the tap tap of her fingers on her laptop keyboard.

They had walked here in silence, which suited him fine. He didn't know why Teal had insisted he be the one to babysit, but right now he would do whatever Teal said. He'd come too far to second-guess what made sense and what didn't, and the clues were all lining up. But fuck, the outcome still looked bleak. Maybe he could talk Teal out of going by himself?

He scuffed his toe along the line between the paving stones. The sound of music playing drifted across from the main hotel and inside throngs of people jostled together. Their heartbeats set his nerves on edge.

'Can't you hurry up?' he hissed through the crack in the door.

Five seconds later, she appeared and swung it open. 'Stop hanging around like you're fixing to break in. I'm going as quickly as I can. The Wi-Fi here isn't the best in the world. Quaint seaside towns don't have that as part of their tourist agenda. Most people come here to get away from technology.'

She glanced back inside as a page loaded. 'Are you coming in or not?'

Moth reluctantly accepted as Olivia pulled the laptop onto her knee and studied the screen. The glow from it turned her face otherworldly. He watched her intently until she glanced up.

'What?'

He shrugged and leaned back against the door, sliding his thumbs through the belt loops of his jeans. Just because he had been sent to babysit her didn't mean he had to play nice. Something poked away at the soft underbelly of his conscience, twisting its way in like a thorn and refusing to let go. It had started in the library when she had thrown her arms around Gabe. She was part of his past and he wasn't.

'I have no idea what your problem is with me,' she said. 'You don't like me. I don't like you. Let's settle on that, shall we, and try and get some work done. If you're done brooding over there I could use a second pair of eyes on this. We're running out of time here, Moth.'

He thought he'd caught the slightest quivering of her bottom lip and then it was gone. Her words stung and part of him wanted to walk right on out of there. But she was right, and he'd have to give her that. He sat on the edge of the bed, but not close to her.

She rolled her eyes and turned the screen towards him. 'This is a photo of the convent from around 1920. It still looks pretty much the same today.' She scanned the lines of text. 'It was used as a hospital in the First World War, but one wing was still kept in use by'—she paused and chewed her bottom lip—'an order of holy sisters who never left the confines of its walls.'

Moth pointed to the far right of the photo, where the domed roof could clearly be seen. 'What's that on the top?'

Olivia zoomed in. 'I can't make it out, it's too blurry. It could be some kind of ironwork, a weather vane maybe?'

'Here, let me see.' Moth moved closer, his eyes fixing on the indistinct shape sitting on top of the dome. 'Get me a pen and some paper.'

She grabbed the hotel notepad from the side table and handed it across.

He sketched the image quickly. 'It's not one hundred percent clear, not even to me, but this is kinda what it looks like.'

Olivia's jaw dropped and she gasped, the sound catching in her throat. 'Moth, that's Hecate's Wheel!' Her eyes darted from the screen to his face and back again, as she opened up another window.

'That means nothing to me. Is that good?' Moth wished he had Teal's knowledge from books, or Gabe's schooling. Learning hadn't been big on his things to do as a kid.

She pointed out the symbol as it loaded slowly on the blank page. 'It's the emblem of the lunar goddess, Hecate.'

It wasn't identical to what he had drawn, but it was close enough.

She continued, her cheeks flushed. 'There's an ancient text called the Chaldean Oracle and it describes the symbol as a labyrinthine serpent. It refers to the knowledge about power and life. And it's another link to the rebirth angle that keeps cropping up.'

From where he sat Moth could see the reflection of the screen in her eyes. 'But what does it mean? I get that it's all tied up to the labyrinth…'

She grabbed his arm, the heat from her fingers seeping into his skin. 'Moth, I think The White Witch came from the convent. The labyrinth as the pentagram, the Wheel of Hecate, there's too many links for it to be circumstantial. The "holy sisters who never left the walls"? I think it was all a front.'

He picked up on her excitement, slightly dizzy on the sound of her blood as it rushed through her veins. 'But why would they bury her?'

'I think she knew something that was considered a threat, but her sisters wouldn't have wanted her blood on their hands. Teal said they couldn't kill her. But what if she still needed to be silenced.'

They both picked up on the truth as soon as it had left her lips.

'Do you think there might be a way to D'Grey's house from the convent, underground?' she asked. 'If this place was doing double duty as some kind of coven then there must have been other entrances out of sight.'

'It's worth a try. Let's go back and tell Gabe and Teal.' He was halfway to the door already, desperate to get back. Something gnawed at his insides that wasn't hunger.

'You cracked it, you know? I wouldn't have been able to join the dots if you hadn't seen that symbol.'

'Glad that I was useful.' He half smiled as she slammed the laptop lid and followed him out. She was so smart; no wonder Gabe loved her. That now-familiar barb sunk in even further and its name was jealousy. He wondered how long it would be before it swelled and became infected. He didn't need this, not with everything else that was going down.

They walked side by side as a fog rolled in from the sea, creeping like shadows through the back alleys and unlit streets. A plan was unfolding, but it was like an old game where the rules are missing and no one knows what the winning hand looks like.

CHAPTER SIXTY-SIX

Her voice guided Teal to the house. It whispered against his conscious thoughts, both calming his heart-pounding fear and prodding any part of him that tried to hold back. He had gone past the point of no return. But it was the terror of the unknown that latched around his heart, its bony fingers squeezing without empathy. What did the ruling body do to a mutation? Teal knew it was horrible. Knew he would die. He didn't feel brave enough to die.

The hunters closed ranks on him as he walked, keeping at a distance, rounding him up like a stray deer from the herd. Their presence played on his heightened senses, their heartbeats, the smell of old blood and triumph, the sound of their bones. He shivered. He had tried to live his dark life to the best of his abilities, using kindness in all but his need to kill, but underneath he had always known he was different.

The house came into view, an innocuous-looking dwelling for what was about to happen. What had he expected, a woodland clearing with skulls hanging from the trees? Something that could have been a smile touched his lips. He thought about Gabe and Moth, his brothers who had done everything they could to protect him. They could have saved their own skins by running. How much more could he have asked from them? Only trust and belief in his voices, and they had given that even when Teal himself had thought he was going crazy. Moth, who had always had his back, right from the start. Who had been there to lean on and talk to, who had never looked down on Teal's meagre fledgling powers. And then there was Gabe, newly born to this life and dragged through his first year without grace because he had to learn, fast. Who had lived with the memory of what had happened at The Manor, and of the sure-fire knowledge that the demon would return. But nothing could have prepared him for this, for her guile and deception.

But, as with everything, there has to be a light to the darkness, and their blossoming love was that light. Teal had seen it long before the first seeds had ever sprouted in their minds, had seen the way sparks flew even when they argued. Opposites attract, say the laws of the universe. They fought it still, both afraid of what would happen if they dove in too deeply and their heads and hearts were submerged. Or maybe they thought there was no point. The hopelessness of the situation didn't walk hand in hand with love. Teal bit his lip and ran the edge of his tongue over a fang. If he had to, if it came down to it, he would fight.

You do not have to fight, her voice rang in his ears. *You are the well and they are the thread and all will prevail...*her words trailed off into an echo, and for an instant he saw through her eyes again. But no, not her eyes. Her conscious thought, spiralling off into the Bloodvyne. Because she was blind. They had taken her eyes.

Teal's breath hitched in his throat as a dark figure loomed behind him.

'What you waiting for, mutant?' A waft of rancid breath floated past Teal's ear.

'Someone to read 'im a bedtime story, I reckon,' another voice added, and laughed at its own poor excuse for a joke.

The door creaked open. Teal tipped his head back and took one long look at the stars. Orion looked down on him, his hunter's belt glistening like diamonds. Teal prayed that this hunter was on his side.

CHAPTER SIXTY-SEVEN

Clove sensed Teal's approach long before D'Grey. The ring-master and the demon sat together, Nekhbet charming his old lover with conversation. Occasionally, she fondly touched his arm. D'Grey, the prize manipulator, was too far in to see how she was manipulating him. This would be amusing in any other scenario, Clove thought, but not this one. The fact his boys had made them wait another night gave him an uneasy satisfaction.

Clove sat on a hard-backed chair, his spine ramrod straight, stealing a few precious seconds to send his own probe out into the night to try to find his children. He found Moth, with Olivia. There was a confused excitement about his presence, but Clove did not linger. He would not risk anyone else picking up on his image. Gabriel was harder to find. His own blood had cloaked himself well, and a flutter of pride ran across Clove's skin. Where? Surrounded by darkness. Surrounded by books. The shape of the room? Yes. The old convent. Clove swept from there quickly. Too close.

And now Teal, about to give himself up. But there was something different about him.

D'Grey shot him a dark glance from across the room and Clove blanked out the thought. Nekhbet leaned over and whispered into D'Grey's ear. He threw back his head and laughed, then jumped to his feet, striding across to where Clove sat.

'At long last, your mutation has realised the folly of his actions. He's here, you know, right outside?' D'Grey bent down and fixed him with a razor-blade smile. 'Yes, I think you did know that. Bring him in!' This last he shouted to the front room. It had all the theatricals of an old performance, all he needed was a whip, and Clove would not have been surprised if he suddenly produced one.

Clove turned and checked on Noah. The priest stood in the corner of the room, his wrists tied together by a hank of old rope. Dark circles ringed his eyes, but his mouth was set in a firm line. Was he expecting Gabriel? Something spiked inside Clove's head. What was Gabriel doing in the convent?

The door opened and Teal stumbled through, his entry aided by a rough push from the tall vampire. D'Grey strode across and grabbed Teal's arm, pulling him to where Nekhbet sat. A slow roil of fury churned in Clove's veins.

D'Grey clamped Teal's chin between his fingers and lifted his head. An exclamation of glee rang from his lips. 'Oh, yes. There is no doubt this one is a rare example of the rogue gene. Those eyes. So pretty in their mutated state.' He glanced across to Nekhbet. 'Such a pity you need this one.' A feral hunger gleamed in his grey eyes.

'Bring him closer.' She smoothed down her silks and watched closely as D'Grey dragged Teal across.

Clove couldn't pick up any fear from his fledgling, not even a ripple, and that both concerned and elated him.

'You have led us a merry dance,' said Nekhbet, 'but you must have known it was merely biding time. Anomalies such

312

as you cannot be allowed to exist. The vampire council will not harbour such a vile example of the blood, and as such, I will bring you before the full senate of the ruling body, to be destroyed at their will. Have you any questions?'

Nekhbet's words came quickly and, Clove thought, a trifle impatiently. *She's playing a game here, and she's not quite got what she wanted.*

A small frown crossed over D'Grey's brow. *He sees it too.*

Teal stood tall before answering. 'I ask that you free Clove and the human. You have me now, and I will go along with your wishes.'

D'Grey laughed, but was silenced by a look.

'I fear it is not as simple as that. Clove has broken a most important rule. He harboured you when he knew of your condition. That cannot go without punishment. What do you suggest?' She inclined her head towards D'Grey, as if his opinion was the most important thing in the world.

Clove rose from his chair. A few long strides took him to Teal's side. The young vampire stared straight ahead, as though his mind was somewhere else, but the glow from his eyes lit up the shadows in this part of the room. Whatever mutation was within him had multiplied like a virus over the past few nights. Clove inhaled softly. There, unmistakably, the scent of Moth and Gabriel, and...something else. A dampness, like a moss-covered memory.

D'Grey had the good grace to look away for a second, but then his eyes fixed on Clove, his tongue wetting his lips. 'We bury him. Alive. So he has an eternity to remember the sin he committed. I will make it known what became of him so no other vampire will dare to challenge what the ruling body holds as truth.' A thin sheen of pink-tinged sweat dotted his brow.

Clove stared at him, trying to read what was behind his eyes, but D'Grey was giving nothing away.

'There is still the chance another could find and free him, is there not?' Nekhbet's voice held a trace of irritation.

It's not final enough for her, Clove thought. *She means to see me destroyed.*

Shadows moved on the periphery of the room. He didn't need to look to know all of D'Grey's hunters were gathered like pack wolves. Even he didn't stand a chance of breaking through them all. A shimmer of a plan birthed in his mind. But it was dangerous. He weighed up his options, aware D'Grey was pacing along the line of his hunters.

'Bring me the other two. I want them to see what happens to those who rebel. All of you, go!' D'Grey dismissed them with a wave of his hand.

Clove had hoped that with Teal there, Moth and Gabriel would be forgotten.

Nekhbet laughed, a cruel, hard sound. 'I commend you, Master D'Grey. It is of great importance we do not leave any ends dangling. Gabriel comes with me. You can do what you want with the other one.' She winked, and the gesture, on the face of Gabriel's mother, sent a wave of repulsion through Clove.

It was time he took control of the situation—especially with the possibility his other two children could be brought here. 'Is that all you've got, ring master? I expected something with a little bit more flair from you. What happened to the young rogue from the time of our youth? I recall he was unique in his ideas for those who broke our rules.'

D'Grey's brows knitted together and he inclined his head slightly, coming up behind Clove and staring at his profile. 'What game are you playing? You can't win, you know, so don't bait me. This is your final warning.'

Clove flashed a hint of fang and gazed back as though he was examining something on the sole of his boot.

'Enough.' Nekhbet's voice rang out. Clove sensed a shudder as it ran through Noah. The priest was a forgotten pawn, for now.

'I tire of you goading each other like small children. I wish to be on my way back to the elders with this mutation before the night draws to a close. I have made provisions to travel in the daylight.'

D'Grey's surprise at this was tangible. No vampire ever travelled once the sun was up, not even one attached to the ruling body. It was pointless to attempt to read his mind, all shields were down and locked in place, but surely something must be rippling in his instincts.

'We burn him. Here. And scatter his ashes in the sewer. That's better than he deserves.' Nekhbet's words dripped with malice.

For one moment, Clove thought D'Grey was going to object, but his old lover graciously bowed in Nekhbet's direction. 'As you wish.'

'I will wait until your hunters return, and they had better not return empty handed, Emron.'

D'Grey's mouth twitched in anger. She was treating him like a minor player, and D'Grey was finding that role hard to swallow.

Clove stood his ground, his expression betraying no emotion. But Teal had not moved throughout the whole cat-and-mouse game, his luminescent eyes staring into space. Was this what happened when the mutation reached its peak? Clove made his decision. He would not let Nekhbet take Teal, not with what he knew the ruling body would do to him. If it came down to it, Clove would have to strike first.

It was an abominable thought.

CHAPTER SIXTY-EIGHT

I met them at the entrance to the convent library. Moonlight skimmed the walls, painting surfaces with a pearl-like glow. When Teal left, I had paced the corridor, away from the lanterns. I wanted to think, and I did that better in the dark. I always had done.

'We found a link, Gabe!' Olivia's voice carried across the darkness, followed by a muttered curse as she stumbled. 'A little more light would be good, for those of us with normal eyesight.'

I forced a smile.

'Where is he? Where's Teal?' Moth was at my side, his hand on my arm, questions in his eyes. But he knew before I opened my mouth. 'Fuck it, Gabe! Why did you let him go alone?' The pain etched on his face made my heart drop into my stomach.

'Because I couldn't stop him. Because something bigger than either you or me is driving him.'

He lowered his face and dug his fingers into my arm. His shoulders trembled and I wrapped my arms around him, aware for the first time just how vulnerable he was. 'It's okay,' I whispered against his hair. 'We need to go find this White Witch of his and let her take her revenge, whatever that means.'

Olivia ran her fingers through her hair impatiently. I could smell the perfume from her shampoo. 'We found something else that ties her in to this place, Gabe. I'm hoping there's a tunnel system somewhere that will lead us to D'Grey's.'

Reluctantly, I released my hold on Moth. A small, questioning sound vibrated in Olivia's throat. It didn't take long for the words to follow. 'So, I guess you two are a thing now?'

It was a rhetorical question, but still it hung in the air. The weight of Moth and Teal cloaked my thoughts.

Moth curled his fingers around mine as his answer, and my heart flipped over.

Olivia lifted one of the lanterns, and the light bathed our faces. A soft glow came from her eyes. She knew. But this wasn't the time for giving in to any kind of personal emotion.

She led the way from the library along the page-strewn corridor, the lantern held high like a beacon in a storm. Moth and I had no need for it, but the light was comforting and God knows, there wasn't much of that around right now.

'There must be a basement in this place somewhere.' She paused. 'Moth, on the photo we saw, where does your gut tell you a tunnel might be?'

His fingers tightened and he turned suddenly, gazing back to where we'd come from.

'Exactly what I was thinking.' She back-tracked, the lantern in her hand causing ghostly shadows on the wall that rippled as they walked with us.

From inside the library, I thought I heard a woman's whisper. The hairs rose on the back of my neck and I turned to Moth. As we came to the doorway, I slipped in front of Olivia, leaving Moth to follow her. Shards of moonlight shone directly onto the labyrinth, the pattern gleaming like silver threads in the dark. All of our clues had come from this, so we gravitated towards its pull like waves to a shore. Now we knew what it was and what it stood for, it seemed unbelievable it had taken us so long to find out.

'The triangle,' I whispered, looking from Moth to Olivia. 'Three points. Three of us. Teal in the middle.'

The silence deepened.

Olivia bent down and put the lantern on the floor, then she slipped her arm through mine. 'The monster in the centre. What if it's not the demon? What if it's The White Witch?'

CHAPTER SIXTY-NINE

They were close, these dark children of the night. And the one who called to her was closer still—inside this dwelling of old stones and lost time.

Long ago, she had come seeking refuge from the taunts and superstitious heckling from those around her. She was older now, with grey in her hair, and she did not wish to become an old crone mothers warned their children about as they tucked them up into bed. So she'd come to this place by the sea, to the convent of St. Marguerita, drawn by the whispers from passing travellers that it wasn't the holy place most thought it was.

She'd been greeted warmly, the nuns seemingly unburdened by the brightness in her eyes. But they'd led her at once to the wing where the Dark Sisters dwelled. Their welcome had been a little less hospitable. Some of them had eyed her with great suspicion, prodding and poking and gossiping. But her pagan gifts had been welcomed and, in time, an uneasy acceptance grew. She'd taken part in their rituals and blessings, even when some troubled the goodness in her heart. Here, at least, she could come and go without fear for her life. Her sparse appetite, or so they presumed, had been welcomed in a place with many mouths to feed.

On rare occasions, she had stolen out into the night and answered the call of the blood. Once she had left a young girl close to death in the dank cellar of a tavern, but she had no choice as discovery had approached with the hard tread of boots upon the stairs.

She had been drawn to the song of the sea, and each dawn would see her standing by the shore, watching the waves crash against it, the harsh cry of the sea birds in her ears. One morning, in the early spring, a man had noticed her lone figure, the long red hair streaked with grey, whipping around her face. She had wished him a good morrow, then felt the blood drain from her face. She knew him from the village. Despite her pleas, he'd followed her back to the convent gates and she'd spent the day fearful of every footstep. But it was in the dark when her true horror began.

The Dark Sisters had come for her, dragging her to the room where their rituals were carried out. All of their suspicions rolled into a great black ball of hate. *Night creature*, they'd hissed, rending at her clothes. She had been powerless against them, her pleas falling on ears that knew no pity. Once again, she was the outcast. But the rules of the witchhood prevented the killing of one with a gift.

So they buried her here, walling up her body as she screamed, her limbs held fast by thick, black rope, binding knots tied along the lengths. Her dark sisters had taken no chances. But her terror was to take another twisted turn. As the bricks had drawn level with her neck, a figure appeared from the shadows. The man from the village. He'd leered at her through a mouth filled with rotting teeth, then pulled a blade from his jacket. He dug out her eyes.

She remembered his laughter as the blood poured down her face, the pain an excruciating steel circle embedded in her head. The brick dust had filled her nostrils, and as the final stone was tapped into place, she'd made a silent vow that one day those who hunted her bloodline would pay.

CHAPTER SEVENTY

No one spoke as the enormity of Olivia's words soaked in. If she was right, they were going to unleash something they knew little about, apart from the fact it was controlling Teal's every thought.

'Is the devil you know better than the devil you don't?' She looked at Gabe.

Moth didn't miss the shadow passing over Gabe's eyes, and he wanted to tear it away. Gabe might not say much, but he must be so close to the edge right now. How bad would it be to face something like that whacked-out demon head on, when it looked like someone you once loved? How did you get past that conflict of emotions? There was a haunted look in those dark blue eyes.

Moth gazed around the room, his eyes flicking from shadow to shadow. 'Where the hell do we start looking for a tunnel?' As if to reiterate his words, his voice echoed from the walls, disappearing into the dome and the moonlight.

Olivia stood back, her hands on her hips, and surveyed the room slowly. 'Carver says if you're stuck, look at the facts and the answer will be there. Run the facts past me, Gabe.'

'We know the centre of the labyrinth. Teal tells us that's where The White Witch is.' Gabe paused. 'And we have to take that as truth, because Teal hasn't been wrong so far. None of what has happened seems to be coincidence, right back to the fact this is where Clove's ship came in. Back then, this town was a smuggling haven.'

'Go on. Lead with the smuggling angle,' Olivia encouraged him, and Moth could almost see her brain picking over the images Gabe was giving her. That sly, sharp pang of jealousy filled his veins again. Was this what they used to do at The Manor?

'The ports where smuggling survived were the ones with multiple caves close to the shoreline, where goods could be stored until it was safe to bring them out or…' Gabe stopped and whirled around, his hands coming together in a loud clap. 'Or the ones where the goods could be taken through tunnels. I don't think there's one tunnel underneath us, I think there's a warren.'

Olivia grabbed the lantern and headed for the door, the ghostly light swinging from side to side. 'The tunnel has to run under here…' Then she stopped and gazed at Gabe. Moth's eyes followed. It wasn't Gabe she was looking at; it was the fireplace. 'What did Carver say he found when he renovated the library at The Manor?'

Another rhetorical question. Moth was beginning to feel more and more out of his depth.

Gabe knelt and scrabbled around in the mass of paper in the hearth. He leaned in and peered up the chimney. 'But didn't priest holes lead to attic hides?'

'Yes. But what if this one didn't lead up, it led down?'

'Moth, help me!' Gabe dug deep into the debris in the hearth, amidst decades of mouldering paper and dust and old soot from the chimney.

Moth threw himself down, his fingers clawing at the uncovered stones, looking for an edge or a crack in the solid base. Occasionally his hand touched Gabe's, and a jolt of static electricity shot up his arm. Olivia hovered at their backs, the lantern held high.

Gabe stopped his frantic scrabbling suddenly, his fingers moving more purposefully. The sound of crumbling mortar filled the silence, closely followed by the rough movement of stone that had been asleep for hundreds of years. Moth helped him pull the hearth floor across to one side. Immediately, a cool draught lifted the hair from his face.

Below the hearth, a vertical tunnel led down into pitch black.

‡

I'm following two young and probably hungry vampires down into a hole no human has seen for hundreds of years.

The thought bounced off the walls of her skull as Olivia let them lead her. Moth was behind, the lantern slung over his forearm, for her benefit entirely. Dust coated her throat, and for a second the memory of falling down the coal chute flashed through her mind. But she hadn't fallen. She had been pushed by a paranormal force that had been trying to kill her. There wasn't much comfort in the fact it would try again before a new day dawned.

The tunnel narrowed at one point, and she gritted her teeth to squeeze through. How structurally safe it was gnawed at the edges of her conscience. Getting wedged in here would be the stuff of nightmares. But how Ollie would have loved it! An adventure with two creatures instinct told him existed. Wetness coated her cheeks and she was glad of the dark.

Gabe grabbed her hand to guide her and she shivered. His fingers were cold. The closeness of the low roof gave rise to her galloping fear. Panic gripped her throat as her brain went into 'buried alive' mode, and it was only Gabe's voice calling back that he could see an exit that stopped her wanting to scream.

The smell of moss and cold water greeted their entry into a tunnel they at least could stand upright in, although the roof was only inches above their heads. It branched into two a little further down. Gabe stopped, his head held high, like a deer scenting the wind, then led them down to the right. The tunnel twisted and turned, occasionally forking off in different directions, but Gabe led them as though he had made this trip every day of his life. Their footsteps echoed on the cobblestones paving some of their path, usually at the junction of the rabbit warren of trails, and the bone-chilling cold seeped from the walls with invisible breath.

Suddenly, Gabe stopped, and she nearly ran into his back. Holding her breath, she listened, but the only sound she could hear was the dripping of water somewhere close by. He turned and stared at Moth, his eyes wide in the flickering pool of light from the lantern. They could hear something she couldn't. Gabe pointed to the wall and put a finger to his lips. The war drum of her own heartbeat filled her ears.

They ducked under a low lintel, and in front of them, set into the left-hand wall, stood a makeshift tumble of old wooden planks, fastened together with pine-tarred, frayed rope. Gabe reached out and touched it, then pulled away quickly as though it had burnt him.

From up above, echoing through the roof, came a sharp cry of pain. A man's voice. Even before the sound had registered in her brain, she knew it was Noah. Moth's hand flew from behind, jamming his palm over her mouth. She swallowed the scream in her throat.

Gabe pushed his shoulder against the planks. The wood imploded on itself with a loud crack, dust and splinters shooting through the air. Moth slammed her into the wall, the side of her face making contact with the slime-covered bricks, but it was only when he let go she saw the long cut on his cheekbone. A line of dark blood oozed from it. Gabe disappeared through the settling remains of the door. Finally, his hand beckoned them forward.

'Gabe, that was Noah calling out…' Her voice sounded too steady to her ears.

He grabbed her hand and squeezed it in both of his. Again those cold, cold fingers.

'I know. And that's where I'm heading. I'm going to try and stall for time.'

The fact he was doing something to try and help Noah should have filled her with a little ray of hope, but any glimmer was drowned out by the knowledge he was putting himself in a dangerous position. That thing upstairs—demon, vampire, whatever the fuck it wanted to call itself—was going to bring him to his knees again. She clung onto his hands as he turned to Moth.

'Can you still hear it?'

Moth nodded, his features unmoving, eyes fixed on Gabe's face. She let her fingers fall and stepped back, her cheekbone throbbing from the meeting with the wall. But Moth had saved her from something worse.

‡

I didn't want to go, but I had to. Noah's cry echoed in my head and it was so hard keeping my true feelings from Olivia. She needed me to be strong. I should at least look like I knew what I was doing.

The scratching in the walls came in bursts. Just when I thought I might have imagined it, there it was again. It was a chilling sound, a relentless call from a grave. If I'd had any doubt over the existence of The White Witch, this swept it away. She was here, close by, waiting for us to find and release her. But God only knew what she would do, and Olivia's words about the monster kept prodding the underbelly of my thoughts. This was it, the moment when I might never see Olivia or Moth again. I didn't want to cry, but my heart felt like it was made of glass and about to shatter.

I pulled Olivia into my arms and kissed her cheek, feeling the tremble of her shoulders as she, too, fought for control. 'I'll stall as long as I can, I promise. Don't ever give up on believing in Noah. He saved my life once. I'm going to do it for him.'

Then Moth's fingers circled my wrist and he drew me close, his lips on the line of my jaw, on the curve of my neck, his body pressed tight against mine.

I clasped his face between my palms, his breath coming in short, sharp gasps against my mouth. 'Just tell me one thing before I go. I thought you loved Teal. I don't understand why it's suddenly me.' My voice faltered. 'Are you in love with Teal?'

Those mismatched eyes burned into mine as he wound his fingers through my hair. 'Yes, I love Teal.'

For one second, I thought I couldn't breathe.

'But not like that. He's my friend and my brother and… who the fuck couldn't not love him?' His lips parted, his tongue flicking out, tasting me from the air in that way only he could.

'Gabe.' My name fell from his lips and the sound of it shattered the last chance I had of holding it together.

I clung to him for a few more seconds, then kissed the tips of my fingers and touched them to his lips. Then I dragged myself away until the darkness swallowed me whole.

‡

Up above, the sound of a chair scraping quickly across the floor echoed between the joists. The metallic scent of fresh human blood followed it and saliva filled my mouth. It wasn't something I had any control over, but what if the blood was Noah's?

Behind me, the grating sound of bricks being teased from their resting place filtered through. I wanted to go back there so badly the pull was almost magnetic. Steeling myself, I pushed on. Feeling the wall as I moved, I remembered Clove's words the last time I'd seen him. *No fear.* The dawning of clarity stopped me dead in my tracks. He was telling me for a reason. I could cloak my thoughts, but I was terrified the hunters would smell any panic if I got close.

I took a deep breath and retreated inside my own mind, letting the pure bred in me lead through the twisted corridors of memory and instinct. There was a shadow place and my inner eye rested there, seeing colours flashing through the passages, bright ultra-violets etched in bursts of gold, like lightning. I followed the glow, smelling ozone and damp soil, my skin coated in rain, dirt under my nails. The harsh caw of a bird rolled through the colours and I had to fight to stay there. I was remembering that moment when I'd given up, determined to let whatever was out there have me and be done with it. But I'd never felt as alive as I did then, in charge for a fleeting few seconds and not giving a fuck about the outcome. It was Clove who had found me.

I remembered the fear as his icy fingers had touched my face, sure that death would follow…then I reached out with my mental hand and swiped the fear from the air, balling it up between my fingers. The colours in the shadow place grew, pulsing and twisting inside each other until all that remained was the light. I drew my arm back and threw the lead weight of terror deep inside that light. There was one bone-shaking burst of radiance, and then it was gone.

I opened my eyes for real, my breathing coming fast and shallow. I waited until it calmed, still able to see the light imprinted on my retina. All I felt now was a steely calm. They wouldn't sense me coming, and I could always play the naive fledgling if that worked in my favour.

I ducked under another lintel. A chink of light pricked through the roof up ahead. I sprinted towards it, clawing my way up the wall. My fingers found an edge of wood and I pushed it hard, my hand breaking through, a thin film of dust fluttering down to cover my face. The noise made me wince. I imagined D'Grey waiting for me on the other side, but the thought was only half formed.

Carefully, I broke enough of the planking away to squeeze myself through.

CHAPTER SEVENTY-ONE

This was all going horribly wrong. The feeling was as alien to Emron D'Grey as one of his hunters answering back, and it left a bitter taste on the back of his tongue. He was used to being the one people looked up to, and he had expected a certain amount of thankfulness from Nekhbet. After all, he was the one who had brought the possibility of Teal's existence to the ruling body's attention. But she seemed irritated by him now. Any hopes he had harboured about her passing his name to the council as a possible envoy in the future were dwindling into dust.

Clove knelt over the priest, his arm around the man's head. A pool of dark blood stained the floorboards.

D'Grey hadn't meant to hit Noah quite as hard as he did, but frustration had filled his fist as he had smashed it into the side of that fragile human skull. It was of no consequence. The priest would die at some point, and it did make him feel a little more in control.

He straightened his cuffs and turned back to Nekhbet. She was walking a slow circle around Teal, the rustle of her dress breaking the silence. The boy was unmoving, still in the same position as when he had first entered. Little fool. Nekhbet reached out one thin arm and stroked the boy's face in a loving gesture, her fingers lingering under one eye. D'Grey held his breath. Was she going to do it here? Part of him hoped so, just to watch Clove's reaction.

It would have been delightful to have a few hours with him first, though. He would bruise so sweetly. D'Grey growled deep in his throat. But something needled under his skin. The hunters should have returned by now. Nekhbet was getting restless. The last thing he wanted was her departure with his failure clutched in her hand. Yes, she had the mutation, but he had a feeling she wanted all of Clove's bastards. He didn't understand why. He knew *he* wanted them, but that was history. But what had Clove said about Nekhbet and Gabriel knowing each other? That's when the first stab of instinct had slid into his flesh. He swore under his breath, damning Clove for still having the ability to ruffle his feathers.

'Don't you dare touch him, demon!'

D'Grey spun around, his eyes opening wide in surprise. Gabriel stood, framed in the doorway, bristling with resentment and untamed energy. A slow smile spread across D'Grey's features. At last, a little crumb of triumph to feast on.

Nekhbet's attention was now purely on the newcomer, her head inclined to one side, her pale lips slowly parting. 'Ah, Gabriel. How good of you to join us.'

The temperature in the room dropped a few degrees.

Revulsion sparked in Gabriel's eyes, and D'Grey gritted his teeth.

'Not a particularly polite way to address me, little lion.' Her voice was thick with sweetness; it oozed across each word, but a thin drool of saliva ran from the corner of her mouth. 'Come to me, Gabriel. She's still here you know, your mother. I ate her up, but I know she still loves you.'

A shadow passed over Gabriel's eyes and then they hardened. 'You know you don't want Teal. So quit the act. You came here for me, because you failed last time. How does it feel to know that Clove outwitted you?'

The boy was baiting her with no regard for her power or what she stood for. D'Grey had to give the fledgling ten out of ten for sheer bravado, stupid and deadly as it was. But there was a truth, like a steel wire, running through his words. Clove caught his eye from the other side of the room. He knew that look. It was the same one from their youth when D'Grey got too caught up in the heat of the moment. It said *think*.

'Do I have your full loyalty, Master D'Grey?' The simpering sweetness was now turned on him.

His stomach rolled. 'Of course, Your Eminence.' He swept a bow. 'Do you wish me to silence this one for disobedience?' He motioned to Gabriel.

'Oh no. He's mine. He's always been mine.'

Nekhbet's jaw opened, exposing two long, curled fangs, dripping with venom. The whites of her eyes all but disappeared into a pool of pitch blackness and then she laughed. The sound from her throat was the skittering of a thousand insect feet.

'Bring me the priest. Or what's left of him.'

CHAPTER SEVENTY-TWO

Moth watched Gabe leave until nothing remained but the empty space where he had been. He felt like someone had tightened a steel cage around his heart. They were all separated, and that hurt much more than he ever thought it would. It made sense now, what Gabe had said. It explained his confusion and the way he'd held back. He had thought I was in love with Teal, and he wasn't prepared to spoil it. What was a word for that? Noble. One of those words Moth had never had cause to use, or even to think about.

The slow scratching started again. Brick dust crumbled behind the wall, and in the brave light from the lantern, Olivia turned to face him, the graze on her cheek studded with dirt. He placed his palms against the moss-slimed bricks and felt for some kind of an edge.

Olivia watched him, holding the lantern at arm's length. Tension ran in the hunch of her shoulders. 'If anyone can stall for time, it's Gabe.' Her voice was low, but certain.

Underneath his fingers, he thought he felt a slight dip between two bricks. 'He's good at it. The word thing. Just be glad it's not me up there.' It was a definite dip and he dug at it, pulling out the moss and hoping the old mortar would fall apart quickly.

'I think you'd do whatever you could if you were there, Moth. You love them both, and when we love something we never give up.'

He thought about that as his fingers worked. They were bleeding already. Love. What did that even feel like? He'd never had cause to experience it, unless you counted his mother. The familiar guilt rose like summer heat and he closed his eyes at the sting. He wondered if she had ever got over his going out and never coming back.

'Here, use these.' Olivia dangled something over his shoulder. It was a set of keys, one in particular long and ornate. He took them, then looked at her. 'It's the key to The Manor. Carver didn't want to change all the locks when he bought the place. He said this key had welcomed everyone in since the house was built.'

'I'm not sure it will be any good after this.' Moth began to scrape and the mortar fell away fast. The scratching came again in short, quick bursts.

'He won't care. Not if it saves Gabe and Noah.' She hung over his shoulder, watching his progress until his fingers curled over the top of the brick.

He heaved it out in a shower of dust. He started on the next one, and Olivia took over when it was loosened enough for her to pull it out. They worked together in silence, only broken by the intermittent noise from behind the wall.

'Still think we're freeing the monster?' Brick dust clung to his skin. He could feel it at the back of his throat, but Olivia didn't complain, her only agitation the sweeping of her hair from her face as she worked.

She paused and wiped the back of her hand over her nose. 'God only knows. I'm going on the myth where the monster is in the middle and that's where we are now. But then we have Nekhbet and D'Grey too.' She shrugged and tugged on the next brick. 'Why were you so anti me at the beginning?' Her eyes held his for a moment.

She didn't mess around. When she wanted to know something, she asked, and to hell with the foreplay.

He stopped for a second. 'It's nothing. I don't do new people all that well.' His real reason sounded so fucking childish in his head.

'Quit that, Moth.' She glared at him. 'It doesn't work with me.'

What difference did it make if she knew now? Probably not a lot, as it wasn't likely they'd all get out of this alive.

'I was jealous of the bond you and Gabe have. I thought you might try and take him back to The Manor after you found him again.' There, he'd said it—far too bitterly, but what the hell. It didn't matter.

'He's not part of my world now, Moth, no matter how much I want him to be. You can't ever go back.'

Moth remembered telling Gabe more or less the same thing that night in the cave. He wondered why he hadn't listened to his own head when Olivia had come on the scene. Maybe it was the fear of losing Gabe just when he had learned to find him? He removed another brick and stood back. A row of missing stones leered in front of them like punched-out teeth.

In the black hole beyond, a vibration began, low and deep. He pulled Olivia behind him, his keen eyes searching for some image inside the black. A low tremor rippled under the ground beneath their feet and Olivia swore, her hand on his arm. A crumbling of dust and the shifting of old air.

A smell like a coffin prised open, thick and heavy with decay. Then silence.

Moth slowly inched forward and peered through the line of absent bricks. Something grabbed his throat and yanked his head against the wall. Pain exploded inside his skull and his vision hazed. He flailed at Olivia with his right arm, trying to tell her to run. The oxygen to his brain plummeted. Fuck. She was right. The monster *was* The White Witch.

He couldn't fail now, not like this, not when Teal and Gabe and Clove needed him. With the last remnants of his strength, he called out in his mind, but it settled as a whimper. A high-pitched ringing began in his ears. Then the wall exploded.

CHAPTER SEVENTY-THREE

Noah opened his eyes. He fought his way out of the grogginess, his brain still half frozen. Pain pounded away in his skull. A pale face swam in his vision. Dark hair. Gabriel? No. It was Clove. A strong hand hoisted him up to a sitting position and he winced. There was something sticky on the floor. Blood. It took a moment for Noah to realise it belonged to him.

Clove bent forward until his mouth was close to Noah's ear. 'Keep her attention on you.'

Noah heard the words but couldn't grasp what they meant. He rubbed his fingers against his brow, and found the slightly raised edges of the scar. Resolve sharpened his senses. With his legs shaking, he managed to stand using the wall as leverage.

Emron D'Grey's shadow loomed over him, with the fox like smile pasted in place. Then Noah heard Gabe's voice from across the room and his heart leapt.

Clove blocked D'Grey's way for a moment. They stared each other down.

'Gabe...' He had to force himself to speak, as though talking might make Gabe disappear once again. Pain jack-knifed in his head. He couldn't lose him again, not a second time.

338

Gabe glanced across, his chin tilted defiantly upwards and his mouth set into a thin line. Noah had seen that look before. For the third time in his life, Gabe's back was against the wall, but he was coming out fighting. Noah wondered if he had a plan, or was he only here because he couldn't run again?

A frown suddenly creased Gabe's brow. From underneath the floor came a loud crash and the floorboards trembled. Dust drifted over the surface. Nekhbet's attention shifted from Gabe, her head turning slowly to Clove. She nodded to D'Grey.

D'Grey waved his hand at Saxon. 'Drag the priest over here then go and see what the hell that was!'

Saxon brushed past Clove, their sleeves touching, and grabbed Noah's arm.

With more strength than he knew he had, Noah shrugged him off. 'I don't need any help. I can walk myself.'

D'Grey laughed. 'I do love a man who can walk up to his own gallows. It shows such character. In your case, of course, it's misguided, but I applaud it anyway.' Noah's collar was stiff with drying blood and he didn't miss the way D'Grey's eyes lingered there, before he turned his attention to Clove. 'Now, spice master, I think it is time we left the children to their play, don't you?'

From the edges of the room, the hunters descended as one, their dark-clad forms surrounding Clove like a blanket of death. Noah saw the master vampire's eyes rest for a moment on Gabe before the hunters dragged him into the darkness of the corridor. D'Grey followed, humming tunelessly.

Noah had no delusions about walking out of here alive. The last vestiges of hope had left with Clove. They had relied upon Nekhbet keeping him close, but it seemed she had other plans for the vampire who had thwarted her once before. All Noah could hope for was that somehow Gabe would make it out. And that he would get a message back to Olivia. His heart thundered in his chest as he drew closer to Nekhbet. *Was Beth still in there?* The question repeated over and over again, caught in a loop and snagging on his own panic. But this creature had devoured the spirit of that childlike woman.

Noah drew himself up to his full height and looked her right in the eye. 'Come to finish what you failed to do sixteen years ago, demon?' A bitter bravado, but it felt good.

Nekhbet's eyes darkened. 'I always finish what I began, priest, no matter how many centuries it takes.'

Gabe appeared at his shoulder. 'You think you've been so clever this time, don't you? And I'll give you full marks for ingenuity. We didn't see it coming. But to use one of my brothers to get to me is a mistake.'

Noah realised that in all of this, Teal had not moved an inch.

Cool fingers intertwined with his. It didn't matter what Gabe now was because the essence of him still remained.

Something irritated the back of Noah's throat. He cleared it and swallowed. It lodged again and he coughed, his airways tightening. He was hacking now, bending over double with his eyes watering. Barbs of anxiety clamped his reasoning as Gabe's image swam before him. His lungs started to burn and he collapsed onto his knees.

Gabe's scream of fury ricocheted against his ears. 'Leave him alone! If you want to taunt something, make it me. Or don't you have the nerve for that?'

From under the floor came a bloodcurdling cry.

Noah had forgotten how to breathe. Sweat trickled down his back and his eyeballs felt as if they were going to implode. A red mist hovered in his mind's eye, and as it descended, he groped blindly for Gabe's hand. Then he toppled over into the desolation of the abyss.

CHAPTER SEVENTY-FOUR

In the dark of the tunnel, amidst a pile of broken bricks, something moved. A skeletal figure, skin still clinging to the bones. In the cells of her shrivelled brain, she found the memory of movement. A hand raised, a foot twisted, the slow grind of a spine as it straightened, the vertebrae clicking into place one by one. She was cocooned by a blanket of dark red hair, entwining around her frame like mummified bandages. She ripped at it impatiently, scattering trails of it before her as she walked.

The White Witch did not have sight, but she saw more than those who possessed natural eyes. The Bloodvyne stretched out from her consciousness and the voices of vampires lost to oblivion sang upon it, asking for revenge, for the deaths of thousands simply because a light shone in their eyes.

She moved over the pile of rubble, her mind connected to the one above, seeing through his eyes. And he had a glorious vision. Long she had waited for one such as him, the one who breathed both light and shadow.

She stopped. Her senses pin-pointed into one long beam of hunger. Her sight was gone, but an unfamiliar vampire was close, his clumsy footfall alerting her long after his scent. His fear. Saxon stood rooted to the spot. She heard the muscles move as his eyes widened, the pulse of his pupils fixing in terror. Her jaw creaked open, exposing a mouth with missing teeth. But her fangs were sharp. Her tongue slowly slithered out over her bottom lip. She could taste his blood there, wet and nourishing like mother's milk.

He did not run, but it would not have mattered if he did. She broke his neck as if he were a troublesome rabbit then clamped her jaw over his throat, her fangs piercing the rolls of fat until they found the artery. She closed her eyelids and spoke to Teal.

Behind her, lying under the rubble, were the girl and Moth. She had not meant to harm them.

She inclined her head, listening for minute sounds, aware of every inhaled breath and tremor of movement. Moth's fingers twitched and he curled them into the ground. He raised his head, an instinctive gesture of survival. His blood was weak but his spirit was strong, and he had the thread, she could sense it.

She drank deeply from the hapless vampire, who continued to breathe long after his neck was snapped, then turned her attention to Moth. He was on his knees now, pulling bricks from the body of the prone girl.

The White Witch turned to stare at him, the new blood rampaging through her veins, igniting dormant cells to life. Moth's lips moved as though he wanted to speak, but no words came out. She crooked a finger in his direction, moving past him to the thin light that bled from the trap door, and Teal's whisper.

'I can't leave her like this. Can't you help me?'

She turned, deciding spoken words would have to do. His mind was too full to listen to her any other way.

'Come. Your place is with me, with your brothers. Teal is the quest. You are the finding. And Gabriel is the ability to return. But only if you are together when I call to The Bloodvyne. The girl is still breathing. That is enough.'

Underneath the open trap door, she paused. She did not have to wait long until Moth came to her side.

CHAPTER SEVENTY-FIVE

I was dancing with death yet again. I didn't know what power Nekhbet held in that twisted mix of demon and vampire, but all I wanted was to force it out of my mother's body. Blind anger took me as I stood there, the taunting words flowing from my mouth without a second thought. All of the pain and anguish the demon had put me and my family through boiled through my veins, gathering speed until I hurled them at her like a weapon.

I was done with hiding. I was done with running. Tonight would end with either her destruction or my death. But underneath, I knew that if I died, my brothers would too. And Noah. His body lay motionless on the floor, his head turned towards the wall. Pain sliced through me, wave after wave of nerve-shredding anguish for a man who had been like a father to me.

But she knew my game and threw it back at me, using my memories and the sounds from that terrible night, trying to unhinge me, still using me as the mouse in her feline game even after sixteen years. My mind shield was locked down tight, but my heart kept knocking, wanting to bring up some image of Moth, of what was happening down below.

Someone had screamed. But it wasn't Moth or Olivia. That's all I cared about.

Still hurling insults, I made my way across to Teal. He was out of it, lost in his own world and that which belonged to The White Witch. What if she couldn't be freed? Would she leave Teal like this forever? The thought was too heart-breaking to contemplate.

I had to gamble on what Nekhbet wanted most. Taking Teal back to the ruling body to gain their favour, wriggling her way further into their ranks, or me—the one thing that had long eluded her. If I was wrong, I was screwed.

She came towards me, the rustle of her dress almost as unnerving as the skittering she used so well. There was an eerie calmness about her now, like the stillness before a thunderstorm. She reached out and ran her fingers across my cheek, her dark eyes boring into my skull. All my instincts screamed at me to run.

I looked around for Clove, hoping to see him return, but he wasn't there, and neither was D'Grey. She saw my glance and laughed. 'Your maker has a prior engagement, Gabriel. With his own demise. Such a pity he had to abandon you in your hour of need.'

The saliva dried up in my mouth. Her hand grasped the back of my neck, her fingers like ice. I tried to pull away, but she held me firm, all of the time her eyes drilling into mine. I could feel my mind shield slipping as she chipped away at the barrier I'd built.

Then her mouth fell open and she exhaled against my face. My legs gave way and she pulled me against her body, wrapping me in a vice-like grip, crooning in my ear, 'All the little deaths I've taken, baby boy. All of the last gasps of the damned.'

My mind shield shattered into a thousand pieces and she crawled inside, but still I fought her, holding on for a few more seconds, praying it was enough.

The pressure on my lungs increased as her grip tightened. She smiled, darkly. I was gasping now, my vision hazing at the edges. Teal turned and stared at the door I'd come through. Nekhbet's hold on me loosened for a second and a growl swept out of her throat. *She knows. She's seen my thoughts.*

With a howl of fury, she thrust my head back with the heel of her hand and pain shot down my spine, interlocking with each vertebrae and turning it into a red pool of agony. I saw the light hit the tip of one cruel fang and waited for it to descend.

But the plunge never came.

'Gabe!' Moth's scream of horror rang against my ears.

Nekhbet paused and turned her attention to the interruption. A shadow passed over her face. I managed to draw one long breath of air into my lungs.

The White Witch stood in the doorway. She was skin-covered bone. From her skull flowed a river of red hair. It wound around her chest, her hips, her limbs. Her eyes were black craters in her skull. And then I realised she didn't have any eyes. Moth was by her side, covered in dust. It clung to his clothes and his skin, turning him into a monochrome figure. His fingertips were broken and bleeding. She moved towards us, and I had a weird sensation that she was floating just above the ground.

Nekhbet's fingers jerked my wrist. 'Is this all you have, Gabriel? Some withered pagan creature brought back from the dead?'

Teal moved past me, silently, his hands outstretched in greeting. All he saw was her. Moth wiped the back of his hand over his mouth, his gaze falling on Noah. I didn't want to look because I'd fall apart.

The White Witch took Teal in her arms, those bony limbs wrapping around him, her bones clicking with each movement. Then she kissed him, full and hard against his mouth. Moth shuddered and that same feeling took me. But it was all out of our control.

Nekhbet dragged me across the floor, my knees skidding on the wooden boards, then released her hold with an angry twist.

I knelt there, looking up as they came face to face, the witch and the demon vampire. Nekhbet's stance bristled with authority and barely restrained fury. The White Witch, little more than a skeleton, and inches shorter.

I crawled over to Noah, pushing past the knife tips of pain pulsing down my spine, and took his head in my lap. His hair was soaked in blood and his lips had lost all of their colour. But he was alive. Just.

'You will be the last creature who hunts my bloodline.' The White Witch's voice came in throaty gasps, as though talking was an act she had long since forgotten.

Nekhbet laughed, throwing her head back so that my mother's snow white hair flared over her shoulders. 'And what bloodline would that be? I don't see anything to fear in you.'

The air in the room hushed. The hair in the nape of my neck rose. Moth took Teal's hand and pulled him away. But Teal's attention never wavered. The White Witch held him in her thrall.

'And that is your downfall. The things to fear don't always scream the loudest.' The White Witch looked to Moth, to Teal and finally to me. There was something happening in the sockets of her eyes. I stared, unable to look away. It was a distant flickering, dozens of tiny gold lights swimming in the darkness. They multiplied, growing ever brighter until they filled the space where her eyes had been with a dazzling golden glow.

Moth gasped and I instinctively shielded Noah's face with my arms.

The light burst from her eyes in two golden waterfalls, spilling to the ground, then floating over the floor. The reflection turned everything to sunlight, and joy filled my heart for an instant. I hadn't seen sunlight for such a long time. The light shimmered then fractured into smaller pieces, each dividing then multiplying. Gradually, all that was left were thousands of tiny dancing flecks. The breath caught in my throat. Teal's fireflies.

They swarmed around us, flitting and cavorting with each other. Then they all suddenly stopped dead, suspended in mid-air.

Nekhbet laughed again, but this time it didn't sound quite as sure. Wisps of fine smoke drifted above her.

Slowly, out of the silence, came a whispering, a Tower of Babel cacophony of voices. I turned and scanned the room, expecting to see ghostly figures. But the voices weren't there. They were coming from the fireflies themselves. The White Witch stood motionless, apart from her hair, which wafted like seaweed in an ocean current.

'My children,' she said, and her voice was heavy with sorrow. 'Each little light is one of my blood who was cut down for daring to be different.' Her voice rose. 'I was the first, demon. The mother of the light.'

Drifts of black smoke poured from my mother's eyes and mouth. Her whole body vibrated. Her limbs jerked.

'Too late, I fear,' said The White Witch.

Something snapped in the air and electricity zinged through my veins. The voices rose to a crescendo, a savage, ear-splitting roar. Moth tried to struggle towards me, but he rebounded from the sound as if it was a physical barrier.

Then, it ended. And each tiny firefly light exploded into flame.

They began to merge like they had done before, and each time the flames ignited inside each other, growing stronger. I whirled around and checked the doorways, but all were instantly aflame, the old, dry wood crackling and splintering under the sudden onslaught of heat. In less than a minute, the edges of the room were all alight. The flames crept across the floor, devouring everything in their path. I looked for somewhere to take Noah, but there was nowhere to go.

All the while Nekhbet and The White Witch waged their silent battle. I couldn't tell if the smoke suffocating my lungs was from the flames or from the demon. I prayed it was the first. If I inhaled her poison then she had won the final battle. I forced back the waves of panic, trying to remember how much a vampire could take without dying. But these weren't normal flames, so all those rules meant nothing.

Amongst the suffocating smoke, Moth and Teal were barely visible. Then a voice cut through the roaring of the fire.

'Gabe!'

It was Olivia. I looked down at the floor and heard her voice again, then her finger poked through a hole where a knot had been in one of the boards.

'Get out of here, Liv! Go back down the tunnel!'

'No. Gabe, listen. I know what you have to do.'

I tore at the hole with my fingers, splintering the wood until I could see her eyes peering upwards. She coughed as the smoke seeped through.

'I heard what The White Witch said to Moth. She said Teal was the quest. Moth was the finding and you were the ability to return.'

One of the timbers holding up the roof collapsed, sending a shower of sparks over me. This was one hell of a time for a lesson.

'It's about the labyrinth, Gabe. You're in it now, all three of you. I'm not the third point of the triangle, Teal is. And together, you're the golden thread.'

Smoke clogged my lungs. I couldn't make sense of her words.

'For fuck's sake, Gabe, listen. Join hands with Moth and Teal. I think that's your way back from the middle.'

CHAPTER SEVENTY-SIX

The flames kissed my skin with scorching lips, the smog choking my throat. Somewhere close lay Moth and Teal. If I left Noah, he would certainly die. The smoke would finish what Nekhbet had started. Wiping my fingers over his nose and lips, I lowered my head and breathed into his mouth a couple of times.

The bottom of Nekhbet's dress was alight, the flames licking greedily up the fabric, but I couldn't see her face or The White Witch. My vision swam, tears streaming down my face, but somehow I forced Moth's name from my throat. It came out as a croak. I tried again. 'Moth! Come here, please...'

Another timber creaked overhead and something exploded across the room in a flurry of blue smoke. There was no reply from Moth. No movement. Fuck. It wasn't going to end like this.

Conflict raged inside me. The only way we could link hands would be if I left Noah alone. And that would be one more death down to me. But if I couldn't save Noah, I had to try to save Olivia. Her scent still lingered, she hadn't gone far, and if this whole room collapsed, she would be right in the way.

Taking Noah's face in my hands, I kissed his cheek and then crawled away from him.

Fingers of firefly flame brushed against me—the souls of the ones like Teal, vampires who had been hunted and murdered.

I watched in horrified fascination as my skin began to blister. I wouldn't die from being burned, not unless I turned to ash, but I would feel every tiny agony as it happened.

Sliding on my stomach, I reached out blindly, finding the bottom of a boot just as I thought I couldn't go on. I felt my way up the limb, knowing it was Moth, coughing and spluttering as the noise of the fire roared in my ears. His body was on top of Teal's, protecting him. My fingers found his wrist, then his hand. He didn't move.

His blood is too weak. I pushed that thought away and grabbed for Teal as a terrible cry screeched from the centre of the room. Plumes of dense black smoke whirled into a vortex, spiralling towards the ceiling.

Despite the flames, Teal's hand was like ice as I intertwined my fingers with his.

Moth moved his head slowly then raised it, his dusty hair plastered to his face. 'Gabe.' His lips were cracked and bleeding.

My heart leapt, fuelled by a ridiculous joy. Through the thick, noxious smoke I told him to take Teal's hand.

The roof started to collapse. Splinters of burnt wood fell like rain and the great timbers groaned in pain and indignant fury.

Then, silence. It happened so quickly I thought I had died. All around us, the room was burning, but it was like looking at it through a waterfall, the colours all mixing and the shapes distorting. Moth and Teal looked on in shock, eyes wide, faces covered in smudges of smoke. But where we were, nothing was aflame.

I pulled them both across to where I had left Noah, taking a gamble the safe space would go with us. It did. We made a protective ring around his body. If he was dead, the fire would not have him. It was the only comfort I could get.

A stream of oily black smoke curled towards us and I knew what it was. I tightened my hold on the fingers of my brothers. Olivia had said we were the golden thread, the same thread Theseus had used to find his way out of the labyrinth. But this time it wasn't helping us find our way out; it was protecting us inside. Once again, Olivia had been the one riding in to save me.

The smoke enveloped us, its tendrils encircling our wrists. Fingers of it dug into our flesh, trying to force us apart.

A line of golden flame appeared above us, hovering like the last cry of the sun as it disappears into the ocean. Its edges were tinged with red. I watched it, unable to take my eyes from the way it seemed to breathe with a life of its own. Then it fell towards us, scattering sparks in our hair, covering our shoulders, our skin, before slowly fading to nothing. I could still see them in my eyes long after they were gone.

The pressure around my wrists lifted. All around us, the room devoured itself, the roof crashing down, splintering into pieces on the floor. The walls had turned into charred canvases, our dark night world now a frenzy of light. A hand tightened its grip with mine. It was Moth, his eyes full of flame and wonder.

A tremor ran along the floor, vibrating through my feet and into my legs. The ground quivered and a rush of dank air came up to greet me as it collapsed beneath us.

CHAPTER SEVENTY-SEVEN

Olivia sat by Noah's bedside. He was surrounded by machines and wires and tubes and she hated every single one of them, even though they were keeping him alive.

She had fought to be here, defiantly standing her ground when the nurses tried to get her to go and rest. Noah wouldn't know she was there, they said. She wouldn't be any good to him exhausted, they said. But she wasn't leaving. They would have to drag her away bodily.

She remembered the tunnel. The weight of the oppressive heat as the fire raged above, her own inadequacy at not being able to do anything but stand and wait, knowing Noah and Gabe were in the midst of it all. She felt for Teal, who was the pawn in all of this, and she felt for Moth, even if he was a snarky mass of rebellious vampire blood. He had tried to protect her in the end. And she couldn't fault him for loving Gabe.

Love didn't come with a coat of laughter and sunlight, it crawled along the gutter gathering debris in its wake but flowered anyway. She squeezed Noah's fingers, so cold upon the hospital gown.

The suffocating heat had driven her back down the tunnel, but she had heard the floor collapse and had staggered back through the wall of dust and smoke, with her heart in her mouth and sweat running down her spine. In a tangle of limbs, she had recognised Noah's pale face, the scar so vivid against his skin.

She had bent over double, hacking and spluttering, as her legs refused to carry on, her lungs burning from sheer exertion. A line of light had flared past her. A hand had grasped her shoulder and she'd jumped, wheeling around, to see the masked face of a fireman. His eyes had been kind. Something firm had gone over her nose and mouth and she'd panicked, and then she had passed out.

Her breath wheezed in her chest. The doctors had wanted to put her on oxygen, but she'd refused. It could wait.

Noah didn't have that choice. They had explained about the dangers of mechanical ventilation, spouting long words with the weary calm all medical professionals have. They must learn it as part of the process, along with extracting small objects from kids' noses.

She had convinced them she was Noah's next of kin, a blatant lie, but God knows she aced that. She always had.

Olivia sighed. The plastic tubes snaked through Noah's nostrils, delivering oxygen and a little bit of hope. Wearily, she laid her face down on the bed, trying to block out the noise of the machines. There wasn't a place in her body that didn't hurt, including her heart.

What had happened to Gabe? To Teal? To Moth? She couldn't remember seeing them after the collapse, could only remember Noah's broken body and the stream of heat from above. Had she been right about the golden thread? Please, God, make it so. But He probably didn't have saving vampires on his must-do list, along with members of the church who had wandered away...

'Fuck you,' she muttered under her breath. 'Fuck you!' This time louder, drowning out those infernal machines.

A nurse paused at the other side of the door, looking in with a bag of saline in her hand. Olivia waved her away dismissively.

Sunlight filtered through the protective blinds on the window, and outside, in the distance, a church bell tolled. It must be Sunday. She closed her eyes. Exhaustion seeped through her bones, but she fought it, listening to the sound. A memory surfaced. Standing with Ollie at the front of a small church, the faces of proud parents facing them from rows of dark wood pews. This was their party piece and they had practiced it for hours in front of a mirror, even though she had told Ollie it was stupid and didn't make sense.

Monday's child is fair of face,
Tuesday's child is full of grace,
Wednesday's child is full of woe,
Thursday's child has far to go,
Friday's child is loving and giving,
Saturday's child must work for a living,
But the child that's born on the Sabbath day,
Is fair and wise and good and gay.

Ollie had taken the lead even though he was the shy one. She recalled it had been snowing outside, a couple had come in late, their shoulders dusted with snowflakes. She remembered thinking that they might be angel feathers. They were the only two children with no proud face to watch them.

As sleep finally claimed her, Olivia remembered what day she and Ollie had come into the world.

It was a Thursday.

CHAPTER SEVENTY-EIGHT

It was the anniversary of my death. Instinctively, I knew.

Clouds scudded across a full moon, and the wind danced along the rooftops, skittish at the promise of a new season. I sat by an old chimney, my back to its worn stack, and stared out into the night, just like I used to do. But I wasn't angry. I was grateful. Somehow, against all of the odds, Teal and Moth and I had made it out alive.

I refused to think about Noah. I couldn't let the weight of his loss interfere with survival. Teal kept telling me he might still be alive, always trying to soothe my ragged feelings. He didn't hear the voices anymore, but he was different. I don't think going through what he did could leave you the same.

We had run that night the tunnel had collapsed, with the dawn on our heels. Since then, the calm had been unnerving. Teal felt the rumble of unease sometimes on the mental vampire web, The Bloodvyne. But he didn't tune into it for long. It was too much of a risk. We had committed a sin. I didn't want to think what the penalty was for killing an envoy of the ruling body. Because as messed up as it was, they would still think of Nekhbet as that. The truth had gone up in flames, along with my mother's body. Oddly enough, that comforted me. She was at peace now. Fire purifies. Fire renews.

The window creaked open below me and I heard the scramblings of feet and hands on the tiles. Moth. He appeared beside me, settling down by my side, pressing his weight against me.

'You should have woken me.' He stretched and I leaned across and stole a kiss. His lips tasted like me. My pulse quickened and I looked away, watching an owl in soundless flight.

'I just needed to think,' I answered, and he nodded. He understood. His fingers laced through mine and I gazed at his sleep-foggy eyes. I wanted to lick away the shadow of the death sleep.

'Do you think he knows?' Moth looked up at me and his mouth twisted slightly. We didn't talk of Clove much anymore.

'Without a doubt,' I answered quickly, because it was the truth. If Clove was alive, he would know. I didn't like to think about what might have happened to him. Because it hurt. But I knew we could get by without him now. Sometimes I heard his voice in my head. *No fear.* I couldn't promise him it was gone completely, but I was doing okay. Moth and Teal both looked to me, the pure bred, for decisions, and I made them, as best as I could, always putting our safety and their welfare at the top of the list, because that's what Clove had taught me.

Moth dug a tuft of moss from a tile and rolled it between his fingers.

'Do you remember when you told me that there was no going back?'

He stopped and ducked under my arm, straddling my hips in one quick move. I grinned. The serious moment was gone. The wind wafted his hair from his face. Far too long. Far too unkempt. But I loved it. Just as I loved him.

'I remember.' His face softened and his tongue flickered out. 'You needed that advice. I was so fucking fed up of you wanting to go back to your old life...' He trailed off, as though uncertain if he'd hit a raw nerve. But he hadn't.

'So you pulled me kicking and screaming into yours, right?' I slipped my hand inside his jacket, splaying my fingers across his chest. The beat of his heart was strong, comforting. 'Thank you,' I whispered, for nothing in particular. For everything.

He took my hand and brought it to his lips, kissing along my palm, his tongue exploring. For a split second, I forgot everything but this moment. This gift.

'Did you know your life line has lots of trails running from it?' He showed me, his dirty fingers cradling my hand.

'Now that can only be a very good thing, I guess—'

He stopped my next words, his lips upon mine, his tongue delving, finding truth.

'Gabriel,' he whispered my full name against my lips, knowing what it does to me. I wound my fingers through his hair, clinging to his kiss, and somewhere in the night, a fox barked.

There were still loose threads in what we'd left behind, a knot waiting to be tied. The three points of the triangle belonged to us. Olivia had said the letters stood for rebirth and resurrection. I think the missing word is revenge, but as for whose revenge that is, the jury was out.

A movement below and we pulled away, breathless, need pounding in our veins. But we didn't care. We had time. All the time in the world.

Teal joined us, his blond hair silvered with moonlight. He smiled, bashfully, and my heart flipped over.

Those ocean eyes gleamed back at us, a little less dazzling than our time in the town, but still magnetically beautiful. Moth pulled him up and we sat together in silence, letting the breeze take our thoughts. Moth's fingertips touched mine and I shivered. My lover. My brothers. My world.

Teal turned to me, understanding the date, wanting to support and uplift. Looking at him was like seeing daylight again.

The blue-green of his eyes, so luminous I thought that sometimes I could drown in them. But there was something else swimming in their depths now.

Tiny golden flecks of firefly light.

‡‡‡

ACKNOWLEDGEMENTS

Every book has its support crew, the people who nurture and encourage it in its various fledgling phases, of which there are many. My grateful thanks again to my wonderful editor, Kate Angelella, who teaches and inspires me. My beta readers who received an early draft of this and waded through with comments and suggestions – James Fahy, G.R. Thomas, Matt Rydeen, Martin McConnell and Mia Maxwell. To Andrew and Rebecca Brown of Design for Writers for my beautiful cover design and interior. You are all absolute stars.

Thank you to my friends and loyal supporters on Twitter and the #bookstagram community on Instagram, for showing me the human side of social media. And for believing in Gabriel and his continuing journey. You took my dream and gave it wings.

And to you, for choosing this book.

ABOUT THE AUTHOR

Beverley Lee is a freelance writer currently residing in the south east of England. In thrall to the written word from an early age, especially the darker side of fiction, she believes that the very best story is the one you have to tell. Supporting fellow authors is also her passion and she is actively involved in social media and writers' groups. A Shining in the Shadows is the sequel to The Making of Gabriel Davenport, and book two in the Gabriel Davenport series.

Reviews are gold to authors! If you've enjoyed this book, would you consider rating it and reviewing it on www.Amazon.com or Goodreads?

The first book in this series, The Making of Gabriel Davenport, is available from www.Amazon.com.

Sign up to my newsletter at www.beverleylee.com for exclusive content and the latest updates on The Gabriel Davenport Series.

Printed in Great Britain
by Amazon